CHOSEN OF THE SUN

Trilogy of the Second Age Book 1

By Richard Dansky

Ratcatcher stepped through the door and inwardly sighed. It was clear that this man would be lucky to remember his name, let alone where to find a long-forgotten tomb. Still, the Prince's orders were the Prince's orders, and thus must be carried out.

His gaze took in the cottage, then focused on Bold Hare himself. The man wore brown, unsurprisingly, and had a bit of a paunch. Once he'd probably had a full thatch of hair; now there was just a fringe of it around a bald pate that gleamed in the firelight. His hands were scarred and thick, the fingers clearly more used to gripping a plow than a weapon. Trembling, the man raised his sword and squared his shoulders. "Come closer and I'll spit you!" he dared, the quaver in his voice belying the bravado of his words.

Abruptly, the figure stopped, just out of reach of Bold Hare's best lunge. "You'll spit me? Amusing." Ratcatcher's voice was surpassingly pleasant, the forced jollity of a peddler too long at his stall. "I've a question for you, that's all. Do you know where a weary traveler might find Talat's Howe?"

"The Howe?" Bold Hare narrowed his eyes in suspicion. "No one ever asks for the Howe, 'cept to know how they can avoid finding it. It's a bad place, a haunted place. Whyfore you'd want to go there?"

"Do you really want to know?" The figure chuckled, and Hare took another involuntary step back. The weapon suddenly felt very heavy in his fingers, and Hare became quite aware of how little he knew about swordplay after all.

Chapter One

The tomb they called Talat's Howe was a good twelve days' ride south-southeast of Great Forks, where it rose up near a patch of scrub wood that all the locals knew was haunted. Wiser than strangers, they gave the place a wide berth, and made sure to shut their doors securely once night fell. Shutters were drawn across windows, fires stoked in hearths, and weapons were kept close at hand in case one of the wandering dead decided to make an unwelcome guest of itself. The farmland was good by Talat's Howe, now that the gnarled laurel trees and scrub pines had been pulled from the soil, and life was easier than it might have been in other places. A clever man simply knew not to be out and about after dark for fear of dead men up and walking, and otherwise it was easy for a hard-working man to prosper in those fields. Even when the dead found a village and started pounding on a man's door, it was a relatively simple matter for torches and scythes to do their work and lay the menace to rest.

And so, once night began to fall, the farmers of the villages near the Howe ended their labors and trooped home manfully. Thinking of what lay beyond their cottage walls in the dark was something that few did, and fewer still enjoyed.

Therefore, it was something of a surprise to the farmer named Bold Hare when a mailed fist pounded on his door in the middle of the night.

There were six riders, all heavily armored and riding coal-black horses. They entered the village slowly, their horses' tack jingling with an odd, funereal sound, and the scent of rot and death trailed behind them. Overhead, clouds scudded low and fast across the moonless sky. Smoke puffed to heaven from a dozen chimneys, rising up to meet the clouds along with the occasional wisp of song or conversation that escaped past wooden shutters. Firelight spilled from beneath cottage doors and around the edges of windows, but in the streets nothing moved. Livestock was penned in barns, a precaution that had been taken ever since Old Man Kheleth had found one of his cows dead in its pen one morning, drained of blood but still staring wild-eyed up at the sky.

The lead rider looked left, looked right, and then raised his hand. Behind him, the column halted obediently. The riders bore names like Bonedust and Shamblemerry and Pandeimos, and only some of them could still be said to be, in any sense, living.

Their leader, who styled himself the Prince of Shadows and who had helped to bring slaughter and madness to the ancient city of Thorn, frowned beneath his helm. "We," he finally said after a long pause to survey the scene, "lack direction."

One of the riders broke formation, urging his horse to walk him forward. He, alone of all the Prince's entourage, went helmetless. His black hair was long and held in place with a silver clasp, and his sharp features were pinched with disapproval. A row of crimson tears had been tattooed down his cheek, in imitation of drops of blood, and his eyes were a shocking shade of green. "If we were using a map scribed on something sturdier than a moth's wing, my prince, perhaps that would not be the ca—"

"Ratcatcher? Do not speak." The Prince's voice was high and soft, but it carried with it the unmistakable tone of command. "Whether the map was frail or not is immaterial. It was, after all, over a thousand years old. I at least can find it in my heart to forgive it for being fragile. What concerns me at the moment is the fact that, without the map, finding our destination becomes somewhat problematic. Hence," and he gestured disdainfully at the collection of huts, "our visit to this charming place."

"Surely you cannot think that anyone *here* would know how to find our destination. They don't know enough to scrape the dung from their boots!"

"You have a curious way of interpreting a command for silence, Ratcatcher." The Prince's tone was mild, but Ratcatcher reacted as if he'd been struck. Reddening visibly, he wheeled his horse back into line.

The Prince watched him go with some amusement. "Well, then, if no one else has any thoughts he must share? No? Then, Ratcatcher, be so good to inquire of *that* gentleman"—he pointed with a single slender finger at the nearest cottage—"as to where our path might lie. The rest of you may observe. It should prove interesting."

Amidst low laughter from the other riders, Ratcatcher swung down from his horse. It made neither motion nor sound as he did so. "Good boy," he murmured, and turned to stride toward the cottage in question. Starlight reflected off the black lacquer of his armor, and a cloak of mottled black and gray billowed out behind him. The horse watched him, placidly, with the air of someone grown bored of seeing the same play repeated endlessly. As the thunder of metal on wood cut the night, it whinnied softly, then bent its head to the lush grass. Still in formation, the other riders waited.

Bold Hare nearly dropped his mug when the first knock on the door echoed through the cottage. Until that point, it had been a fairly normal evening; his wife Grey Rushes sat weaving broad-leaved grass into a mat to trade to Kheleth's daughter, who made good fabrics. Hare himself was bone-weary from a day in the fields. His son, who was simply called Rabbit, sat behind him, emulating his father's posture and weary observation of the day's labor.

The pounding on the door changed that. Hare's wife froze, as did his son. Hare himself gently put his mug down and, half-crouching, groped his way to where his sword hung on the wall. He put his finger to his lips for silence, unnecessarily. His wife had already put down her weaving and hastily bundled their son into the corner of the room. Grey Rushes made no sound; she'd heard the dead at the door before.

Painstakingly, Bold Hare took down his sword from where it hung. It was a stabbing blade, perhaps eighteen inches in length and notched from innumerable uses for which it had never been intended. Bold Hare's father had carried it before him, and his father before that, and it had been lovingly cared for down through the generations. The sword was the only one in the village, and thus was a point of pride in Bold Hare's family. Bold Hare even fancied himself a bit of an expert with it. Certainly he'd held his own in dealing with the handful of beasts who'd preyed on the livestock at various times, and more famously in a fight with a pack of woodland barbarians who thought that a passel of farmers would be easy pickings. They'd been wrong, though only briefly, and digging the mass grave for the bodies had taken longer than the fight itself.

The knock echoed again, impatiently, and then a third time. Bold Hare settled into a guard position and glanced over at his family to reassure them. His wife's face was a mask of determination, while the boy was clearly terrified. He was doing his best to hide it, though, and Bold Hare felt a swelling of pride at his son's fortitude. The next morning, he resolved, he'd start teaching the lad how to use the sword. He'd waited long enough already; it was time to train the boy in the arts of becoming a man.

The pounding stopped. Silence hung in the air. Bold Hare held his breath and counted heartbeats. Ten passed, then fifteen, then twenty.

"Maybe it's gone," his wife breathed, so low that the crackling of the fire nearly drowned her out. Bold Hare nodded, and relaxed his stance. The sword's point dipped toward the floor, and he took a half-step back, relieved. "I think so, " he said, in a voice barely louder than his wife's, and then the door exploded inwards.

A chunk of wood caught Bold Hare in the midriff, and he went down, puffing. Another landed in the fire with a shower of sparks. Others went spinning through the cottage, and the boy shrieked, his voice cracking as he did so. As if the cry were a fanfare of trumpets, a figure in black armor strode through the door.

Bold Hare picked himself up and gawked. The figure was over six feet tall, clad in elaborate armor painted in black lacquer and crafted to look as if it were made from monstrous scales. He was bareheaded, with sharp features and an expression of pure disdain on his countenance. A long sword in the shape of a serpent was in his fist, and absently the stranger sheathed it across his back as he stepped forward. The fire leaned away from him, the flames moaning, and shadows crept across the room as the intruder advanced, heralds of his darkness.

Ratcatcher stepped through the door and inwardly sighed. It was clear that this man would be lucky to remember his name, let alone where to find a long-forgotten tomb. Still, the Prince's orders were the Prince's orders, and thus must be carried out.

His gaze took in the cottage, then focused on Bold Hare himself. The man wore brown, unsurprisingly, and had a bit of a paunch. Once he'd probably had a full thatch of hair; now there was just a fringe of it around a bald pate that gleamed in the firelight. His hands were scarred and thick, the fingers clearly more used to gripping a plow than a weapon. Trembling, the man raised his sword and squared his shoulders. "Come closer and I'll spit you!" he dared, the quaver in his voice belying the bravado of his words.

Abruptly, the figure stopped, just out of reach of Bold Hare's best lunge. "You'll spit me? Amusing." Ratcatcher's voice was surpassingly pleasant, the forced jollity of a peddler too long at his stall. "I've a question for you, that's all. Do you know where a weary traveler might find Talat's Howe?"

"The Howe?" Bold Hare narrowed his eyes in suspicion. "No one ever asks for the Howe, 'cept to know how they can avoid finding it. It's a bad place, a haunted place. Whyfore you'd want to go there?"

"Do you really want to know?" The figure chuckled, and Hare took another involuntary step back. The weapon suddenly felt very heavy in his fingers, and Hare became quite aware of how little he knew about swordplay after all.

"Who are you?" Hare tried for defiance, but the question came out weakly. The rider advanced another step, and shadows pooled around his ankles.

"Who am I? Tsk tsk, don't ask questions you don't want answers to. You'll be happier and live longer." In a heartbeat, the smile fell from his face, and his voice grew suddenly harsh. "Now, to business. Tell me where to find Talat's Howe, and I'll leave. Continue to pretend you're braver than you are, and I'll gut your boy in front of you, then whisper a charm that'll make your woman think you held the knife. For the last time, where is Talat's Howe?"

Without waiting for an answer, the rider turned and strode to where Hare's wife cowered. With pitiful ease, he tore the boy from her grasp and held him aloft. Ineffectively, the child beat at the fist that held him, crying for his father to save him. Grey Rushes leapt desperately for the armored figure and was slapped contemptuously aside; Bold Hare heard bone break as Ratcatcher's fist crushed her cheek. Breathing heavily, he stepped forward, sword raised.

Abruptly, incongruously, Ratcatcher laughed. "Oh, you mighty warrior," he said, and dropped into a swordsman's crouch with the screaming boy held before him like a shield. "Come, Sir Dirt, attack me. I'm sure a swordsman of your mettle will be able to skewer me in a single blow." He pretended to stumble, and the hand holding the boy almost dipped to the floor. Bold Hare saw his chance and lunged. With inhuman grace, the intruder brought his kicking, screaming shield up in time to knock the sword away effortlessly. Bold Hare shrieked, but could not stay his hand, and the boy's side caught the flat of the blade with a meaty smack. The child screamed, but no blood spilled and his captor danced back mockingly.

"Care to try your luck again? You didn't quite spit your boy last time, though I'm sure we can do something about that." Enraged, Bold Hare lunged again, and again the human shield was brought down expertly on the flat of the blade.

Overbalanced, the farmer stumbled forward and received a blow on the ear from a mailed fist as his reward. He crashed to the floor, narrowly missing impaling himself on his sword, and grunted from the impact. Weapon still in hand, he scrambled to his knees in time to receive a solid kick to the ribs. Howling with the pain, he crawled forward on hands and knees, buffeted by additional, precise kicks and blows.

Panting, Bold Hare reached one of the cottage walls and turned, holding the sword before him with his knees drawn up tight. Looking down on him was the intruder, child held negligently in his off hand. The boy was silent now, his eyes wide with terror and his jaw slack. Red welts showed against the bare flesh of his stomach where the sword blows had landed, and his tunic was in rags.

"Is there still some fight in you?" the boy's captor inquired, and made a come-hither gesture with his free hand. "Really, I expected better from one of your oh-so-noble stock."

Slowly, Bold Hare stood. He looked from wife to son and then back again, and then dropped the sword.

"You ride south about an hour, maybe an hour and a half. Due south, mind you, straight as you can go. You'll come to a stream that's got a hedge of mountain laurel around it, some of it burned by the roots. That's your sign. Turn left and follow the creek upstream. When it peters out, you'll be at the base of a hill. Climb it, though be careful for wolves. They're thick that way, thick as thieves. Climb the hill and look east. You'll see the Howe, surrounded by old forest. There's dead men that haunt it, though, and I hope they tear you apart."

"Doubtful, I'm afraid. We have mutual interests." Ratcatcher released his grip on the boy. With a cry the child hit the floor and scrambled over to where his mother lay, then looked up at his father with accusing eyes. "However, I thank you for the warning about the wolves." The armored figure bowed sketchily, then turned his back on Bold Hare and strode toward the door.

Grey Rushes saw her chance. The stranger's back was to her, and the sword was within her reach. Slowly she reached for it, then, when her fist closed on the hilt, she sprang up. "You don't touch my boy!" she said, and stabbed with all her might. Bold Hare dove to stop her, but stumbled and fell.

Ratcatcher turned just in time to catch the full force of the thrust on his breastplate, below his heart. He raised a hand out of reflex, but it was too late; the blow struck home.

With a sound like a hammer on stone, the blade broke into pieces. Grey Rushes froze, astonished. Ratcatcher looked back at her with a sad smile, one that promised vengeance for perfidy and a great deal of pain. For an instant, no one moved.

Then the boy screamed. Ratcatcher pursed his lips, then struck Grey Rushes with the back of his hand. Her head whipped sharply sideways, and a sharp crack rang out. She crumpled to the floor and ceased to move.

Bold Hare howled and threw himself on the stranger, who made no move to dodge or resist. Instead, he bore the farmer's pitiful blows and brought his hand to Bold Hare's throat. The man's eyes bulged, and he gave a shriek that abruptly cut off as Ratcatcher's fingers closed on his windpipe. Without so much as a moment of hesitation, the intruder lifted his victim like a child lifting a doll. The farmer's face reddened, and his fists pounded impotently on Ratcatcher's armor as his feet left the floor. "I'll kill you," was all he could choke out, each blow coming wilder and weaker than the last.

"I don't think so," replied Ratcatcher conversationally. "Say good-bye to your boy. He might miss you." Then the stranger squeezed, and Bold Hare started what a generous man might call screaming. It took him a very long time to stop.

Vaguely dissatisfied but no longer hungry, Ratcatcher turned and left the cottage. The interlude that had played out within had not done much for his mood, and he'd found the farmer's Essence vaguely dissatisfying. The man's wife was already dead from the blow he'd struck her, and the boy wouldn't have been worth the trouble—or the screams. Besides, leaving him alive was crueler by half, a practice Ratcatcher followed whenever circumstances permitted. *After all,* he thought, *without witnesses, artistry is nothing.*

Ahead, the Prince waited, the insufferable bitch Sandheart

to his left. She had just told a joke, it seemed, as beneath his helm the Prince was laughing.

"Ah, Ratcatcher. Do you have news for us?"

"I should never have doubted your wisdom in stopping here, my prince. The peasant was indeed acquainted with the location of the tomb we seek."

"Was?" The Prince sounded mildly amused.

"I'm afraid so, my prince. He was a terrible host."

The Prince laughed. "I see. We certainly cannot countenance a failure of courtesy, can we now, Ratcatcher? So tell me, where do we go from here if we are to pay our respects to Talat?"

Ratcatcher bowed deeply. "It is simple, my prince. We ride south until we see laurel trees at a small stream, then turn to follow the stream to its source. From there, we should be able to see the Howe." He paused to brush an imaginary speck of dust from his greave. "I should also inform you that I was warned to watch out for wolves and ghosts. I assured my host that his concern was misplaced, but I did appreciate at least that much consideration from him."

"I'm sure you did," the Prince said dryly. "Mount up. Since you disapprove of this place so much, we will leave it forthwith as a reward for your service." Ratcatcher opened his mouth to say something, caught the Prince's tone, and thought better of it. Instead, he gave another bow and walked stiffly to where his horse waited, patient as always. As he mounted, it chewed prosaically on a mouthful of grass, then tossed its head once, waiting.

With a bone-chilling cry, the Prince touched his spurs to his horse's flanks. It cantered forward, headed south, and behind it the other five riders followed without comment or question. Only the boy witnessed their departure, and he was as wordless as they.

In the morning, the villagers came to Bold Hare's house. They found Bold Hare's wife, dead, with her neck at an angle like a broken marionette. They found Bold Hare's son, silent and mad, clutching his father's broken sword as if it could conjure up the ghost of peace. They found a mound of ash in the fireplace, and shattered furniture, and a smoldering patch on the grass mats that covered the floor.

And in the center of the room, they found a withered husk that they agreed must once have been Bold Hare, and they silently congratulated themselves for not coming to his aid when the shrieking had started. Then they started piling up wood for the pyre, and made damned sure that their own doors were stout.

After all, the least they could do was learn from Bold Hare's example.

It was still two hours before moonrise when the procession left Bold Hare's village, giving them plenty of time to seek Talat's Howe before dawn. Only the jangle of tack and harness, and the sound of extra bolts being thrown across doors, heralded their departure, and soon enough they left the village behind. The path south was relatively smooth. It bore the look of an old game track that men had taken for their own for a while, and then abandoned.

Now, however, it was disdained by animals as well. Neither man nor beast disrupted the small column as it moved steadily forward, and the few pairs of watching eyes in the bushes soon turned away. To the west, a thick bank of clouds blanketed the sky. Their advance was slow but steady, and the night grew steadily darker as they swallowed up the stars. Flickers of white light demonstrated the presence of lightning, and low rolls of thunder drowned out the patient hooting of owls.

Ratcatcher turned to the advancing storm and spat. "Damned if we won't get soaked again. I swear, one of us must have offended the entire West. Why else would we get rained on every damn night?"

Pandeimos muttered something about rain drowning out foolishness. He was a nemessary, an unquiet soul who'd clawed his way out of hell and stolen one body after another in order to wreak havoc upon the living. As each shell either rotted away or was hacked down by enemies, the soul inside fled to another corpse, and then another one. Only hatred sustained such as him, which was why they were drawn to the Prince's service.

There were several such as Pandeimos in the Prince's retinue, Sandheart among them, and the sole trait that they shared was a poor sense of humor. Ratcatcher hated the lot of them, and they hated him right back, though in an impersonal, dull way. They hated all creation, after all, and Ratcatcher was just a particularly annoying manifestation of it.

After Pandeimos's comment, the others—living and dead—ignored Ratcatcher stonily. He paused for a moment, then, undeterred, bantered on. "All this, and for what? Talat's Howe? A myth, a legend, a hole in the ground—and no doubt one plundered already by grubby-fingered men with picks and shovels. I'll wager they brought the treasures of the ages home to adorn their fat wives, or melted them down for coin to buy beer and whores. And yet, here we are at the Elemental Pole of Boredom, of Idiocy, of Sheer Bloody-mindedness. That peasant certainly was an avatar of it, I swear, if such things can be said to exist. After all, the sages are still debating as to whether or not a shadow that falls in the forest creates darkness, while—"

"Silence."

The single word cut across the chatter like a whipcrack. In its wake thunder rolled, much closer now.

"Your Majesty, I most humbly apologize. I was merely—"

"I believe I called for *silence*."

There was silence. The rider at the front of the column stopped, and an instant later, the rest of the riders stopped as well. A cold wind whipped over them, the herald of the coming storm. One of the horses whinnied anxiously, and stamped its hoof upon the turf. No one spoke.

With slow deliberation, the lead rider turned his horse and walked it back along the line. When he reached the spot where the complainer's steed stood, he stopped. None of the other riders moved, hands tight on the reins to control their mounts.

"Your observations, Ratcatcher, are not amusing." The voice that issued from the Prince's hyena-shaped helm was no longer light. Instead, it was flat and weary, with a brutal undertone. "Do you understand why I gave you the name that I did?"

The man called Ratcatcher slumped in his saddle, very carefully not meeting his master's gaze. "No, my prince."

"It is because you are here to serve me in the same way that a small dog serves its master, namely, by ridding the pantry of rats. Your services are welcomed, but not indispensable, and should you prove troublesome, there are always much larger hounds than you about who'd view you as a morsel. A *snack*. Am I not correct?"

"You are correct in all things, my prince."

"No, I am not, and idle flattery is not going to get your paw out of the trap you've set it in. But in this small thing, at least, I most certainly am." Ratcatcher began to respond, but the Prince waved him to silence.

"No, no, we'll have no more of that. Now, give me your crop."

"My crop, my prince?"

The Prince's words were icily precise. "Yes. Your crop. The small device made of leather and bone you use when you wish to make your horse run as fast as your mouth. Give it to me."

"Of course, my prince." Ratcatcher handed the whip over, nearly dropping it in his eagerness. It was black, with a bone tip that was cruelly barbed, and it bore signs of hard use. The Prince examined it, then held it up so that he might see it better.

"Yes, this will do," he remarked to the night, and brought his hands together. He spoke a word of power, and then another one, and something considerably darker than the night flared between his fingers.

Then, abruptly, it was done. The Prince lowered his hands and offered the crop to Ratcatcher, who took it, gingerly. Experimentally, Ratcatcher tested its heft, thwacking it thrice against the palm of his hand. There was no effect save the dull clang of bone on metal and the swish of the leather in the night air, and several of the other riders laughed. The Prince joined in the merriment, head cocked to one side as he observed Ratcatcher's predicament.

Finally, uncomfortably aware of being the object of scorn,

Ratcatcher made a great show of straightening himself in his seat, and bowed his head formally. "I thank you, my prince, for returning my crop to me. I trust its service to you was most satisfactory." At this, the laughter rang out louder in the night air, and Ratcatcher's posture stiffened.

"Oh, quite satisfactory, I assure you—at least to me. You may find it less so."

"My prince? I don't understand."

"That's to be expected. I have not yet explained to you how matters now stand." Again, there was a general round of laughter, and Ratcatcher turned wildly from left to right, in vain hoping the force of his gaze would silence his tormentors.

"Oh, do stop that," the Prince barked irritably. The laughter cut off, its last echoes mixing with the thunder. "You look like a drunken puppeteer's last wish. Now, take your crop and strike your steed."

"Will it not bolt if I do so?"

"Not if you are any kind of horseman, it won't."

"As you wish." Ratcatcher tapped his horse's flank lightly, to no effect. Dubious, he raised his whip hand and brought the crop down harder. Again, the horse stood stock-still, with only the ugly slap of bone on flesh marking the impact.

"Harder, you fool," the Prince snarled. "Pretend you might actually want your horse to move."

Fearfully, Ratcatcher raised the whip up over his head and glanced once more at his Prince, who nodded once.

Ratcatcher was no coward. He had descended into the vaults that lay beneath the Underworld and there pledged his service to the dead gods in their restless slumber, dreaming foul dreams of corruption and hatred. He had seen battle, and had slain so many foes that the blood had coated his armor inside and out, and he himself was crimson and wild-eyed when he emerged. He had made sacrifices of villages, and had bartered with spirits whose names it was not good to say in daylight. But Ratcatcher feared his Prince, and he feared his Prince's whims most of all.

The crop descended, meeting horseflesh with a sickening crack. The horse moved not at all. The Prince of Shadows watched impassively, any smile or concern hidden by his monstrous helm.

It was left to Ratcatcher, then, to scream. Searing agony burned through his side, and a warm stickiness along his ribs told him that he was bleeding. The riding crop lay innocuously in his hand. He lifted it and gazed at it, and there could be no mistaking what he saw. Its barbed and vicious tip was wet with fresh blood, and surely not the blood of a horse. With a howl of rage, he drew back his arm to fling it aside, but the Prince reached out and caught his wrist, just as a father might catch the wrist of an erring child.

Incredulous, Ratcatcher looked up at his master. "My prince?"

"This is yours, I think, for a while longer." Gently but irresistibly, the Prince brought Ratcatcher's hand down. "Now, I think, you'll pray for a slow pace, for every blow you strike with this will paint itself on your body. At least, until I decide otherwise." The Prince sniffed the night air and shook his head. "You're too hard on your horses in any case."

"As you say, my prince." Ratcatcher bowed his head and switched the crop to his off hand. "I have no wish to delay our journey further, and I humbly beseech your forgiveness for having cost you this valuable time."

"One more thing, my little terrier: We will have no more of your comments about the road, the food, the labor or indeed anything else until our journey is complete, and then not for a year and a day after that. If you manage to obey that particular command, then you'll be suitably rewarded. If not, I'll cut your tongue out and burn the stump, and then make you sing for your supper. Do we have an understanding?"

Ratcatcher nodded, dumbly.

"You are finally learning. Excellent. Now let's ride on, without any more foolishness. Ratcatcher, drop back in line and take the rear. Shamblemerry, take Ratcatcher's place behind me. The rest of you know your place, I trust. Let us ride, before we run out of night." He trotted to the front of the line, then gazed back over his shoulder at his followers. "And we most certainly don't want to get wet."

Thunder boomed, much nearer now. As one the six horses leapt forward, their riders pressed low against their backs for speed. All save the last went for the whip within seconds.

The creek, as Bold Hare had called it, suffered from the local population's delusions of grandeur. It was scarcely three feet across, and the shallow water it contained gave every promise of being muddy and unpalatable even to the horses. Fat raindrops broke its surface at odd intervals as the Prince's column cantered up to the banks, eyes anxiously scanning for the promised laurel trees. Ratcatcher brought up the rear, haltingly, his horse picking its way among the exposed roots of the creekside with slow dignity.

A few moments' diligent searching was all it took, aided by a fortuitous flash of lightning.

"There, my prince." Sandheart dismounted easily and walked lightly down to the water's edge, as if her armor were no more of an encumbrance than a summer tunic. Her helm was crafted to mimic the visage of a fanged stallion, and her armor was hammered with patterns like crashing waves. "Someone's been here before us."

She had not been long in the Prince's service, but her eye was keen and her counsel good, and she held a place close to the Prince's throne. The other riders feared and hated her, and for her part she returned their hatred with cool disdain. In the presence of the Prince of Shadows, however, such jealousies were pointless; the Prince could destroy any and all of them at a whim, and if it was his wish that they journey together in peace, then journey peacefully they would.

Advancing along the creekside, she knelt and pointed. Behind her, the Prince and two other riders dismounted. The others, including Ratcatcher, stayed mounted and turned their steeds around, the better to keep watch through the thickening rain. Low shrubs and tall grass covered the landscape, leaves bending under the rain and bowing to the wind. Across the muddy ditch the landscape was the same, rising to a low wooded hill. No sign of human habitation marked the hillside; for all the riders knew, the trees might have been undisturbed since the Contagion.

None of the riding party were in the slightest bit moved by the scenery, the Prince least of all. Clearly displeased, he strode to where Sandheart knelt. "Explain."

"Here, my prince." The knight gestured to a row of burned and blackened stumps, cut low to the ground. "This is mountain laurel, or was. It's a strange place to find it, but we've all seen far stranger. No wonder the farmer used it as a landmark; it doesn't grow anywhere else around here."

"Yes, yes, I'm quite certain it's fascinating" the Prince said impatiently. "The farmer warned Ratcatcher that they'd be burned, but gone? What happened?"

"Gone for at least a half-dozen years, my liege. The cuts on the stumps are smooth and old; I'd say they were hacked down, though there's precious little use for that wood. The burn marks are older than that, though, and by the looks of them, no natural fire made them. I'd not venture a guess as to how they survived."

The Prince made a dismissive gesture. "Unimportant. The trees were a signpost, not a destination, and I don't care if they were cut down, torn up by the roots or devoured by deranged gnats. So tell me why you think we're not the first on this track?"

"Here," she said, pointing at some long lines across the top of one of the stumps, "and here. Scratches on the stumps, made with a knife. Fresh, too, though I can't understand why." She looked up and shook her head. "If we'd been half an hour later, the rain would have washed away all sign of this passage. It's a good thing we made the pace we did."

"Indeed," said the Prince with a smirk. He glanced only briefly at Ratcatcher's back, then returned to the task at hand. "Hmm. Are you sure?"

"I would not dare suggest such were I not sure, my prince. And if you look by the water's edge, you'll see a half-sandal print. Someone's not taking good care to cover his tracks."

"Sandal. But no hoof prints?"

Sandheart shrugged and stood, careful to let the Prince

rise first. "I see none, and the ground's barely disturbed. I'd say we're following one man, two at most. On foot, and traveling light, but tired and careless. He probably thought the rain would cover his tracks. The level of the water is already rising. You can hear it." And indeed, the gurgle and rush of the stream was far louder than one would think such a small rivulet would make.

The Prince swung himself back into the saddle. "He is alone, or nearly so, and on foot. And we are many, and well armed. 'Tis a pity for him that we did not arrive here first."

Sandheart mounted and turned to look at her liege. "Pity, my prince? From you?"

"Only because I've run out of contempt," he replied, and touched his spurs to his horse's flank. It snorted and turned, and began the careful process of picking its way along the creekside in the dark and the rain. One by one, the others followed. One by one, raindrops obliterated the single footprint in the mud.

Beneath the shadow of the trees, a tall man did his best to make himself seem much shorter. His name was Eliezer Wren, and he was by profession a priest, though not a very good one. He was lean and strong, with a long face that seemed incapable of more than half a smile, and light brown stubble grew on a scalp that normally was clean-shaven. His only garment was a simple robe, belted at the waist with rope, and woven sandals were on his feet. One of them was, despite his best efforts, muddy.

"Are they gone yet?" he asked of no one in particular. His voice was low and quiet, nearly drowned out by the spatter of raindrops on leaves. Nevertheless, something heard and answered.

"They're not gone yet, but they're leaving. Now hush before they notice that I'm about. There's power on the other side of the water, wild power, and it's hungry."

The speaker was not a man, nor would it ever be mistaken for one. It was a shambling effigy of woven reeds and grasses, with sinews of climbing vines and eyes of shining water. With a creaking of branches, it rose up from the creekside and strode to where Wren squatted upon his haunches. The apparition was easily eight feet tall, and its maw was wide enough to take a man in a single gulp. Rough hands on its rough hips, it stood before the priest, waiting.

"They're less likely to find us if you'd see your way clear to being less conspicuous, Rhadanthos. Not that I'm not grateful for your gift of shelter, but I'd rather live to pay it back." There was a hint of wry amusement in Wren's voice, but a very real urgency as well.

"If you insist," the spirit grumbled, and sank back toward the earth. In seconds, it was little more than a rough mound, though its eyes and mouth remained. "If I had a tenth of my former strength, you'd not speak to me thus. You owe me a boon, priest. Remember that while you order me about."

"I'm a priest, Rhadanthos. I take oaths and bargains rather seriously."

"You are a very poor priest, Wren, and according to some of your fellows, should not be making bargains with the likes of me at all." The spirit chuckled. "Then again, four hundred years ago there were men dwelling here who'd castigate me for speaking to one such as you. Wheels turn, Wren. Wheels turn."

"Indeed they do. That is part of why I'm here." Satisfied that he and the spirit were alone, Wren stood carefully and reached into his belt pouch, searching for something. "And for whatever it may be worth, it is a tenet of the faith that due reverence is to be shown to spirits and lesser deific beings by those most appropriate to show it, namely the priesthood. You, of course, are worthy of my friendship and respect, but precious little reverence, and thus it is entirely fitting that I treat with you." He paused thoughtfully for a moment. "If you'd like, I can quote the appropriate passages."

Rhadanthos roared with laughter. "I see. No need for that, I think. And since your unwelcome companions are gone, I'll take my fee for hiding you."

"I can't give you it all right now, Rhadanthos, but I'll pay as much and as dearly as I can. You wanted a word, a deed and a gift, yes?"

"You know the terms of the bargain, Wren. A word, a deed

and a gift, and in exchange I hid you from prying eyes, muffled your breath so that unfriendly ears would not hear you, and lifted up the reeds that lay broken in your track. Now give me what is owed, or you'll see that even old godlings like myself are not to be trifled with."

Wren sketched a rough bow. "I'd not dream of cheating you or your kind. Now let me hold up the first part of our bargain. I owe you a word; what tale would you have of me?"

Rhadanthos rumbled and drew himself up to full height again. "It was a simple favor, so I'll settle for a simple tale. Two days ago you trod on my banks; now you return and things with the stench of graves ride on your old track. Give me the story of those two days and I'll call the first part of our bargain finished."

"There's not much to tell," Wren said with some embarrassment, briefly venturing far enough out from under the canopy of leaves to ascertain that the rain was indeed still heavy. "But if that's what you wish…"

"It is."

"Very well. Two days ago I first found your banks, and as I had been instructed to do by a friend whose name I prefer not to utter, I turned my course upstream to where my destination lay. You no doubt have heard tell of a mound that lies beyond where your spring arises. Men call it Talat's Howe when they feel kind, or Talat's Hell when they are drunk."

"I have heard of it," the creek-spirit rumbled. "Needless to say, I have never seen it."

"It's quite unremarkable, in truth. It's a hill, as this is a hill, and it is green with tall grasses and taller flowers that fight to claim their share of sunlight. There are even trees on it, though they're not what I'd call fine specimens of such. But it is perfectly round, and on its crest is a single standing stone, and thus men and things that deal with men know that it is no natural hill. If they come by night, they learn this lesson but briefly, as there are dead men that haunt it, and they don't take kindly to the living."

"I know it is not a natural hill, and I've never cast eyes on the thing, Wren."

"You are cleverer than most men, Rhadanthos." The spirit bowed its head in acknowledgment, and Wren went smoothly on. "Set in the stone is a lock, though not a lock that takes any key ever forged or cut. Beneath that stone is a passage, and at the end of that passage is a burial chamber. Buried in that chamber is, according to legend, song, and several of the Immaculate Texts, something that was once known as Talat."

Rhadanthos chuckled. "And who no doubt was buried with untold treasure and riches, not that a priest would have any use for such."

Wren spread his arms wide in a beneficent gesture. "Not I, but I am in service to others. You will notice, I trust, that I bear no treasure with me."

"I had noticed." The spirit stepped back, out into the rain. Rivulets of mud washed from its flanks, and it raised its arms to the heavens as if to supplicate for an even heavier squall. "Curious, that," it said, burbling.

"That was, of course, because someone had found Talat's burial chamber before me, and had emptied it of everything, including Talat, in a manner of speaking. But now I get ahead of myself. Let me speak more plainly. Having obtained the key to the lock in stone some time previously, the details of which I shall not bore you with, I approached the Howe by day and used it, pouring first a libation of blood to the spirits of that place from a rabbit I'd caught. This being done, I was not surprised to see the stone itself sink into the Howe. The strange movement of the stone revealed a passage down into the mound, and I followed it cautiously. There was no need, however. The Howe was empty. There was but an empty tunnel and an empty chamber, with a single coin on the floor."

"Preposterous!" Rhadanthos roared. "A burial mound with no burial? Such a thing would be an affront to the heavens! Stealing bones? What wretch would do that?"

"Or," said Wren quietly, "there never were any bones in the first place."

Rhadanthos blinked. "No bones? Then the entire mound...a ruse?"

Wren nodded. "Exactly. The coin dates to the first days of

the Empire. I suspect it was left as earnest of the architect's rather poor sense of humor. The lock, the riddles leading me to this place—all were designed to keep the curious searching for a way into the Howe, and never to wonder why they were doing so."

"A fine jest indeed. So, you entered empty-handed, and you left behind an empty tomb?"

"That is not quite the case, I confess."

"Oh?" The monstrous figure leaned forward, curious. "Explain."

"Well, I took the coin. It was left as my fee, after all. And it would have been shameful not to leave something in return."

"Something?"

"Something." Wren adopted a supplicant's humble posture. "Though I don't suspect it will be to the liking of those who rode after me."

"You've more assassin in you than priest, Wren, and more thief than either." The spirit shook its ponderous head slowly. "I'll not trouble you for the details as to the traps you laid; I know that they are deadly to men, and that is enough. Now, for the rest of your tale?"

"The rest you know. I hied myself back here, and cut some ashes from the stump to summon you when I heard the riders approach. It seemed prudent."

"It did indeed. Consider the first portion of your debt paid. Now, as to the second."

In response, Wren took from his pouch a single coin. It was golden; that much was clear in the brief flickers of lightning. "A gift," he said, and threw it with all his might toward the rough valley below. A distant splash told him that it had found its destination, the center of the creek.

"Very clever, Wren," the spirit chuckled. "Your gift is accepted. I'll let the coin from the heart of Talat's Howe lie in the muck, and laugh every time another fool rides past to seek the fabled treasure. Now you just owe me a deed, and one of my choosing."

"May I point out that if I labor here in service to you, I am rather likely to meet with the riders whose stench you disliked so much, and thus am most unlikely to finish my task." Wren spoke softly, choosing his words carefully. What he was attempting was dangerous. Spirits were rarely open to re-negotiation, he knew, and while Rhadanthos seemed jolly enough, he could easily take Wren's flesh off his bones in a matter of seconds.

"I hear your words, priest, and I do not like what they say. What are you asking for?" the spirit growled.

"Time. And in return, I shall work a greater labor for you than the one you might receive from me now."

"Hurrum. By all rights I should bind your feet with roots until you served me, and set biting flies to dance on your eyes while you labored."

"And you'd get poor service from me that way, Rhadanthos. You know better than that. Grant me this, and I swear by the love of the Five Dragons, you'll not regret it."

"That is not," growled the spirit ominously, "an oath of which I am particularly fond. But," it said, straightening its form until it stood, willow-like, upon the hillside, "you have made me laugh, which I value greatly, and you tell a good tale. Go. Find your way, if you can, and then return to me to settle your accounts. I'll give you seven years, Wren, but with each year the debt you owe me grows. Pay it sooner and your service is light. Pay it later and your labors will have songs written about them. Seek to avoid paying it, and I will have my vengeance."

"Thank you, Rhadanthos," Wren said, heartfelt relief in his voice. "I will not disappoint you. If nothing else, it would be bad for the priesthood if one of us broke that sort of promise. It would cause no end of talk."

Despite himself, Rhadanthos roared with laughter again. "Go, priest, before I change my mind and keep you here as my jester. The rushes will part for you until the edge of my domain, and all that grows will hide your passing." With that pronouncement, he sank into the earth and vanished. But all the grasses and weeds of the long hillside now bowed to where the priest stood, regardless of the direction of the wind.

Wren noticed this and quirked one eyebrow in amusement. Hopefully Rhadanthos would remember to withdraw his power before the riders returned, else he'd have some unpleasant explaining to do. Wren had not gotten a good look at his pursuers from where he'd crouched, but even from a distance he'd been able to tell that they were Anathema, and worse. He seriously doubted that the traps he'd left at the Howe would be enough to do more than annoy them, but annoyed monstrosities of that sort could no doubt do him—and the spirit—quite an injury.

Sighing, he took stock, rescued his pack from the tree branch he'd hung it on, and then set a course south and west, over the crest of the hill. The slopes ahead looked to be thickly wooded, tough country for men on horseback, and he'd take every advantage he could get. Eventually he'd have to cut back to the north, but he was confident he'd be able to find ship passage to Nexus, and whatever assignment awaited him there. That is, if the little joke he'd played back at the Howe didn't catch up with him first.

Perhaps it had been pride, a desire for the ages to know him. After all, it had been hundreds of years since Talat's Howe had been raised, and never once had it been disturbed; how could he have known that others were searching for it not two days behind him? He'd never imagined that the token he had left behind would be found in his lifetime, or indeed found at all.

And thus, he was very worried about the fact that he had left a token with his mark on it amidst the lethal traps he'd strung up in the corridors and chambers of the empty burial mound. A clever man might be able to decipher the token, discern its origins and hunt down the one who had left it there.

The Five Dragons alone knew what Anathema of that power would be capable of.

Rather nervous, Eliezer Wren walked faster.

"What is the name on the token, Ratcatcher?" asked the Prince of Shadows. Sandheart's unmoving body lay at his feet, and it was none of his doing. His anger was terrible, and his anima flared around him like the beating heart of some great nightmare beast.

Ratcatcher did not answer. Rather, he cautiously approached

and, bowing, placed the token in the Prince's outstretched hand. Behind him, the others murmured amongst themselves and kept a sharp eye out for more snares like the one that had claimed their companion. She lay on the floor, a narrow blade neatly protruding from her eye, and there could be no doubt that she was in fact dead.

This was a lesson, one that Ratcatcher understood. He could see plainly that power is useless if it is not guarded, and that a clever assassin may succeed where an army cannot. He also saw that Sandheart had gotten cocky, and thus had gotten herself killed, and that the Prince's anger was as much directed at Sandheart for her foolishness as toward her killer.

They had called upon their powers to tear open Talat's Howe while dead men made obeisance to the Prince. The ghosts had stood at the base of the Howe, never drawing nearer, and whined their devotion as he strode past. Behind him, the others had followed, and the ghosts had watched fearfully as they did so. One called out a warning to Sandheart, but she ignored it. *More fool she*, Ratcatcher thought. *More fool she.*

Power, raw power had shattered the lockstone and sent great gouts of earth geysering into the night. One by one, they had descended into the gaping maw of the tomb, and in the distance they could hear the wolves howling in fear. The wolves, Pandeimos had noted, were wise. He'd seemed uneasy, Pandeimos had, as he'd entered the tomb. Shamblemerry had made some comment about it, and Pandeimos had snapped at her. He'd said that he'd entered his own tomb once already, and that this place had the same feel. The walking dead among the Prince's retinue were sullen after that, and the living were thoughtful.

They had come seeking a dead man and a sword. The dead man was one against whom the Prince bore some sort of grudge, and it was always wise to indulge the Prince's hatreds. The sword was the one that this Talat had borne, and in passing Ratcatcher had gleaned that it was of a vintage and a craftsmanship to put the mace the Prince bore to shame. Thus, it behooved them to find this place, to sack it, to desecrate the bones of the one who lay within and to make off with his grave goods as a final insult.

Alas, then, that they had found a tomb empty save for a maze of hasty traps. Sandheart had triggered the first one, striding confidently forth into the dark, and she had paid the price for that arrogance.

Ratcatcher had seen the trap, of course. It would have been nigh impossible not to, so amateurishly had it been set. But calling out a warning would have required him to speak, and he was not willing to risk the Prince's ire in this matter any further.

The fact that he had hated Sandheart with a loathing so pure as to be luminous had, he decided upon reflection, played some small part in his decision as well.

The Prince had been furious, and in the tomb little withstood his fury. By the time the least edge of his rage had been abated, the rest of the impudent thief's traps lay in ruins, as did much of the interior of Talat's Howe.

Ratcatcher had not been terribly surprised to find it empty, once he'd finished picking through the ruins that the Prince had created. What had surprised him, however, was finding a token the thief had arrogantly left behind.

If the thief had been clever, and had found a deep enough hole to hide in, he might have survived his cleverness and its consequences. Leaving the token, however, was too much. It was bragging, and it was a gauntlet thrown at the feet of the Prince of Shadows.

The Prince did not like braggarts. The Prince did not like those who murdered his servants. And most of all, the Prince did not like those who thwarted his plans, and the man who had left this token had done all three.

Ratcatcher found himself feeling sorry, briefly, for the unknown assassin. Then he put the thought out of his mind, bowed, and backed away while the token was examined. Long seconds went by while the Prince stared at it, then suddenly, it was over. He closed his fist on it, and crumbled it to powder.

"That token was temple-made," hissed the Prince, "And it belonged to a priest named Eliezer Wren. I'll have his heart on a spit. Bring it to me, any of you, and you'll be rewarded. Now go!"

The others left and rode off slowly, the Prince's stallion with them. A few seconds later, a deafening explosion shook the hill, and the Prince strode forth from the wreckage. He dusted his hands and mounted, his body ramrod-stiff in the saddle.

"A fitting tomb," he said, and was silent for a moment. "She will not rise again. There are enchantments on this place to prevent such things. No doubt Eliezer Wren was unaware of such when he left behind his little toys, but he'll pay for it nonetheless. Let us leave this place, then, and do our best to find this unfortunate priest. Ratcatcher, Pandeimos, ride at my flanks. We are leaving, and may the gods and spirits help anyone who makes the least move to thwart us."

A flash of lightning split the sky, freezing everything in a tableau of grim determination for a single moment. Then it was gone, and the thunder rolled in, and with it came the clamor of hooves, galloping.

Chapter Two

The Most Learned and Venerable Hai Sholosh took his duties very seriously, which is why Tanak Milam didn't take him seriously at all. Had Sholosh known this, he probably would have disciplined his acolyte severely, but since he was fundamentally absorbed in his work, it worked out for the best for all concerned.

Sholosh was an Immaculate of the Fourth Coil, who had given long years of service to the Order and as a reward had been given a post in a secluded shrine near Chanos. The temple was a small one, housed in a building that had once been a family chapel on a minor estate belonging to House V'neef, and a posting there was regarded as quite the prize. The accommodations were spacious, the duties light, and the temple grounds harmonious to mind and eye.

It had been suggested to Sholosh when he accepted the post at Trae Chanos that he devote his time to teaching human acolytes the art of translating and recopying the Immaculate Texts. A devotee of the path of Hesiesh, Reciter of Loud Hymns and Efficacious Prayers, Sholosh was a past master at the art of the illuminated manuscript, and the precision of his brushstrokes was legend. One story often told to ambitious acolytes was that of Shraeash Cynis, who fancied himself an artist until he first saw a manuscript in Sholosh's hand. At a single glance, Cynis understood that his work would never equal that which he saw before him, and so he took a knife and slashed the palm of his drawing hand, lest he be tempted to try the impossible.

But Sholosh would have none of that. Gracefully, firmly, humbly, he declined every offer and averted every entreaty. Old in service, comfortable with the contribution he had made, and intimately aware of his fading strength, he wished nothing more than to attempt the path he had turned away from in his early days in the Order.

"For is it not fitting," he had said to the Mouth of Peace herself, "that at the end of all things, when the pattern of one's life is woven, is it not fitting to string the loom for the next life?" And to this even the Mouth of Peace acquiesced, and decreed that he might live out his days performing the duties of holy divination, and thus assisting the natural order of the world.

"After all," she confided in one of her advisors, "what harm could it do?"

Tanak Milam was a bastard's bastard, which was why House Mnemon had been only too glad to see him enter the Order. Of moderate talent and immoderate temper, he had been gently but firmly guided into the ranks of the priesthood. This was done both in the hope that the Order would teach him mental discipline and the certainty that, once the Order of the Immaculate Dragons took him, Tanak would be safely out from underfoot.

And so he had entered the Order, his feeble powers harnessed imperfectly to Heshiesh's path. Within a few short years, he had acquired an admirable reputation for efficiency in his labors and diligence in his studies, along with a less admirable one for being an officious, overbearing, ambitious loudmouth.

Thus it was that a brilliant plan was conceived. To teach Milam humility, he would be placed under the authority of the humble Sholosh. To teach him patience, he would be removed to the sleepy temple at Trae Chanos. And to teach him that his elders and betters in the Order had seen a thousand like him come and go, and that he had best learn to behave himself if he ever wished to achieve a more desirable posting, he would be sent packing with no notice and less consideration.

In the end, it was decided that Milam, who had just attained the First Coil of the mysteries, would be sent to "study" under Sholosh, to assist him in his labors for the foreseeable future. Milam had accepted this with good grace, at least publicly, and had taken up his position with Sholosh in good time.

Rapidly, however, he learned the exact nature of the predicament he was in. For it happened that Sholosh was obsessed with divination and astrology, and with reading the stars and omens to pinpoint the location of Anathema when those ancient powers were spat back into the world. Sholosh approached his labors with grave solemnity. After all, his task was one of vigilance for the Realm entire, and the slightest lapse in discipline could have disastrous consequences. The fact that there were diviners and astrologers of much greater expertise and skill laboring toward the same end meant nothing to him; he would carry out his duties as best he could. After all, he reasoned, sometimes the child who sees the flower for the first time is the only one who can see the butterfly nestled within.

Milam, for his part, thought this to be arrant foolishness, and as a result thought Sholosh to be an arrant fool. Thus, it was with less than good grace and spiritual equilibrium that he brought the instruments of divination to the temple's small central garden as the sun rose on an unseasonably chilly morning. Sholosh stood there, wearing nothing more than a plain robe of white cotton and sandals. Milam, for his part, was garbed in a heavy robe surmounted by a wool cloak, and he was shivering. As he pushed the cart with the ceremonial implements into the tiny garden, Milam mentally cursed the old man for demanding a reading outside instead of within the comfortably warm sanctuary. Most days this garden was pleasant enough, and cool, but during the morning it was always quite chilly. Sholosh was fond of observing the stars from its confines, no matter how cold the nights might be, and apparently the old man had seen something in the last night's vigil that had excited him tremendously.

"Is the water pure or salt, Tanak?" Sholosh's voice was clear and surprisingly strong, a stark contrast to his frail form. "Pure works better for this sort of thing."

"I know, Most Learned Sholosh." Milam was taller, bulkier and heavier than his putative mentor. His face was handsome, in a sullen sort of way, and he missed the black locks he had sported before joining the Order. "I have brought you the Five

Instruments of Divination, and should you wish it, I have prepared a sanctified knife, a hare and a chicken so that you may read their entrails if you so desire."

Sholosh waved. "No, no, none of that will be necessary. The signs were quite clear last night. A pity you did not join me, though I understand that it was a cold night for young bones." He chuckled with artless condescension, and Milam found himself irrationally hating the old man for a brilliant moment. Instead of replying, he simply wheeled the cart forward, and bowed.

The cart itself was made from some dark wood not native to the Realm, and it had seen long centuries of use. On its top rested an intricately carved crystal bowl. Next to it was a pitcher of silver, an inkwell of jade, a golden brazier and a rod carved from five different woods so cunningly that it seemed to have been taken whole from a single, miraculous tree. Sholosh examined the items, clucked to himself, and then selected the silver pitcher. Chanting quietly, he poured the bowl full to the brim with clear water. Milam joined in the chanting half-heartedly, which drew a raised eyebrow from his mentor.

When the bowl was full, Sholosh pointed to the wooden rod. "Take it, Milam. It's time you participated in this."

"I would not dare to presume, Most Learned. I am untrained in the arts of divination, and would not dare interfere with your scrying."

"You are also quite certain that I am an ancient fool, and that all this is the fantasy of an old man who has spent too long on the Wheel." There was steel in Sholosh's voice now. "That may be. But for the moment, unworthy one, I am still Most Learned, and you are my student. Take the wooden rod."

"Yes, master," Milam mumbled sullenly, and reached for it. Before he could take it in his hand, Sholosh caught his wrist in a grip like a circle of steel. Try as he might, Milam could not move his arm a hair's breadth, and unthinkingly drew back his other hand as if to strike.

"That would be very foolish," Sholosh said softly. "Very foolish indeed. I have walked my path far longer than you have been alive, you silly boy, and you have not learned all of your lessons well. Now," and he adopted a more pedantic tone, "before I let you do this, let us see if you are worthy to attempt divination. We shall see how well you heed your studies. The wooden rod before you—what is its purpose?"

"It is the wood that binds the world, that draws life up from the earth and light down from the sky." Milam gave the answer perfunctorily, but Sholosh seemed satisfied and released his wrist. Wincing, Milam took up the cylinder of wood and gazed at it. Apart from its unique composition, it seemed quite ordinary. A swift blow to the back of his hand brought his attention back to the present, and he tried to look contrite as Sholosh quizzed him further.

"So much for the wood, aimless one. Now, what of the water?"

"It is the sea that holds secrets, and which gives birth to mystery on the shore."

"You might have studied after all. The bowl?"

"Air, which brings whispers to the ear, and which shrouds the world."

"Very good. Now perform the ritual."

Milam bowed his head, in part to hide the look of disdain on his face. Apparently he had successfully hidden it from Sholosh, as the old man was smiling. "As you wish, Most Learned," was all Milam could trust himself to say. He took the bowl, into which a long-dead craftsman had painstakingly etched the shape of a map of the Realm, and rang it five times. Ripples formed in the water, and they did not subside even after Milam once again laid the rod down on the cart.

"Ah, superb." Sholosh's voice was wry, as if he had expected this result all along. "You do have some talent after all. Tell me, then, what comes next?"

By way of reply, the younger priest once again took up the rod and held it to the brazier. "Fire, which illuminates mystery, and devours that which has been hidden." The wood smoldered, and Milam quenched it in the still-rippling water. Ash washed from the stick floated to the bowl's surface and danced in patterns. Against his better judgment, Milam found himself leaning closer, peering at them in an attempt to make sense of the ever-shifting patterns they made. "What does it mean, Most Learned?"

Sholosh's face split in a wide grin. "Ah, so you do care! There is hope for you yet, young one. Now, pay careful attention to the patterns on the water. Do not attempt to make sense of them. Let them explain themselves to you. Make no effort. *Accept.*"

Milam nodded, and tried to still his racing thoughts. Never before had he taken part in a divination, and now the results promised to be spectacular. No doubt, he would be called upon to explain what he had seen, perhaps before the throne of the Mouth of Peace herself! He would be called back from this dreadful posting in honor, and never see Trae Chanos again. Smiling, he looked down on the bowl.

To his horror, the waters stilled, and the ashes sank. He looked up, and his eyes met Sholosh's.

"Well?" the elder priest asked quietly. "What did you see?"

"I saw..." Milam's voice trailed off into nothingness under the Most Learned's gaze. "I saw nothing."

Sholosh nodded. "Good. You admit your failure. Why is this, do you think?"

"My thoughts were of myself, Most Learned." There was a note of genuine humility in his tone, which surprised him. "I did not see what the ashes held."

"Fortunately, I did." He smiled warmly, and Milam felt his spirits rise. "You are a quick study, and you have taken the first step on an important road. But for the nonce, you have journeyed far enough. Give me the last instrument." Wordlessly, the young Immaculate gave him the inkwell.

"Do you know why we are performing this divination, student?"

"No, Learned One."

"If you had observed the stars with me last night, you would know. They speak plainly; soon the Wyld Hunt must ride again."

"Another abomination is born?"

The old man nodded. "I am afraid it is true. And so the ink, which is the darkness that follows in Anathema's wake, will show us where this abomination will rear its head." With infinite care, he unstopped the ink bottle and let a single drop fall into the water. Immediately it began to dart back and forth, looking like nothing so much as a tadpole created from the stuff of night.

Milam watched, fascinated, and Sholosh watched Milam. "What will it do?" he asked curiously. "I confess to never having seen this before."

"That is because until now you could not be bothered with the old fool's foolishness. Remember that before you surrender to your pride again; you know very little, but knowing how little you know is the greatest wisdom you can achieve. Now, if all goes well, the ink will find the spot where the Anathema will rise, so that we can call forth the Hunt to descend upon it in fury and wrath. Keep a sharp eye. This is no time for thoughts of yourself."

"Of course not, Learned One." As Milam watched, the droplet of ink spun faster and faster, then suddenly turned and slowly made for the bowl's side.

"That is it, yes. Watch where it strikes the crystal," murmured Sholosh. "Can you see it?"

"I think so."

"Do not think. Do!"

Abruptly, the surface of the bowl began to steam. Sholosh jerked back as if he had been scalded.

"Is it supposed to do that, Learned One?" quavered Milam, retreating in alarm.

"I...I do not know. I do know that it has never done this before."

"Learned One!" Milam looked back at the water and gasped in horror. The single dot of ink had been transformed. Where it had been was now a cloud of darkness spreading around the outside of the bowl, and the surface of the water now boiled and hissed.

"This cannot be. This *should* not be! Get back!" Milam threw himself to the ground a second after Sholosh did. An ear-splitting whistle rose from the bowl, followed by a series of sharp retorts. A geyser of black water fountained upwards and the bowl shattered, sending crystal fragments in every direction.

As the water crashed to earth an instant later, the cart toppled as the other Instruments of Divination hit the flagstones of the walkway with a clatter.

Milam broke the silence, scrambling to his feet and exclaiming, "Learned One! Are you hurt?"

Sholosh rose gracefully, and dusted himself off. "I am well, though I fear that we will need to commission new Instruments. These are…no longer suitable."

The younger priest surveyed the devastation. "Yes, I can see that. But did you see what you needed to learn? Did the divination work?"

The older man fixed his student with a gimlet eye. "What I needed to learn? No, this was to discover what the Realm needs to learn. This is horrific, unnatural, a crime against the natural world. What we have seen is the harbinger of evil, Milam. I only hope that we have seen it soon enough to allow us to prepare."

Milam persisted. "But did you see where the evil will come from? Where shall the Wyld Hunt ride?"

Sholosh shook his head sadly. "I almost saw, before the waters went black. But all is not lost. The crystal itself should bear some mark of the power that shattered it. If we can rebuild the bowl, we can see from whence the evil came, and arm ourselves with that knowledge."

"But, Most Learned," Milam said with dismay, "the bowl is broken, the pieces scattered all across the courtyard. The task is hopeless!"

"Then you had best begin it quickly, yes?" said Sholosh, and departed into the depths of the temple.

"I knew there was a reason I hated that old man," said Milam to no one in particular, and began picking up pieces of crystal. A second later, he paused and asked of the air, "Prepare for what?"

The wind gave him no answer, and no comfort, either.

"How goes the work?"

Tanak Milam did not turn around. He sat, cross-legged

on a reed mat, before a low wooden table that had been transported to the garden for this very purpose. On the table sat a partially reconstructed crystal bowl, and around it were various fragments. The shards ranged in size from tiny slivers to pieces the size of a man's thumb, and they were painstakingly arranged from smallest to largest. "It goes well, Most Learned. If you will grant me another four days, I believe I will be able to complete the reconstruction of the bowl."

"We do not have four days." Sholosh glided into the room, his strides noiseless as always. "Your progress is excellent, but simple excellence is not enough."

"I am doing my best, Most Learned," Milam snapped, a bit peevishly.

"I am quite certain you are." Sholosh strode over next to where his student sat and folded his legs underneath himself to sit. "You do good work, I think. What are you using to hold it together?"

Milam gestured to a pot and brush at the end of the table. "One of the acolytes makes glue from snails he catches here. I don't understand it, but it works, so long as you don't pour water on the seams that you have joined." He grinned briefly. "I, at least, do not think we'll be doing that again."

The elder priest shook his head, smiling. "I think not, at least not with this bowl." Abruptly, he sobered. "Your work is very important, you know."

"I know. Have you sent word yet to the Mouth of Peace of the vision we were shown?"

Sholosh stood, shook his head to the negative, and began pacing past carefully tended trees and the precisely minded flowers.

"I have not, and I will not until you finish your labors. The Mouth of Peace is wise and learned, but she is wise and learned enough to demand proof. Even an Immaculate of the Fourth Coil, an august and noble personage such as myself," and at that he chuckled, "may be required to bring forth evidence supporting his claims in her presence. I would hope that other diviners, astrologers and sages saw the same thing that we did—surely something so potent, so dangerous could not have passed by unnoticed—but one takes no chances in matters like this. No, when we go before the Mouth of Peace, we shall do so with all our arguments in perfect harmony, our evidence in undeniable display."

"And if we are still not believed?"

Sholosh stopped, looked over his shoulder, and affected a beatific expression. "Why, then we raise our voices."

Milam burst out laughing, and Sholosh sketched a deep bow. "You honor me with your laughter. I shall leave you to your task, and make provision for our journey."

The younger priest turned and half-rose to his feet. "Our?"

Sholosh nodded. "Our. You'll be coming with me. You will of course report what you have seen, corroborating my story, and you will bear and care for the bowl that you reconstruct. It is nothing less than fitting."

"Thank you, Learned One."

The old man shrugged. "Do not thank me. I do not do this for you. I do this for us all." And with that, he departed, leaving Milam to run through an entire series of breathing exercises in order to be calm enough to take up his labors once more.

It was a bare six hours later when a new acolyte brought word to Most Learned and Venerable Hai Sholosh in his chambers that he should hurry to the garden. The acolyte, who could not have been more than a dozen years of age, was as insistent as he dared to be, and once had the effrontery to grab Sholosh's hand in an attempt to pull him along.

Sholosh, perhaps wisely, gently removed his hand from the boy's grip, giving him a reassuring glance as the acolyte turned pale with terror realizing the enormity of what he had done, and strode unhurriedly toward the garden.

The sight that met his eyes as he reached his destination was not entirely unexpected, though it saddened him nonetheless. Milam lay sprawled on the mat, his form unmoving and his fingers curled into claws. The skin of his hands and arms was stained pitch black, as if he had drawn all the darkness the scrying bowl had contained into himself. On his face was a look of wretched agony, his eyes wide and staring.

Sholosh dismissed the boy and knelt next to the corpse. It was cold, far colder than it had any right to be, and when he manipulated Milam's arms to grant him a posture of peaceful repose, the dead man's limbs were as stiff as if they were frozen.

Sholosh frowned. While Milam's self-absorption and petulance had made him a less than perfect member of the Order, he had begun to show promise of late. The successful divination, odd though it had been, had sparked something within the man which, if given time, might have made him a worthy Immaculate.

But that, it seemed, was not to be. Behind him, Sholosh could hear other monks gathering in silence, all curious but none willing to shatter decorum by asking what had occurred. They, at least, were disciplined.

Sighing, Sholosh put forth a hand to close the cadaver's eyes. Doing so would enable Milam's spirit to rest more easily, and Sholosh did not want the Underworld gaining any kind of a foothold within the temple walls during his tenure here.

Abruptly, he jerked his hand away as if it had been burned. Looking down into Milam's dead eyes, he realized with a shock that a message had been left there, and that it had been left for him to deliver. In elegant and tiny characters, an unknown hand had scribed a warning in characters of blood on Milam's eyes. The message was simple enough, a combination of dire threat and ominous prophecy, and it commanded its reader to bear word of its existence to the Mouth of Peace.

Sholosh committed it to memory, then closed Milam's eyes for the last time. He stood, and turned to the gathered monks. "Postulants Surus, Ishi, Lofol, my brothers, I would be most grateful if you would take the body of our brother Milam and dispose of it by fire. Do not look at it after the flames have caught, and use cedar wood for his pyre. Afterwards, cleanse yourselves before you return to prayer. Beyond that, I most humbly require that you forget the tale of what you have seen ere you leave this place. That is all."

Arms folded across his chest, Sholosh stood and watched

impassively as the crowd filed out, decorously. Three monks came forward to lay their hands on the corpse and remove it for burning, and each gasped wordlessly when they felt its chill. Walking in effortless lockstep, they ferried Milam inside, while deeper within the building voices called out for pitch, for torches, and for the purifying wood of the cedar tree.

Alone once again, Sholosh turned his attention to the table. In its center sat the rebuilt bowl, but instead of clear crystal, it had been stained entirely black.

Gingerly, the priest lifted the bowl and made a small sound of surprise. It, too, shared the chill of Milam's corpse.

Frowning, he examined it. On the whole, the reconstruction had been a success. Pieces were missing here and there, but the world was clearly recognizable even in the fractured crystal. *Here* was Lord's Crossing, and *there* Arjuf, and further toward the edges of the bowl the familiar shapes of the coastline and forests of the Threshold.

Suddenly, pain stabbed through the ring finger of his left hand. Resisting the urge to drop the bowl, Sholosh instead cradled it in his right hand while he examined the source of the pain. It was a cut, no doubt inflicted by one of the rebuilt bowl's jagged edges, and it was perfectly semicircular in shape. Even as he watched, a single drop of blood welled up from it, but no more.

Moving very slowly, Sholosh brought his injured hand over the bowl. "Perhaps," he whispered to himself, "perhaps this is what it really wants."

The drop of blood fell. As it struck, the bowl rang like a bell, tolling for uncounted dead. A charnel smell filled the air, and the entire bowl turned the color of blood. Then, as quickly as they had begun, the scent faded and the bowl's chiming ceased.

Frustrated, Sholosh set the bowl back down. It was only then that he noticed that in the midst of the crimson was now a single spot of black.

To the untrained eye, it would been nothing at all, or perhaps a chip in the much-abused crystal. But to Sholosh, it was a banner of darkness proudly waved, a sign that something foul was brewing in the wilds between Great Fork and Sijan.

"But there's nothing between Great Fork and Sijan," he said, puzzled. "Curious."

With steps that seemed entirely too slow, Sholosh paced down the temple's corridors to its venerable and overstuffed library. Various of the Immaculates studying or scribing within made a tremendous show of not looking at him, and he returned the favor by ignoring them as he searched for a map of sufficient detail to unravel the mystery. With surprising impatience he went down the long shelves of scrolls, passing a thousand years of collected wisdom in a heartbeat. The space that had been devoted to maps and cartography was now filled with the Immaculate Texts penned by one Sullen Tiger of Yane, as well as scrolls of interpretation of his works. Of the maps, however, there was no sign.

Finally, one of the younger initiates approached him. She was short, with a round face and eyes too close together to be beautiful. "May I help you, Most Learned One?" she inquired hesitantly.

"You can make me more learned by telling me where I can find a map," he snapped, and instantly regretted it. "You have my apologies. That was unworthy. Still, the library seems to have been rearranged since my last visit. Who authorized such a thing?"

"It was," and she hesitated, "a project of the Most Studious Milam Tanak. He was quite certain that this would be easier."

"Of course it was," Sholosh said softly. "Would you do me the honor of showing me where I might find maps more easily today? Then leave this place and rest, for your labors tomorrow will be heavy."

Her face showed puzzlement. "Tomorrow, Most Learned One?"

He nodded significantly. "Tomorrow you begin putting everything back where it was."

Much later, Sholosh sat on a wooden bench in the library, alone. Stumpy, fat candles burned in every corner. In the shadows cast by their dancing flames, the priest could almost see the forms of his teachers and predecessors watching him, waiting to see what he did.

The map that young Taphat had led him to had been made over three centuries earlier, so he could no longer be sure of its absolute accuracy. Villages died and borders changed, after all, and a thriving metropolis of a hundred years gone might be little more than towers poking from sand today. The fate of the city of Thorn, which in living memory had been overwhelmed by the forces of the Abyss, served as mute reminder of that inescapable fact.

The work itself was beautiful, and Sholosh suspected that more than a little Essence had been spent in long-forgotten ways to make the colors more radiant, the penstrokes of the mountains sharper, the picture itself more real. Gazing down on it, Sholosh could imagine himself a bird, soaring unimaginably high over the landscape with the entire Realm spread out below. But, alas, he was no bird, and he had a task before him.

The area between Sijan and Great Fork was mostly barren of civilization and its trappings, a hodge-podge of small villages and farmers' steadings that had been passed down from time out of mind. Careful searching, however, revealed a single name; a small hamlet that had been immortalized where its neighbors had been ignored. Next to the village's name was the symbol that denoted an Immaculate shrine, and nothing else. Roads, Guild caravan routes—nothing passed anywhere near the place.

"Qut Toloc." He pronounced the name carefully, as if saying it too loud might conjure something untoward. "A small temple, a small town—nothing more. What could possibly emerge from that? This is someone else's riddle to unravel, I fear." Carefully, he rolled the map up, then called for an acolyte to bring him parchment and ink so that he might write to the Mouth of Peace herself and advise her of what he had seen. "Younger legs than mine will have to make that journey, I think," he said, and waited.

Later, when he had finished the missive and chosen an initiate to bear it to the Palace Sublime, Hai Sholosh was informed that the divination bowl had miraculously crumbled to a pile of red dust, which had been swept up by the wind and mingled with the smoke from Milam's pyre. While no one could claim to have seen this miracle directly, everyone who knew of it agreed that it was a very bad sign.

Upon due reflection, Hai Sholosh decided that he agreed with them.

Chapter Three

"Tracks?" asked the Prince of Shadows. Ratcatcher shook his head mutely, then spread his arms wide to indicate that he was at a loss. The Prince looked at him narrowly. "You're doing your best to make me regret the geis, aren't you? I warn you, now is most emphatically not the time to test my patience."

Ratcatcher bowed low and backed away, perturbed that his motives were so plainly transparent. Up ahead, Pandeimos thrashed about in the woods ineffectively, cursing the damnable trees at every step. The corpse Pandeimos's spirit inhabited had been clumsy when he'd first taken control of it, and time and hot weather had done nothing to improve its coordination.

"Pfaugh," the man spat when Ratcatcher joined him, and Ratcatcher's nose wrinkled at the smell. "There's not a trail here made by anything bigger than a squirrel. Tell the Prince that this Wren may as well be a bird, for all that we're going to find sign of him here. Damned if I know why we even stopped to look for him."

Ratcatcher looked curiously at him. Pandeimos was a heavyset man, well-muscled and broad of feature. His hands were huge and his beard was black, and he had long since removed his helmet because the steady rain dripped relentlessly down inside it. Like the others, he wore armor that had been lacquered black, though his was styled so as to make it seem as if he were some sort of nightmare beetle, stalking the land ponderously. The rain had washed his hair over his forehead and into his eyes, and it was with a half-hearted gesture that he brushed it back.

"Cold fire, I forgot you were under geis not to speak. I'll tell him myself." With that, the larger man shuffled off downhill, cursing once again as he moved from under the canopy of the leaves into the open downpour. Downslope toward the creek, the Prince sat astride his horse like a statue carved from ice. The rain seemed to shy from touching him. Boneshadow was down by the creek, doing something spectacularly ineffective, and Shamblemerry stood and tended the horses.

On the whole, it was not an auspicious beginning to their pursuit of Wren.

With a disgusted sound, he retraced Pandeimos's steps, looking to see if the man had missed anything. Privately, he considered the possibility unlikely. The forest floor was thick with leaves and soaked through, and any trace the mysterious fugitive had left would most likely have been washed away by now. As for the forest itself, it was so dense that it would be impossibly easy to miss a single footprint in the undergrowth and gloom. In addition, a nagging voice at the back of his mind warned Ratcatcher that they had no proof that Wren had ever passed this way at all, and that they were wasting precious hours searching for phantoms.

Resolutely, Ratcatcher ignored that voice and pressed further into the wood. The trees grew closer and closer together until he could scarcely fit between them, and overhead the canopy of leaves was thick enough that the furious rain sounded like a gentle rhythm played upon a child's drum. From down the hill he heard Shamblemerry calling his name, but he ignored it and pressed on, in search of he knew not what. There was something here. He could feel it. The signs at the Howe had been too fresh for the mysterious Wren to have vanished so completely. Something else was at work here. He could feel it.

Frowning, he tore vines out of his way, the stink of fresh sap in his nostrils. Underfoot, dead leaves swallowed his footsteps. An owl, or something that looked very much like one, peered at him from its perch in a tree trunk and warned him against going farther. He fixed it with a stare, and felt mildly gratified when it blinked, twice, and then turned its gaze elsewhere. It was a small victory, but tonight he'd take what he could get.

"This is pointless," he grumbled, low lest someone hear him and bear the tale back to the Prince. "This forest hasn't been disturbed in decades. Wren couldn't have slipped through here without an axe, let alone do it so neatly." From afar, he heard his name called again. Resigned to his failure, he turned and headed back. The trees thinned rapidly as he did so, and Ratcatcher could not shake the feeling that the woods were glad to see him go. Indeed, the vines that had barred his path into the woods were now entirely gone. For a moment he thought he'd simply hacked them to the ground, but a quick glance showed that there were no tatters of greenery there, either. They had simply vanished.

"Aha," he breathed. "You've overplayed your hand, whatever you are." Crouched low to the ground, he ran his fingertips along the soil. His eyes darted left, right, looking for anything—a footprint, a scrap of cloth, anything—that would betray Wren's passage. The others, he noticed distantly, were all watching him. Let them, he thought. This was his hunt now. This was what he had been made for.

Right at the edge of the trees, he found it. Pressed into the mud was the unmistakable outline of a sandal.

Or rather, half the outline of a sandal. The rest of the print was filled with a gnarled tree root, one that clearly could not have been there when the footprint had been made.

In an instant, it all made sense. The tree could not have been there when the footprint had been made. Therefore, the tree had moved. The whole forest had moved to cover Wren's tracks. Spirits had been at work here, had aided the fugitive, had played the Prince for a fool. Wren had summoned one down at the water's edge to help him, and they'd missed it. But now the evidence was clear. If they could not catch Wren, they could at least bring to heel the spirit that had aided him, and burn answers from it.

Triumphant, he lifted up his head to shout, then let his cry die in his throat as he realized that doing so would be foolish. At the edge of the creek, the Prince and others stood, waiting for him to finish his fool's errand. Shamblemerry was actively calling out halloos, while Pandeimos was having trouble controlling his restive mount. For a moment, Ratcatcher clearly imagined the sight of Pandeimos's horse rearing and dumping the man, armor and all, into the muddy creek, but nothing came of it. With as much dignity as he could muster, he stood and gestured urgently for the Prince and his company to join him, to see what he had discovered.

None of them moved. Through the rain, he could hear snatches of their conversation.

"...being insolent, my prince..."

"...was over that ground myself and didn't see a damn thing..."

"...could use the extra steed..."

As for the Prince himself, he sat stock-still in his saddle. His helm was tucked under his left arm, and his right hand held the reins loosely. His eyes sought Ratcatcher's, challenged him, commanded him.

Yes, my prince, he thought, and headed down the hill.

The Prince was not smiling when Ratcatcher reached him. Shamblemerry and the rest were, but they had positioned themselves strategically so that the Prince could not see their smirks. Boneshadow had gone so far as to replace his helmet so as to stifle his chortling, and booming, choked sounds echoed from beneath his helm whenever laughter got the better of him.

Ratcatcher found none of this amusing. Bowing extremely low, he simply turned and gestured to the spot where he'd found the priest's track. Hopeful that he'd gotten his point across, he loped a few steps up the slope and listened for the sound of the Prince following him.

Instead, he heard the rain.

Slowly, Ratcatcher turned. The Prince had not moved. Behind him, the other three were helpless in the grip of hilarity. Grimly, Ratcatcher lifted one foot off the ground and pointed to the sole, then knelt and indicated the ground. Slowly, he turned and pointed very deliberately at the spot where he'd found the footprint. Desperately hoping his face would not betray his true emotions, he knelt, then looked up at the Prince.

The others were helpless prisoners of hilarity. Shamblemerry was making rough gestures in the air in imitation of Ratcatcher's rough capering while the other two egged her on.

The Prince, however, merely sat stock-still. Gradually the laughter faded, until the only sounds were the rain and the thunder. Still, the Prince did not move. Miserable, Ratcatcher knelt before him.

Then, wordlessly, the Prince urged his mount up the hill. Ratcatcher scrambled to his feet and staggered after him, terrified that the Prince's mount would obliterate the footprint and thus leave him empty-handed before his Prince.

The Prince was waiting when Ratcatcher reached the spot where he'd first found the footprint. He had dismounted, and bore a look of extreme displeasure on his face. "Well?" was all he said.

Ratcatcher bowed again, then gestured emphatically toward where he'd seen the footprint. The Prince nodded, then leaned forward to examine it. He clucked to himself under his breath, turned to look at Ratcatcher, then peered at the ground again. "Fascinating," he finally said. "You have done a remarkable job of finding a telltale root."

Horrified, Ratcatcher stepped forward and stared at where the footprint had been. It was gone, replaced by a swollen and twisted tree root that, by all evidence, had been there for years. Any sign of any footstep other than his own was gone, grown over in the few moments he'd spent playing the clown to lure the Prince up here.

In the sound of the wind through the trees, he distinctly heard soft laughter.

"I do hope you have a very good reason for showing me this tree root, Ratcatcher. Does it perhaps remind you of your mother? A favorite pet? Shall I guess, or will you act out charades?"

"My liege, there was a footprint here a minute ago, I swear it!"

Ratcatcher's words echoed in sudden silence. The rain seemed to stop, the thunder to hold its breath. The Prince looked up, eyes blazing, and a stab of fear gnawed at Ratcatcher's guts.

"You spoke," the Prince said, his anima flaring out behind him like tattered dragon's wings. "You actually dared speak. And why? To lie to me." He advanced a slow step, shaking his head sadly. "I think, Ratcatcher, you have made a terrible mistake."

Ratcatcher was instantly aware of his danger. Tendrils of the Prince's anima wrapped around and caressed him, their touch burning cold against his skin. The Prince himself was too calm, too peaceful for his intention to be anything but murder.

"No, my liege." Shuddering, he dropped to one knee and bowed his head, exposing his neck. "If you disbelieve me, then take my head. But I swear to you as I swore in the tombs of the dead gods that I saw the mark of a man's foot here, and that the very trees of the forest work against us here."

"You would dare make that oath?" The Prince's voice held faint amazement. "The dead gods hear when such things are sworn. They know who honors them and who forswears them. They *listen*, Ratcatcher. Know this: If you have lied to me now to save your wretched skin, there will be a reckoning that will last ten thousand years. The ones you have named do not take oaths sworn in their name lightly."

"I swear that oath, my prince." Ratcatcher closed his eyes, felt the touch of the Prince's mace at the back of his neck. Along his arms, the hairs stood on end, and it was all he could do to avoid fleeing. Then suddenly, the pressure was gone. The Prince stepped away, and he could hear rain falling once again.

"Get up, Ratcatcher." The Prince's voice was tired. "Get up, get on your horse, and get out of my sight. I'll find you when I need you. For now, though, it is best that you are far, far away from me."

"Yes, my liege," he mumbled. He pulled himself erect, not daring to meet the Prince's eyes, and walked stiffly over to where his horse waited. The others watched him in silence, and for that he was grateful. They had seen this before, a favorite dashed to humility. They also knew that in the Prince's service, the humble could rise very quickly, and it was best not to make enemies who might one day return as their betters.

They also knew precisely how unlikely this was, and in

their minds they thought of Ratcatcher as if he were already among the dead. And so as he rode north, only the Prince stared after him, and he did so with narrowed and suspicious eyes.

"Go," he said, "and catch a bird for me."

Chapter Four

Upon due reflection, Wren decided that he was in trouble.

He stood on an open road in the middle of a pleasant and sunny day. Behind him, the road stretched up and over a low hill, and beyond it into the distance. Ahead of him, he could see a distant haze where Nexus should be, and the blue ribbon of a river scrolled in and out of view. Trees dotted the landscape in a most picturesque fashion, and the sky was a pleasant shade of blue. A soft wind rolled down from the hilltop, ruffling the sleeves of Wren's robes and making him wish, irrationally, that he had a kite.

Indeed, the only element in the scene that was not suitable for preserving as a landscape or tapestry was the clutch of armed men standing on the road perhaps a hundred feet from where Wren stood, leaning upon a makeshift staff. They wore belted red tunics and loose blue trews, and bore a motley collection of swords, maces and less identifiable weapons. It was quite clear that they were officially waiting for Wren, and just as clear that they intended to do him harm as soon as they were finished waiting.

Wren counted. There were five of them, all looking reasonably accustomed to causing mayhem. He saw no bows, though, and nothing that indicated that they'd had formal training in anything beyond a basic understanding of how to use a sword. This, he thought, was a good sign, or at least as good a one as might be expected under current circumstances.

Experimentally, he took a step back. The band in front of him took a single step forward. Had he been watching it from afar, Wren would have deemed it comical, something out of a puppeteer's catalog of stock scenes. In real life, it was less amusing, though it gave him another measure of the men facing him. They were, beyond a doubt, amateurs.

Wren exhaled sharply. There was nothing for it, then. If he retreated, they'd pursue, and finding a route around them offered no guarantee that he'd not find others like them. The bull had lowered its horns; it remained for him to grasp them.

Accordingly, he fixed a cheery smile on his face and strode forward. "You look ridiculous, you know," he said, and advanced as if the warriors before him were no more substantial than air. Glances darted back and forth between the men. They had not expected this, and were unsure of how to deal with it. Meanwhile, Wren continued to advance.

"Furthermore, I must say that you look quite nattily turned out for bandits," he prattled. "Did you rob a traveling haberdasher?" He spread his arms wide, to show that he was unarmed. "What could you possibly want with a poor initiate of the Order, though? My robes don't even match your trews."

Uncertain, the ruffians took a step back. One, presumably the leader, half-stepped and was half-shoved forward. She held a thick oak stave, which she thumped into her palm nervously, and on her head was a red turban. "We're not bandits," she said, almost apologetically.

"Oh?" Wren smiled pleasantly. "Then you must be Official City Gardeners, here in the name of the Elemental Dragons to tend the flowers along the road. Your labors seem to be bearing fruit. I congratulate you."

"We're here to take a toll for using this road."

"Ah. So you're uncommon bandits, then."

The woman looked flustered. "We're toll collectors. Now halt, and you won't get hurt," she finally said, then "Halt!" again, as Wren refused to stop. "I'm warning you," was her next pronouncement, and she dropped into a guard position. Behind her, the men readied their weapons.

"Don't be ridiculous. This is Nexus territory, and you're not wearing Nexus city guard uniforms. If the city guard knew you were extorting from travelers this close to the city, they'd have your guts on a string. Do be sensible, and just get out of my way." Wren was within a few steps, and showed no sign of slowing.

The woman jabbed her staff at him, and took another step back. "We're legitimate toll collectors for this road."

Wren stopped and yawned. "Nonsense. At best you're brigands in uniform, at worst you're lousy liars. Besides, I'm a penniless monk of the Immaculate Order, so what you think you're going to get from me by way of a toll escapes me." He let his walking stick fall to the ground. "Not that you could take anything from me I didn't want you to, in any case."

The taunt had the desired effect. With a shout, the woman brought her staff around in a low sweep designed to catch Wren across the shins and knock him to the ground. He leapt over it easily, landing a kick to her chin in the process. Her head snapped back and she stumbled backward, losing her turban. The others charged forward, yelling hoarse battle cries that Wren refused to take the time to try to understand.

One thrust high at him with a sword. He ducked forward and grabbed the man's sword arm, then straightened and flipped the man over his shoulder. A thump and a yelp behind him told Wren he'd managed to trip up yet another attacker. He spun to the side, sparing a half-second to land a blow to the leader's ribs, then ducked away from a wild swipe with a mace. The mace wielder, a short woman with a long braid of brown hair down her back, swung again. Wren caught the handle of the weapon in his right hand, then twisted it before his assailant had a chance to let go. The sound of something snapping filled the air, and suddenly she was stumbling backwards, clutching a ruined wrist and a hand that dangled at an odd angle.

Wren turned. A sword thrust cut the air where he had been, as a bearded man with a curved blade chopped downward in hopes of landing a crippling blow. Wren extended his arm, palm flat, and struck the side of the blade as it descended. The sudden shock jarred the swordsman into dropping his blade, and in that instant Wren landed a pair of side kicks to his gut. The man whoofed as the air was knocked out of him, and he sat down heavily in the middle of the road. Behind him, another maceman circled left, ready to try his luck if Wren's attention wavered. Wren matched strides with him, keeping an eye out for the man he'd thrown, who even now was groggily climbing to his feet.

The maceman saw his ally recovering and grinned, bright teeth in a dark beard. He feinted left, then right, trying to buy time for his friend to pull himself together thoroughly enough to attack Wren from behind. When footsteps sounded behind him, though, Wren simply dropped to the ground. The sword whistled harmlessly overhead, and as the mace-wielding brigand rushed forward, Wren spun on his heel, delivering an elbow to the swordsman's knee. The man crumpled forward, onto Wren's back. He landed heavily, and Wren staggered for a moment, but then finished his spin and straightened up. The swordsman flew forward and hit his friend with the mace. Both went down in a tumble of limbs, and Wren distributed kicks where appropriate as he strode past.

The leader was attempting to stand again as Wren reached her, and had gotten so far as her hands and knees. Wren considered his options for a second, then kicked her under the chin. She collapsed with a satisfying thud, the staff rolling from her grip.

Wren looked around. The woman whose wrist he'd shattered had run. The others were all down, and blessed with the sense not to attempt to rise. He briefly pondered killing them, so they'd not afflict other travelers, but thought better of it.

"It's too beautiful a day," he said. "Pick yourselves up when you can, and run. I might be taking this road again, and you don't want to be here when I do."

He heard a single moan, which he took as assent, and followed the road into Nexus.

As he headed down the gentle slope toward the city, Wren reflected that it was highly unlikely that these bandits were nothing more than a cluster of brigands trying to capitalize on the road traffic to Nexus. Still, the presence of the uniformed thugs so close to the bustling, eminently civilized city was mildly troubling. It was yet another sign that things were unraveling all over. Still, that was more the concern of the city fathers of Nexus, if they could be bothered to look up from their counting-tables and scales. His duty, and that of his fellows, was protecting the world itself.

That, he told himself, was why he'd followed his circular path to Nexus. After his flight from Rhadanthos's domain, he'd gone southwest for several days, then turned west until he struck the Rolling River. Men he avoided during this time, and beasts he only saw when he trapped them for his supper. Spirits he spoke to when they seemed benign, and he'd bargained with one to send a message through intermediaries to the Palace Sublime. It has cost him his pack, but he felt little need of it here. The land was rich enough for him to survive without it, and the nights warm enough that he needed no blanket. A few times he saw what looked to be evidence of barbarian raiding parties, but he felt disinclined to investigate, instead redoubling his own pace.

Once he found the stream, he followed it north until it met the Yellow River at Great Forks. This was his signal to take passage on a barge that would take him downstream to Lookshy. There he booked swift river passage down the Yanaze toward Nexus where no doubt the Most Illustrious and Illuminated Chejop Kejak had a message and a new task waiting for him. Three days' travel outside the city, he'd disembarked with the intention of walking the rest of the way. His head told him that it was to avoid the possibility of being seen at the docks, but his heart knew that he simply wanted to avoid his next assignment as long as possible. While the two debated, he strayed south from the river, and found himself approaching the city from an entirely unexpected direction.

Still, he reflected, it was indeed a beautiful day, and he was alive, and Kejak's missions were infinitely more fascinating than sitting in an Immaculate scriptorium, copying out the Texts until he saw them in his dreams.

In that, at least, he was content, and he might even have considered himself happy as he strode down toward the river.

Chapter Five

Thousands of silkworms would have wept, were they able, had they seen the chamber in which Chejop Kejak received his visitors. Silk curtains of an envious shade of green hung in every alcove, and silk cushions were strewn carelessly across the polished marble floor with its cunning inlay of jade. Crystal chimes hung from the azurite dome of the ceiling in imitation of the stars and planets; each was hung on a silken thread and repositioned daily by meticulous, fearful slaves. Kejak read the stars from this chamber on occasion, and the punishments visited on those who misaligned his makeshift orrery were terrible and swift. Equally spaced around the room were five braziers made from hammered bronze. Each stood as tall as a man, and had been lovingly fashioned into the shape of a dragon. Each had gemstones for eyes and had been constructed so that fragrant smoke curled from its mouth. So detailed was the craftsmanship that many a visitor swore that they seemed to be resting rather than wrought, and glanced nervously at them on occasion for reassurance that they had not moved.

In the center of this room sat Chejop Kejak and his guest, each seated upon a pillow that matched the blue of the ceiling and was embroidered with an intricate geometric pattern. Slaves hovered around them, offering wine, sherberts, and sweetmeats. After a moment, each would swoop away, to be replaced a few minutes later by another. All moved silently and none spoke; Kejak had removed their tongues years previously, so they would not disturb his meditations. Like wraiths, they vanished behind the silk curtains noiselessly, and barely a ripple of silk marked their passage.

Kejak sat on the higher cushion, as was his right by rank. He wore robes of blue silk, tied at the waist with a green sash, and on his wrists were bracelets of copper and white gold. He was tall and slender and sat at perfect ease in the lotus position, his head high and his gaze clear. Those who had seen him compared his face to that of a hawk, and there was some truth to it, for his eyes were bright and his face narrow. A caste mark was prominent on his high forehead, and on occasion he brushed it absently with his hand. What remained of his hair was steel-gray, and it hung over his left shoulder in a ponytail wrapped in a device made from black leather and silver beads. His hands were long ones, with fingers that a harpist or a surgeon might have put to good use. One hand held a glass of wine, the other nothing at all, and he was smiling.

Opposite him sat his guest, whose features were coarser and whose hair was darker. Shajah Holok was a burly, heavyset man, whose hands were callused with labor in the fields and whose scarred arms showed that his toil had not been easy. He wore simpler robes than Kejak, linen instead of silk, and his bare feet still had some road dust on them. Holok's beard was thick and black, and his eyes were equally dark. His visage was that of a mystic, or perhaps a fanatic, and he did not suffer fools gladly. Holok had no wine, but a wooden cup filled with water sat on the stone in front of him, untouched.

"So what is the news?" Kejak's voice was strong and assured. It had power behind it, the confident power of a man who was used to having his voice heeded. The tone of his question indicated that it was not in fact a question; that he already knew everything that Holok would say to him and was simply checking the accuracy of the man's recitation.

Holok grunted. "The news is about what you'd expect. V'neef and Cynis ships setting on each other just out of the harbor at Cherak. Some damn fools off siccing the Wyld Hunt on a wendigo up in the northlands when they've got more pressing problems at home. There's a new crop of acolytes just in, none of them worth a damn. Oh, and this might interest you: There's more Deathlord activity every damned night. I'd swear they're seeding the land with ghosts. They've gotten bold as brass, and they ride to and fro as they please. There's word that they set an ambush for a Wyld Hunt three days south of Nexus, but that's just alehouse rumor."

"It's not an alehouse rumor of the sort we can afford. A great deal of the Wyld Hunt's power is tied up in the fact that everyone knows it is invincible. The inevitability, if you will, that it *will* run its prey to ground, come fire or flood or the next breaking of the world. But now we have a rumor in an alehouse." He unfolded himself and stood, his gaze a thousand miles away.

"It starts like this, it starts small. A rumor in an alehouse, a story that a Wyld Hunt failed. A drunk, or a man pretending to be drunk, staggers to the next inn over and repeats the story. The process repeats. Men bring the story home with them and tell their wives, who gossip it to their lovers and friends. It spreads. It becomes," and he paused to inflect the words with particular bile, "common knowledge."

"So?" Holok took a noisy sip of his water. "Everyone knows. Do you think that will make a difference when the Hunt rides next?"

Kejak shook his head. "Not the next time, or even the time after. But slowly, it becomes part of their lives. They are conditioned to believe that the Hunt is fallible. That it is weak. That there are other powers out there greater than the arm of the Realm. And that, Holok, is where they slip the dagger in."

Holok shook his head. "If you say so. It's just one tale that no one believes, Kejak. You're growing anxious in your old age."

"I'd like to reach an even older one, Holok. That's why I pay attention to these things. Look around you when you leave this place. Look for rot. You'll see it. Our Realm has enemies, and this is the moment they've waited a very long time for. Without the Empress to command their allegiance, the Houses are turning on one another. With the Houses marshalling for strife, the armies and fleets are neglected, and the territories at the borders discover that they like keeping their tax monies home. That's how an empire becomes a memory. What's holding the Empire together, Holok? Tradition, and momentum, and the very few things that the Dragon-Blooded and the dung-on-the-boots peasants can agree on. The fact that the Dragon-Blooded saved us from Anathema. The Order. And the Wyld Hunt. It's flimsy thread to stitch together the fabric of the Realm, but it's what we have to work with. And this little alehouse story of yours is a seamstress's knife."

Holok grunted and shifted on the cushion. "If you say. I'm a simple man, Kejak, and I have been for as long as I've had a beard. If you say the tale's a danger, then I'll see to it that it's stamped out. I'll call out the Hunt and send it past every tavern in town, and see who dares to mock it then. I'll find the men who spread the tale and have them exposed as frauds, and denounce the notion of the Hunt's fallibility from every altar for forty leagues. What I am, is the Order's. You know that. But I don't see the danger in this."

"No, you wouldn't." Kejak's back was to Holok, and he did not turn as he spoke. "Fortunately, it is enough that I did. Your suggestions are excellent. I expect you to implement them upon your return. You are a craftsman, Holok, and the Order is the better for having you help shape it."

"You honor me—" Holok began. Kejak put forth a hand to stay his thanks.

"It is nothing more or less than your due. Now, what other news do you have for me?"

"Little enough worth reporting. Salaos prepared a scroll and has long since given it over to your servants."

"Ah, I should have remembered. How is Salaos?"

"Well enough, for an ambitious man. Meticulous and clever, but too eager to have my rank by half." Holok snorted, half in amusement. "He thinks he's too clever for his, that's for certain."

"If his ambition fuels his excellence, I am not concerned. Your place is secure, and you at least should well know that. Come, walk with me a while."

"Of course, Kejak." Holok stood and bowed precisely, bending slightly at the waist and deeply at the neck to denote the proper attitude of respect to an honored superior. Kejak returned the bow, inclining only his head as was proper, and gestured his guest forward.

"You honor me," Holok said, and stepped through the curtain. Kejak followed.

A quartet of slaves prostrated themselves as the two men stepped forth into the temple. Kejak ignored them and trod leisurely down the corridor, Holok falling naturally into a position a step behind. The walls they walked past were adorned with mosaics, each depicting a scene from the Order's scriptures. Here the Five Dragons coiled protectively around the throne of the Realm; there the Empress personally slew a chaos-spawned monster with a howdah of Fair Folk lords on its back. Each was painstakingly crafted from sparkling glass and gemstones, the result of decades of labor by dedicated, devout craftsmen. Such was the skill that created them that, with the cunning placement of lights, the figures in glass and stone seemed to move as one walked past them, bringing the Order's doctrine to shining life.

Kejak strode past them without a second glance. Off in the distance, a gong sounded, calling monks to their chores. The sound of chanting mixed with the distant shouts of monks at their daily martial-arts regimens, off in one of the courtyards. Now and then a gong was struck, and the telltale whirring of prayer wheels was omnipresent. Hints of a hundred different types of incense wafted on the breeze, making the air a heady mix of scents.

Holok paused to close his eyes and breathe in the potpourri of offerings, then realized that Kejak had not slowed his pace. With as much dignity as he could muster, he hurried down the hall in pursuit. A handful of acolytes, heads bowed respectfully, walked past in the opposite direction and then burst into giggles. Holok made a mental note to have them reprimanded, then abandoned all pretense and pelted after Kejak's receding figure. Belatedly, he found himself wondering if this was exactly what Kejak had intended.

Holok finally caught up to his host at the entrance to a massive sanctuary, pentagonal in shape and curiously unadorned. Rows of priests of all ranks sat on prayer mats, cross-legged. Some chanted, some meditated. Most had their eyes closed. Kejak motioned Holok to hush, and gazed out across the room.

"Why have you brought me here, Kejak?" Holok's voice was a harsh whisper that carried. Across the room, heads snapped up in surprise.

Kejak shook his head. "First Coil priests. You'd think they would have mastered themselves sufficiently to ignore even your whispers, Holok." A few upturned faces showed embarrassment, and Kejak smiled. "Ah, they will learn. They will have to,"

"Yes, yes, very good, but I am assuming you didn't call me all the way here to show me that you can impress students." Holok was caught between puzzlement and irritation, but reserved judgment as to which he'd allow free rein. "I do assume there is a point to this?"

"There has been a point to everything I have done for two millennia, Holok. You, of all of us, should know that." Holok's face reddened, but before he could say anything, Kejak smoothly continued. "There is something here I want your opinion on. It troubled the illustrious Mouth of Peace, may her enlightenment shelter us all, and so she sent the problem to me."

Holok's expression demonstrated ample disbelief, but Kejak continued. "The matter troubled me as well, and so I wish your interpretation."

"Of course," Holok said wryly. "I shall be happy to confirm whatever course of action you have already decided upon."

"It's not like that, Holok," Kejak said wearily. "For once, it's not like that." He raised his voice. "Eager Student Hinnah!"

One of the priests chanting in the third row looked up. She was short, and she was round, and she was unlovely. Her ears were large and her mouth was small, and in her eyes Holok could plainly see a fervent, unwavering devotion. In this, she was much like hundreds, if not thousands, of other acolytes Holok had seen over the centuries. He could not possibly imagine how she could be in the slightest way troublesome.

"Arise, Eager Student Hinnah, and approach." Kejak's voice was musical now, cajoling and commanding, and it washed out over the rows of priests. There was magic in that voice; there always had been. Fifteen centuries ago it had been enough to start a war against those ordained by the heavens. It still was a formidable weapon, and Holok found himself idly wondering if it was wasted on these children. But Hinnah had approached and was already speaking, and Holok mentally wrenched himself back to the present.

"—ost Learned Hai Sholosh sent me to the Mouth of Peace with these tidings, Most Enlightened Ones. Having been sent here by the Mouth of Peace, I felt it best to spend time in meditation for guidance regarding my next duty, as I had not been instructed how to proceed."

"An excellent decision, and one demonstrative of your devotion." Kejak's voice was all honey and cream. "It would honor me, Most Eager Student, if you would share with the Most Enlightened Holok what you have shared with me. But first, let us repair to someplace more private, so as to avoid disturbing the meditations of others."

"I would be honored to oblige, Most Enlightened," Hinnah said, and Holok reflected that she almost certainly would be. He heard Kejak murmur something unintelligible, and then the three of them were walking back toward a small, empty chamber that was furnished with wooden benches and nothing more. Kejak entered first, followed by Hinnah. With a scowl Holok brought up the rear and closed the chamber's thick wooden door behind himself.

And so Holok listened as the young initiate told a story of prophecy and murder, and of the other strange events at the temple at Trae Chanos. She recited it in singsong fashion, chanting it as if she were chanting passages from the Immaculate Texts. For all she knew, Holok reflected, she could be.

Eventually, the recitation ended. Hinnah looked up at Holok, a little breathless. "That is all, I think. At least, that is all Most Learned Hai Sholosh charged me with bringing to the attention of the Mouth of Peace." She looked slightly embarrassed. "There was a letter as well, but I left it at the Palace Sublime. Elsewhere in the Palace, that is. But I just told you everything that was in it."

Kejak smiled. "You have done very well, Most Eager Student. Worry not about the letter. Instead, I would ask that you return to your meditations until such time as we call for you again."

"Of course, Most Enlightened One." Hinnah got up, bowed deeply, then fumbled with the door and left. It shut behind her with a dull thud, and the two men were alone.

"What do you think?" Kejak asked lazily.

Holok snorted. "I think you could ask her to walk on clouds, and pick flowers from a Deathlord's garden, and she'd skip off to do it."

"Probably," Kejak shifted in his seat. "I was referring to her account, however."

"I don't know what to say. How long have you known about this?"

"She's been here over a month, flitting from one functionary to another. She arrived the same night Wren's message about the goings-on at the Howe did, come to think of it. Odd, that. In any case, it was sheer luck the Mouth of Peace actually stumbled across her, and another bit of luck that she was sent to me. I think the Mouth of Peace rather enjoys making me deal with the impossibilities."

"That's because you're impossible yourself, or perhaps because she likes tying you up with mysteries like this so you stay out of her plans. Bah." He swiped at the air irritably. "This story bothers me. If it's true, we should probably send someone to Qut Toloc posthaste. Have any of the other seers confirmed this?"

"Not a one."

"Hmm." Holok hunched his shoulders and leaned forward. "It is entirely possible that Most Learned Hai Sholosh is not nearly so learned as he would like to think when it comes to the delicate art of divination. What exactly are the other augurers discovering?"

"That's what disturbed me. Every reading they have taken has been full of boundless optimism. There is, according to their star charts, nothing but glory and wonder ahead."

Holok half-suppressed a bitter laugh. "Well, we know that can't be the case. Do you think it's possible that Sholosh saw something they missed?"

"Or that something was hidden from the known diviners, but Sholosh was able to discover it because he was...shall we say, unique in his approach?"

"An excellent way to put it. I trust that you have the letter in your keeping?"

Kejak nodded. "Of course I do. She got it mostly right, but there are a couple of details our over-eager acolyte neglected to pass on. The unusual temperature of the corpse is one, as I recall. It was quite chilled, you know."

"Interesting. Who penned the letter?"

"Sholosh himself, and in quite a hurry. There's actually a misplaced brushstroke."

"That *is* a sign of impending doom." Abruptly, Holok stood and paced. "You know that you cannot afford to ignore this. Send a rider to Qut Toloc. At best, you've shown interest in the initiates in that sky-forsaken place. At worst, you have someone there to deal with things when the storm sweeps in."

Kejak nodded, tiredly. "I agree. The whole matter puzzles me, though, in a way I've not been confounded in centuries."

Holok frowned. "You know what's buried at Qut Toloc, my friend."

"I know *who's* buried there as well, and what she was capable of," Kejak snapped wearily. "If it's her spirit up and about again, then a dead bastard and a broken bowl are the least of our worries."

"On the other hand, no sense causing a panic."

"Agreed. So this is done quietly, at least for now." Kejak yawned, and for a brief instant looked almost frail. "I'll send someone in the morning. It's too late to begin today, in any case."

"Is Wren back?" Holok tried to sound unconcerned, and failed. "I understand he was off causing trouble again, but you seem to enjoy enlisting him in this sort of thing."

"I have word that my clever Eliezer is alive and well, but being detained by other business on his way to Nexus. His message was not the most complete—I'm certain your Saraos could do better—but it was quite interesting. You can read it if you like."

"Thank you, but no." Holok's annoyance was palpable. "I still fail to see why you use him when one more..."

"Powerful?"

Holok nodded. "Exactly. He's but a man, and yet you favor

him over those who have a hundred times his worth."

"Ahh, but you miss one telling detail." Kejak rapped Holok's shoulder with his fan. "None has done me a hundred times Wren's service. He may be but a man, but he is a most resourceful one at that, and profoundly attached to his own continued survival. As such, he is more likely than some to return after his task is completed, and more likely than most to complete it. And besides, he has no idea whom he really serves, other than the Order, and so his head is untroubled by thoughts that might distract him from his duties. A more perfect servant in these troubled times? I could not imagine one."

"If you say so, Kejak." Holok's voice was still troubled. "I still say your little songbird is going to end up a pile of entrails and ashes one of these days, and sooner rather than later."

"And if that's the case, Holok, then he's a dead man, and there are many more men where he came from.'" Kejak grinned like a schoolboy who has just confounded his teacher. "But in any case, it is irrelevant. Wren is otherwise engaged."

"Most Eager To Get Herself Killed Hinnah?"

"Don't make me laugh."

Holok shrugged. "There are several thousand monks within the Palace, and several thousand more within a day's walk. I'm sure you'll be able to find someone. Just do it quickly, and make it someone you trust. Even most of the initiates at Qut Toloc don't know what they're standing watch over. There's no sense sending someone out there just to add to the confusion."

Kejak bowed slightly, from the neck. "Your advice, as always, is excellent, Holok. I shall take it to heart, and confer again with you in the morning." He left the chamber, and after a moment, Holok did the same.

Morning came, and with it came a message for Holok from the Most Enlightened Chejop Kejak. It read, simply, "I look forward to your observations of the Qut Toloc shrine," and nothing more.

"Most Unreasonable Bastard is more like it," said Holok, and called for an acolyte to help him prepare for the journey.

Chapter Six

Ratcatcher had a certain theory about horses, namely that they, and not his liege lord, were the true servants of evil in the Realm. His current steed was doing nothing to allay that suspicion, picking its way at a too-leisurely pace along a narrow dirt track that seemingly led from nowhere to nowhere. The land on either side of the pathway was green and bland, marked by occasional farmholds and nothing more. Of civilization, of inns and hostels and good wine, there was no sign.

"Damn you," he said absently to the horse, which whickered but otherwise ignored him. "Where have you led me this time?"

The horse did not answer, and neither did the surrounding countryside. Cursing his luck, Ratcatcher rode on through the pre-dawn gloom. He'd chosen this route, north toward Sijan, back when the Prince had exiled Ratcatcher from his company. He still couldn't say what had made him pick this path, save that it ran directly counter to the course he'd seen Pandeimos charting, and that was enough reason for anything.

Initially, his plan had been to make the river crossing at Lookshy, then angle west when a propitious omen told him to head for the coast. Ratcatcher sincerely doubted that Wren had fled to this particular bit of trackless wilderness. The man was an Immaculate, after all. The priests tended to run for home when they were spooked, to hide under the wings of the powers that lurked in the Palace Sublime. The chances of Wren's deciding to take refuge in Sijan instead were somewhere in the close neighborhood of nothing. Still, something unspoken told him that this path was worth following, and so dutifully he had gone.

That unspoken voice, Ratcatcher dully resolved, was a liar, and if he ever found a way to embody it, he'd do so just for the pleasure of killing it. Since leaving Lookshy he'd seen nothing but smaller and smaller towns, bigger and bigger fields, and less and less interesting scenery. Only the knowledge that he was putting more leagues between himself and the buffoons who still traveled with the Prince kept him from turning back; that, and the potentially unpleasant consequences of returning to the Prince's presence without any success to report.

Ahead in the distance, something shimmered. Ratcatcher straightened in his saddle. It flickered like torchlight, and torchlight that could be seen from this distance meant that someone had lit a great many torches.

"Hopefully, this will be amusing," he said to himself, then spurred the horse forward. It snorted its disdain for anything Ratcatcher currently felt like proposing, but set off at a brisk trot regardless.

As he got closer, the hazy glow became more distinct. It was indeed torchlight, mixed with a steadier glow that must have come from oil lamps. Feeling vaguely excited by the prospect of a comfortable bed and anyone's cooking but his own, Ratcatcher pressed forward. The horse protested, having no wish to maintain any kind of fast pace in the dark, but Ratcatcher was insistent, and so they traveled on.

Eventually, shapes loomed up out of the dark. Most were cottages roofed with thatch, their walls made from dried mud. Taller buildings lurked behind them, presumably made from more mud and the odd wooden beam. And behind that, illuminated by the torches that had called to him across the dark, was a temple.

The building, from what Ratcatcher could see, was made entirely from a dark, smooth stone. That in and of itself was enough to arouse his suspicion. He'd seen no quarry anywhere on his journey. Where the stone for this fane of the Immaculates had come from was a mystery.

The exterior of the temple was awash in light. Torches in sconces and great oil lamps illuminated it, making shadows dance and writhe all along its many columns. Like all Immaculate shrines, it was unadorned, elegant in its simplicity. The sweeping grandeur of the entranceway, the breathtaking simplicity of the columns supporting an overhang, the clean lines of the roof—all had been crafted to please the eye and calm the mind.

"So maybe my little bird ran here after all," Ratcatcher whispered to his horse. "I certainly had no idea this place existed. I think it bears closer investigation, don't you?" Without waiting for the unlikely possibility of an answer, he turned the horse around. "But not right now. Let's find somewhere to rest for the day, and then tomorrow night we'll pay the Immaculates a visit to see if Wren's fluttered his way here."

Obediently, the horse picked its way through the dark. Dimly, Ratcatcher spotted something that looked like a rock formation, and resolved to use that for the day's repose. Close inspection revealed that the formation was in fact a chunk of an ancient and broken tower, and that it should serve nicely to shelter him and his steed from prying eyes. The land around it was uncultivated, and Ratcatcher had the definite feeling this was the sort of place yokels regarded as being "cursed."

Sighing with relief, he slithered out of the saddle and proceeded to tie the reins to a particularly convenient outcropping. Satisfied, he removed his blankets from his saddlebags and, eschewing the removal of armor, settled in with his back against the stone in preparation for a few hours' rest.

Beneath him, something howled.

Ratcatcher leapt up, somehow managing simultaneously to turn in midair and draw his sword. His eyes pierced the fading dark, looking for any sign of an enemy. There was none, just a gentle breeze.

The howl came again.

This time, Ratcatcher was prepared for it. Now that he could listen attentively, the moan sounded less like something living, and more like wind forcing its way through a narrow chamber.

"There just might be something down there after all." Ratcatcher rummaged around in the dirt until he found what he was looking for: a well-hidden opening into the earth beneath the wrecked tower, fringed with tall weeds. The hole was large enough to admit a man in armor, and bruising on the weeds' stems showed that someone had passed this way recently.

Looking up at the sky, Ratcatcher made his decision. "Try not to get eaten by anything," he implored the horse, and then he slid through the cavern entrance into the deeper darkness.

Chapter Seven

Unforgiven Blossom was alive, which meant that she was a genuine rarity among the servants of the Prince of Shadows. She also still had her tongue in her head, which made her even rarer. And most uncommon of all, she had the privilege of entering his throne room unannounced when she felt she had news of sufficient import to pass along to her liege. As Unforgiven Blossom was not a stupid woman, she exercised this right very rarely, but the mere fact that she possessed it demonstrated that the Prince held her in very high esteem.

Once, she would have been considered beautiful, but years in the Prince's service had flensed her youth from her. Her face was angular where once it had been striking; her figure thin instead of slender. She had seen barely thirty summers, yet her hair was entirely silver, and her gait was the measured, careful pace of a woman who awakens one morning and realizes that she no longer wishes to recognize the stranger in the mirror.

Such was the price of service to the Prince of Shadows. Yet she had sought him out of her own free will, and gladly vouchsafed him her loyalty. He, for his part, had been intrigued by her boldness and impressed by her talents, and had taken her for his own.

Now Unforgiven Blossom tended the Prince's orrery and was considered chief among his diviners. Indeed, so efficacious were her readings that, one by one, his other diviners had been dismissed, destroyed or otherwise removed from his service. Now she, and she alone, consulted the future on the Prince's behalf, and this she did with skill, with artistry and with an eye ever toward advancing the Prince's fortunes.

Today she wore a blue robe, embroidered with a speared dragon and belted with a sash of black silk. Her hair was tied back with blue cord, and her feet were bare as she labored at her task. Above her, the orrery whirled and spun, stars and planets dancing by with alarming grace.

A fool might look at the device and wonder how it worked, as the five planets darted and swooped amongst a host of greater and lesser celestial bodies in imitation of the motions of the heavens. A knave might gaze at the prince's engine of divination and wonder at the cost of its making, for the stars and planets were made from gems, and the orbits and epicycles upon which they moved were hammered from silver and gold. And a wise man might worry about what the stars had just whispered to Unforgiven Blossom, as she checked and double-checked her hastily scribbled notes against the humming machine.

"Something interesting, I hope?"

Unforgiven Blossom whirled, dropping the scroll that she had been studying. "My prince, I did not hear you enter."

The Prince of Shadows gestured artlessly. "It was not my wish that you do so. I wanted to observe you at work. Unless, of course, you object?"

"Not at all, my prince." Stooping to retrieve the scroll, she was once again effortlessly cool and unfeeling. "You may wish to examine this," she said, and extended the parchment for him to peruse.

The Prince smiled, as much at the failure of his attempt to rattle her further as at his pleasure in having such a servant, and took the scroll. "Your latest prophecy, I take it, my unwilted flower?"

She nodded, and backed away. The Prince unrolled it and strolled about the room, ducking instinctively to avoid an unfortunate collision with a careening planet, or a celestial catastrophe in miniature as Luna veered by in all her glory. "Fascinating," he said at one point, and, "Are you sure?" at another.

"Quite," Unforgiven Blossom replied. "The signs are quite plain, but there is no clear oracle to be divined from them. Never before have I seen such confusion among the stars."

The Prince nodded. "Indeed. It seems that we stand on the brink of times that may prove most auspicious—if they do not destroy us first." He paused in mid-stride and mid-thought. "What is this?" he asked, one long finger stabbing at the parchment. "A name?"

The diviner approached. "May I, my liege?" The Prince nodded and handed her the notes. "Ah."

"Ah?" The Prince quirked one eyebrow. "Would you care to expand upon that, or shall I simply wait for wisdom to descend from the skies?"

"It already has, my liege," she said, disconcertingly, and rolled up the scroll. "This much I can tell you: Great things were set in motion today. Jupiter's path was altered by an unseen star *here*," she turned and gestured to the orrery, "while a new comet manifested itself *there*, and scribed for itself a path uncomfortably close to the sun. It may be destroyed, or it may flare into prominence; the omens are uncertain as of yet."

"Please let me know when they become more certain, then." Ghost-like, he dodged between two rapidly orbiting globes and set each one to spinning with but a touch. "And the name I saw written in your hand?"

Helplessly, Unforgiven Blossom shook her head. "It is no name I have ever heard before, my prince. The stars insisted on scribing it, but…I do not know what it means."

"Then find out." His voice was silky with menace and low with command. "Or I may yet decide that dismissing my other augurers was a mistake, and add another to my service. One who reads entrails, perhaps?"

"Yes, my prince." She bowed very low and made no other sound. The Prince waited for her another moment, then strode off with almost unseemly haste. The door to the orrery chamber closed behind him, the crash of heavy wood swinging shut echoing throughout the room.

Unforgiven Blossom sank to the floor, and was still for many minutes. At last, she roused herself and made her way to her master's library, which held many thousands of scrolls. Hours later, she re-emerged, grateful that she had been able to discover the information she sought but still befuddled as to its ultimate meaning.

Still, she thought, *this is a beginning. Wisdom will follow. And* she sat down so that she might prepare a document for her master, one that would contain all there was to know about the town called Qut Toloc.

It would be, she suspected, a very short document indeed. But that was not her concern, at least not yet. Head bowed, she dipped a reed brush in ink and began writing.

Chapter Eight

Yushuv was an ossuary rat, which meant that the one thing he knew how to do was run. He pelted down the narrow corridor that he'd long ago named "Bonebreak Lane," his bare feet slapping on the floor with a sound that echoed far too loudly off into the dark. There were no torches here, and the dust lay thick on the bones to either side of the boy's path. The only light came from patches of fungi growing on the piles of broken bones that he sprinted past, cold green or angry red. Old statues with the heads of beasts and the bodies of men scowled as he went past, but the boy paid them no heed. Ahead of Yushuv lay only shadows, but he knew that behind him was death.

On the left, a semicircular opening yawned wide, and Yushuv ducked down into it. Bones were spilled in the path here, and he stumbled over what felt like a dead man's thighbone. Desperate, his hands scrabbling on the stone of the floor, he drunkenly righted himself and kept on. Echoes of bone scraping across stone trailed behind him, however, letting his pursuer know where he had gone.

Fear lending wings to his feet, Yushuv put on a burst of speed. He knew that if the man—if it was a man that was following him, and not some kind of ghost or demon—would kill him if it caught him underground. What he had seen was a creature of darkness and death. But Yushuv was sure that if he could just get out of the corridors, up the stairs and into the sunlight, he might get away. Yushuv no longer even cared if the priests who tended this place caught him, though an hour ago he would have feared nothing else so much in this world. Maybe the priests could do something to hold back the monster he had seen.

Maybe they could slow it down for a few seconds, the voice in the back of his head whispered and, terrified, Yushuv hushed it. Even his thoughts seemed too loud in this place, where the only sounds were his feet on cold basalt and far off, the steady tread of iron-shod boots.

Fortunately, Yushuv knew this part of the catacombs well. A turn to the right up ahead, followed by a fast turn to the left, and he'd be at the foot of the winding stair that led to the basement of the local temple. There would surely be an Immaculate priest there who'd wonder how a young boy had slipped down into the tunnels, but he was sure he could tell a story that would withstand scrutiny for a few precious seconds, and then allow him to run.

So great was his haste that he nearly missed the turn to the right. Sliding on the smooth stone, he reached out to grab the edge of the arch and instead found himself clutching at a precariously balanced pile of partially disassembled skeletons. The tower hung in the air for an impossibly long moment, then collapsed into the center of the archway.

"No!" Yushuv heard himself screaming, and in the distance, a peal of cold laughter. Desperately he tried to shove bones out of the way to clear a path, but each attempt simply brought more crashing down. A nearly full skeleton toppled over onto him. He struggled, but his tunic caught on the jagged edges of some broken ribs and he couldn't break free. Nearly blind with panic, he tried to rise, but that triggered a new avalanche of cracked skulls and fingerbones.

When the last of the bones had finally come to a halt, Yushuv was buried. Experimentally, he tried to move first his left arm, then his right. Neither would budge. His left leg was free, and so, panting with fear, he arched his back and pushed up with it, in an attempt to free himself. For an instant the pile shifted, and then collapsed back on him. He was trapped.

From down the long, empty corridor he heard footsteps again, and louder. They were slow and deliberate, the tread of a hunter who knows that he need not hurry to catch his prey. Faintly, Yushuv could hear his pursuer's voice now. The man was singing, his voice deep and full of mockery. The song was in a language that Yushuv couldn't understand, and it ran in time with the echo of boots on the black stone of the floor. But the song didn't speed up, and the pace of the damnably slow footsteps remained the same, and so Yushuv found himself waiting in the dark.

He'd seen the man by accident. Like the other children in the village, Yushuv had long since learned how to sneak down into the catacombs under the temple. His older brother Sijanar had shown him the secret staircase that the priests who guarded the catacombs knew nothing about, and taught him the maze of passageways so that he could find his way in total darkness. Thus had the knowledge of the tunnels been passed down for hundreds of years, and Yushuv was just the latest heir to it.

And like all of those children who had come before him, Yushuv had discovered the tunnels' secret: Not every skeleton had been stripped of its treasures. Here and there, a golden torque still hung from a bony neck, or rings still adorned skeletal fingers. Rumor had it that the Immaculates were supposed to confiscate all of that before laying the bones to rest, but that they'd gotten lazy over the years and stopped bothering. Yushuv didn't know if this was true; he just knew that the skeletons near the staircase had been long since picked clean, so that if he wanted to find something to sell he needed to travel far from the light to do so. Until today he'd been remarkably successful, finding jewels and bracers with ease, and handily avoiding the cursory, panicked patrols the priests sent to look for people like him. None of his friends would venture as far from the stairs as he would, and none would go as far into the dark. He laughed at them when they turned back, and then loped off easily into the far tunnels. Until today, he'd considered himself a prince of the catacombs.

Today was different, however. He'd gone searching to the east in hopes of picking up another dagger to sell like the one he'd found a few weeks back. It had been made of something that looked like gold but which felt lighter, and Malaky the Guild factor had given him a good price for it. So he'd headed back to those tunnels, intent on finding something else to sell. Instead, he'd found the stranger. Coming around a turn, torch in hand, he'd seen the figure of a man where no living man should be. The stranger was tall, with raiton-black hair and fair skin. His eyes were black, and he wore black armor covered in cruel spikes and hooks. Across his back was slung a long black sword with a thin blade carved in the shape of an asp. He was hunched over a pile of bones, talking to them, and occasionally his voice rose to an angry shout. When it did, more often than not a mailed fist came down and crushed a skull to powder, and the man's voice trailed off into a string of curses. Then he'd rummage through old, dry bones and find another grinning skull, and begin the interrogation all over again.

Yushuv knew that he was looking at something unholy. He knew that he should flee, and that if the man saw him there he'd be broken and left here for another ossuary rat to find. But something about what he saw held him fast, and he found himself unwilling to go. He told himself that it was safer to stand where he was and stay quiet, and to let the stranger leave first. He'd be safe that way, he was sure, and with that assurance in hand, he hunkered down behind a pile of what looked like armbones, and watched.

He never knew what it was that gave him away. Perhaps it was a chattering of teeth, for the thin gray tunic he wore was no match for the cold in the deeper chambers of the catacombs. Perhaps he'd dislodged a bone that was on the verge of falling, and the stranger heard him. Or perhaps the stranger was just not human, and knew things in a way that only demons and monsters could. But heard him the stranger most certainly had, for he looked up from the fistful of bones he held and smiled at Yushuv where he hid.

"I see a boy who's far from home," he said in a mocking singsong, and Yushuv felt himself shiver. He said nothing, however, and held as still as he could in hopes that the stranger would overlook where he cowered. For a long moment there was silence, and Yushuv almost dared to hope. Then the man laughed, and Yushuv felt his heart turn to ice.

"My business is with the dead today, not the living," the stranger said, and unraveled himself to stand in the center of the chamber. Yushuv gasped. The man stood tall, and he moved with the grace of a hunting cat. Silently, casually, he reached over his back and drew the asp-bladed sword that hung there, and Yushuv could swear he heard it *moan*.

That had been enough. Whatever spell had been cast on him was broken, and Yushuv fled, back toward light and life as fast as he could go. Behind him, he heard the unhurried tread of the stranger, and he knew that if he turned to look back, he'd never be able to run again. So Yushuv ran, and ran hard, and hoped that he'd lose his pursuer in the maze of dead men's bones beneath the ground.

But as hard as he'd run, he'd failed. Somehow, the stranger had kept up with him, always on the edge of hearing, and no matter how fast Yushuv had gone he'd been unable to escape. And now he was pinned in the cold and the dark, and he could do nothing but close his eyes and wait for the stranger to find him. The crunch of bone breaking underfoot was closer now, and so was the singing. Yushuv screwed his eyes up tight and whimpered. His bladder felt very full, and the stone he lay pinned on was very cold, and he could suddenly feel the slightest hint of breeze shuffling over his skin. No doubt it was coming from the staircase. He'd been so close…

Just in front of him, the footsteps stopped.

"You can open your eyes, boy. Closing them won't do a damned thing to protect you." The stranger's voice was almost amused, but not gentle. Yushuv stifled a moan, and looked up.

What he saw was the stranger's feet, as well as the tip of the man's sword. It swung back and forth in a hypnotic rhythm, and a cold light shone from it. Yushuv's eyes followed the blade back and forth, slowly. He said nothing, clamping down on his tongue with his teeth so hard he could taste blood. He would not speak, however; he promised himself that. He didn't trust himself not to beg for mercy, and there was no way he'd let himself beg. Not here, not in his tunnels.

"You know," the man said, seemingly aware of Yushuv's inner turmoil, "the reason I followed you was that I was certain you'd run straight for home, and would lead me out of this godsforsaken place. Where's the exit, little rat? I can smell warm earth on the wind. Tell me, and I'll let you live." When Yushuv failed to respond, he brought the blade closer. "Tell me, or you meet my friend."

With horror, Yushuv saw the serpent's head on the blade somehow move. The sword regarded him for a moment, then very distinctly hissed. Yushuv shrieked. The stranger laughed at the sound, and brought the blade still closer, so that the snake's tongue flickered over Yushuv's face. Its touch was cold, and where it passed Yushuv could feel blood welling up.

Suddenly, the stranger squatted down, his face close to the boy's. "You're brave, boy. I've talked to live men and dead ones who wouldn't hold their tongues from me as long as you did. But there's no sense in being brave now. I can find the way out, with or without you. Just give me a reason not to leave you here, trapped, in the dark. You'd go mad down here before you died, you know. That is, if the rats didn't get you first. Nasty things, rats. Can't stand them. That's why they call me Ratcatcher. Once they find out you're trapped, they'll go right for your eyes. Clever beasts, rats are, and they learn fast. No, soon enough one will come snuffling around, and he'll find you. You'll feel him soon enough, and then you'll feel his friends. And do you know what the best thing about rats is? They don't care if you're dead or not before they start eating." He smiled. "I'll give you a moment to think about that. I can be very patient when I need to be."

Yushuv looked up, tried to look away, but he couldn't. His ears strained. Were those claws on stone he heard off in the distance, or just his imagination? His breathing rasped in his ears, and he shuddered. "I'll tell you," he said, "but you have to set me free first. Then I'll show you the way."

Ratcatcher threw back his head and guffawed. "Marvelous! Why don't I set you free, so you can run away again? You're in no position to bargain, boy, but you've got brass. I can admire that in a man, even more in a child. So let me make a counteroffer." The sword whipped out, and the bones that pinned Yushuv fell away, cleft neatly in twain. Before the boy could move, his tormentor stooped down on him and lifted him by his tunic front. His feet dangled off the ground, helplessly, as he stared into the man's dead eyes.

"Now," the man said, holding Yushuv up effortlessly, "why

don't you tell me where those stairs are? I've had enough of this place."

"Through there," Yushuv said, pointing. "Through there, and then to the left. You'll find the stairs there."

"And at the top of the stairs? What there?" Ratcatcher's voice no longer held the slightest trace of amusement. For half a heartbeat Yushuv considered lying, then thought better of it. Besides, he owed the priests nothing.

"Priests. There's a temple there, at the center of the village."

"Ah. I should have expected such. If you can't put a fortress over a Solar Exalted's grave, put a temple down and fill it with Initiates of the Immaculate Order. They're bigger fools than they know." Yushuv looked at the stranger, puzzled. "Anathema, boy," the stranger spat. "You've been creeping around in the tomb of what those piss-drinking priests call an Anathema. All this," he gestured about with his sword, "is his honor guard into hell. That'll make you think twice before you rob any more corpses, won't it? Pfah!" With that, he flung Yushuv against the wall, hard. The boy hit with a sickening thud, then slid down into a mound of skeletons. Bones clattered on the floor as Yushuv whimpered and tried to rise.

"Here's a last bit of advice, boy," Ratcatcher said as he stalked off. "If I were you, I'd stay down here for a little while yet. Just keep moving. It will keep the rats away, at least until they figure out that you're defenseless." With sword unsheathed, he kicked away the remains of the pile before him and walked off into the dark.

As the light faded, Yushuv huddled in the shadows and listened. He could hear the clanging of the stranger's boots on the endless staircase up, and then what could only be the sound of men screaming and dying. This went on for several eternal minutes, then gradually faded away. Then there was only silence, and in the distance, quiet sobbing.

Yushuv stood. A flare of pain shot through his side from where he'd hit the wall, and he almost fell. Gingerly, he reached down and found, miracle of miracles, a length of wood that must once have been a spear-haft. He leaned on it, and it took his weight. With infinite care, Yushuv began walking toward the other staircase, the one he'd used to enter the ossuary. After all, he needed no dead priests haunting his dreams—or him.

And in the darkness, a rat watched the boy shamble off, and fled into the deeper tunnels in fear.

Chapter Nine

The dead men were waiting for Yushuv, down in the dark. And he had no choice but to go down and meet them.

It would have been too much to hope that the stranger would have left a torch behind, and Yushuv was in no shape to look far for one. The stabbing pain in his side told him that he'd probably cracked a rib, and every step sent a flare of agony racing through him. Still, it was better to retrace his steps in the dark than to follow the stranger up the staircase—of that, Yushuv was certain.

And so he hobbled off in the darkness, leaning dangerously on the broken spear he'd found by chance. Once or twice, when the pain had grown too great for him to continue, he'd examined it as he rested and tried to figure out what sort of creature it might have belonged to, but his mind rebelled at the images and so he abandoned that line of thought as best he could.

The path went left, and then right, and then left again as it sloped down, and it got darker with every step. The stranger's passing seemed to have done something to even the feeble life in this place, and the fungi that had glowed so vividly before were now dull and weak. In many places there was no light at all, and Yushuv was reduced to pressing forward blindly. Had he not known the catacombs so well this would have been troubling, but Yushuv had once bet his brother Simeon that he could run from staircase to staircase with a cloth tied over his eyes. Simeon had scoffed, and so he'd been forced to make good on his boast. Not only had he done so, but he'd done so fast enough to leave his brother behind him in the dark, sobbing for someone with a light to come and rescue him.

Simeon was gone now, though. He'd fallen ill, and then the Immaculates had come for him, and that was the last he had seen of his brother. There was no one down here to rescue him the way he'd gone back for Simeon. There was no one, Yushuv decided, down here at all.

And that was when he heard the voice for the first time.

"Bbbbbbooooooyyyyyyyyy."

He stopped, closed his eyes, and listened. In the distance he could hear something that was probably rats, but little else. He heard no breeze, no water dripping, and most emphatically no footfalls. Then the sounds of the rats died away, and he was left in perfect quiet, except for the rasp of his own breathing and the pounding of his own heart.

"Boooooyyyyyyyyy."

The voice came from everywhere and nowhere. Yushuv spun as best he could, looking around to see from whence it came, but there was no one there.

"Boyyyyyyyy."

It was whispered, drawn out and howled all at once. The voice that spoke was oddly discordant, as if a dozen voices were all speaking from the same throat. Yushuv turned again, frantically, and his left foot landed on something that might have been a pebble, might have been a bone. It rolled out from under him and he fell, crying out. The sound echoed down the corridor, and then there was nothing. Sprawled out on the cold stone, he painstakingly reached out and found his makeshift cane, then hoisted himself to a sitting position. "Who...who are you?" he finally dared, once the last echoes of his cry had died away.

"We have something to show you, boy. Come with ussssssssssssss." The words slowly grew more distinct, as if the speakers were unused to using their voices aloud.

Yushuv crossed his arms. "Not until you tell me who you are."

"We mean you no harm. If we meant to hurt you, you'd be deeeaaaddddd." The voice was behind Yushuv now, and very close.

"I don't care. I'm cold and I'm tired and I hurt, and I'm not going on until you tell me who you are."

"You'll die down heeeerrrrre"

"And then you won't get what you want, either." Suddenly Yushuv felt very alone, and very young. He closed his eyes and hunched over, and found himself almost wishing that the stranger had killed him. His voice sounded very small and weak in the dark, and the notion of his bargaining with or threatening whatever monster was out there struck him as funny. He started laughing, raggedly, and the sound bounced off the walls until it seemed as if all of the skulls that lined the catacomb walls were laughing with him. And as he laughed, a golden glow appeared in the center of the tunnel ahead and grew stronger, until the light was as bright as day.

"This is who we are, boy," said the voice. "We died heeeerreeee. We died for yoooouuuu."

"I don't understand," said Yushuv, as he clambered to his feet. "I didn't ask you to die. Why would I do something like that?"

"We fought a great battle here." The golden glow grew brighter, and it collapsed on itself to form something roughly man-shaped. As it did so, the voice grew more distinct, and it clearly emanated from the figure ahead. "We fought an abomination."

"And you died?" Yushuv hobbled forward.

"We all died. But it died, too, and was buried here with ussssss. Follow me. I will show you a marvel." With that, the glowing shape turned and began walking off. Yushuv, after a moment's consideration, followed.

Their path was ever downward, and Yushuv was surprised at the turn of speed they made. Beside them, bones lay in tangled disarray. Men and woman lay interred here, and for the first time Yushuv could see how many were clad in rotting remnants of armor or had broken weapons by their side. "Were these all warriors?" he asked.

"Soldiers. Led by those with the blood of the dragons in their veins. They hunted something far greater than themselves, and they used us like arrows. In the end, the monster was slain, but we constituted her escort into oblivion. And now you are here, and we will show you where she rests."

"Why me?" Yushuv's voice was plaintive.

"Because you are here." The voice grew testy. "Is that not enough, boy?"

"My name is Yushuv, not boy."

The figure stopped and turned. "You should not have told me that. Names have power, Yushuv. Be very careful whom you give power over you." Yushuv got the uncomfortable sensation that the figure was staring at him, and then it began moving again, more quickly.

"So we're going to where she's buried? Why?"

"So you can find it again."

"Why would I want to do that?"

"You won't. Others you meet will." And with that, silence returned. Yushuv tried speaking several more times, but either the ghost could no longer answer or, more likely, didn't want to. Eventually their path led down a flight of stairs and into a great chamber, and when the glow from the figure illuminated the room completely, the boy gasped.

The room was over a hundred feet across, completely circular, and with a ceiling that soared overhead. In the exact center of the floor lay a skeleton clad in the remains of intricate armor, marked by flame and pierced in a hundred places. Next to the skeleton lay a riven shield, and still clutched in a bony hand was a sword longer than any Yushuv had ever seen. It was made of golden metal, and it shone brightly in the ghostlight. The blade was hooked, and intricate sun designs had been worked into the metal so skillfully it looked as if the metal had been drawn from the earth already shaped thus. Around the body lay heaps of bones. Some were blasted as if by fire, some hacked and hewn, and some looked as if they had simply melted. Yushuv gasped, while the glowing figure strode to the middle of the room and, hovering over the sword, extended an arm and beckoned the boy closer.

"This," it said in a voice full of dust, "is orichalcum. You see around you some of the destruction it helped create. You must never allow this to fall into evil hands, Yushuv. The stranger you met must never find this."

"What if he does?"

"What happens if a wolf finds a flock of sheep with the shepherd away? What happens when the entire town drinks from a poisoned well? It is the same question."

Yushuv edged closer and looked at the sword. The shimmer of the metal that comprised it looked familiar, and something told him that it would be warm to the touch. He looked up. "I found a dagger made of this same stuff. I took it with me, and I sold it to Malaky."

"Malaky?" The ghostly voice was full of concern.

"Malaky. He's the man who works for the Guild. He comes around once in a while to see if there's anything here worth trading for." Yushuv paused for a minute, thoughtfully. "He always makes sure to talk to the children, to see if we found anything down here. He seemed very happy with the dagger."

"I'm not surprised," said the ghost, dryly. "It may be a very dangerous thing for this Malaky to have the dagger."

"I don't understand, though. Why is it so bad? And how did the dagger get to where I found it? I've never been here before."

The ghost paused, and looked thoughtful. Others, also glowing, faded in around it, until the room was so bright that Yushuv had to squint and half look away. The dead men began conferring amongst themselves, their voices rising and falling in the sonorous whisper that the boy had first heard in the dark. Then, satisfied, most faded away until only one remained in the suddenly dimmed room. It might have been the one who led Yushuv there; it might not. Yushuv couldn't tell and, alone with the dead, honestly didn't care.

"Yushuv, what I tell you now is old knowledge, and rare. Orichalcum is the metal of those who serve the sun. It holds power for them, and it serves them well. It is more precious than gold in the same way that diamond is more precious than glass, and a fool who sells it as golden makes for himself a poor bargain. In the proper hands, it can do much good, or much harm."

Yushuv nodded. "So the dagger is dangerous, too?"

"It is, though not half so much as the daiklave—the sword you see before you. The dagger itself was forged to match it, but was stripped from its wielder during battle. The man who

took it from her was very brave, but did not survive to brag of
his deed. He fell, and the blade fell with him. I cannot tell you
more."

"Can you answer one more question for me?"

"If I must."

"Why are you telling me all this? You fought her," Yushuv
waved in the vague direction of the armored figure on the floor.
"Why bring me here?"

"Because things change over eight hundred years, boy. Even
for dead men, they change."

And with that, the ghost vanished.

Yushuv sat down in the dark and shook his head. He'd been
expecting something of the sort since the ghost first appeared,
and was not really surprised to be left thus. The ghost, while
more forthcoming than the stranger had been, had still left him
with many questions. Not the least of them was why he had
been shown this. After all, it would surely have been safer if
no one had ever come here; how they expected a single twelve-
year-old boy to safeguard this ancient horror's tomb was beyond
him, especially if they didn't show him the way out.

Unless, of course, they had a reason for bringing him here
and then abandoning him. Yushuv ran down a few of the
possibilities for why that might be so, came up with a short list
of unpleasantries, and tried very hard to think about anything
else. Eventually, he succeeded, though not before giving himself
several severe frights, and at one point becoming convinced
that he'd heard one of the nearby skeletons move.

Patiently, he sat and waited, and eventually his eyes
re-adapted to the dark. The fungal glow was stronger here,
away from where the stranger had walked, and as such he
could dimly make out the skeletal figures on the floor. The
sword caught and dimly reflected patches of red and green
light, shining somehow brighter than it had any right to do. It
beckoned to him. *Touch me*, it whispered. *Know me.*

With a look to the left for watchful ghosts, and another one to the right, Yushuv did so, and the world came rushing in on him. He screamed, once, and then there was silence.

Yushuv opened his eyes. He was lying on his back, on fine black sand. It was warm, but not unpleasantly so. Above him the sun was blindingly bright, so bright that he saw it even when he closed his eyes. He propped himself up on his elbows, marveling at the fact that his side no longer hurt, and took a look around.

He was in some sort of arena, that much was clear. He'd heard stories of such from Malaky, though his father had warned him not to talk to the Guild factor about such things. He knew that men fought here for pay, sometimes against beasts and sometimes against other men. He wondered if he was supposed to fight, and if so, how? He had no weapons, and the only fighting he knew was the savagery that boys practice amongst themselves, the combat of the thumb in the eye and the bloody nose.

Somehow it didn't seem like that would work well here. Fearful, he got to his feet and explored his surroundings further. The arena itself was carved into the earth, and it was lined with stone benches as white as the sands were black. No one sat on them; he was completely alone. Above, the sun shone down from a cloudless sky. A lone black bird circled above him. Otherwise, nothing broke the perfect blueness of the sky.

"Hello?" Yushuv called. His voice echoed from the stone. The crow cackled a response, but there was no other sound. "Hello?"

He walked forward. The sand crunched softly under his feet. Suddenly, the sound of his footfall changed, and he looked down. Instead of his own ragged sandals, he suddenly wore boots. His hands were encased in gauntlets, his body in armor. Astonishingly, it was light enough that he could move unencumbered. Experimentally, he faked what he imagined was a sword-thrust. It was smooth and fast, and it felt right. He laughed aloud, and his laughter bounced from the empty benches.

Ahead, he heard metal creaking. He looked up, and where there had been solid stone before, a gate now appeared before him. Unseen hands winched it ever higher, and behind it he could see a figure. Instinctively, he knew it was the stranger he'd seen in the tunnels, the man who called himself Ratcatcher. The sun beat down on Yushuv but, strangely, he felt no heat. Instead it filled him with strength. Still weaponless, he strode forward confidently.

The gate finished its journey upwards, and Ratcatcher came forth to meet him. He was clad as Yushuv remembered, but a line of bloody tears ran down one cheek now , and a strange mark stood out in high prominence upon his brow. Instead of his own sword, however, the stranger held the blade Yushuv had seen in the catacombs. The sun caught it, and it flared in the light.

"Come to play, little rat?" said the stranger as he circled left. The sword danced in his hands, cutting shining arcs in the air. "Come to Ratcatcher. I'll show you what's waiting for you." He lunged. Yushuv dodged him, barely, and the man laughed.

"You're slow, boy. This won't even be a challenge." He brought the daiklave down in a two-handed sweep, and Yushuv rolled to the right. Behind him, the blade cut deeply into the black sand. With a whispering sound, Ratcatcher pulled it free. "That's two. Third time is the charm, boy!"

Yushuv came to his feet, assessed his chances, and ran. Behind him Ratcatcher sprinted gracefully, the wind humming over the daiklave's blade. Ahead yawned the black expanse of the tunnel from which the stranger had emerged, and while Yushuv didn't know what it held, he knew that staying on the sands would be certain death. He put his head down and sprinted, and the heat of the sun lent wings to his feet.

A sudden crash made him look up. Perhaps a dozen feet ahead was the gate, a black iron portcullis marked by cruel spikes. It had swung down abruptly, though he could see neither winch nor chain by which it had been lowered. Regardless, his path to escape was blocked. He looked up, but the walls of the arena were a dozen feet high, much too far for him to jump.

Despairing, Yushuv turned. Ratcatcher advanced on him,

step by deliberate step. Menacingly, he twirled the daiklave. "What's the matter, boy? No sword? It's a pity. You shouldn't come into the arena unarmed. You shouldn't come here *human.*" He brought the blade around in a lazy swing, not really intending to hit, and Yushuv backpedaled anyway. That brought his shoulder blades in contact with the portcullis, and suddenly there was nowhere left to run. Yushuv feinted left, then right, but each time the daiklave was there. Ratcatcher smiled, the sun somehow behind him and surrounding his helmetless head with a golden halo.

"This is how it ends, boy." He brought the sword down, painfully slowly, until the very tip touched Yushuv's forehead. "This is how it ends for all time."

Yushuv screamed. Where the sword touched his skin burned like fire. The sun flared around Ratcatcher's head, filling Yushuv's vision and then somehow filling Yushuv himself. Ratcatcher jerked the sword away and took a step back. "What in the name of nine dead gods is this?" he said, rising alarm in his voice.

Yushuv felt the fire filling him, felt the burning on his forehead subside. He raised his right hand, and in it was the dagger he'd sold to Malaky. It was light in his hand, and he thrust effortlessly with it. Cursing, Ratcatcher parried, and took another step back. He swung, and Yushuv lifted the dagger to parry. The daiklave bounced off, harmlessly, and the boy took another step forward.

"Who are you?" asked Ratcatcher, fear in his voice. Again he swung, more clumsily this time, and again Yushuv parried.

"I am Yushuv," the boy said, and advanced.

"Yushuv is dead in the catacombs. Who are you?" The daiklave came crashing in from the left, and Yushuv flicked it aside.

"I am Yushuv, who is Exalted in the eyes of the Unconquered Sun, and I wield the blade of one who came before me." The words were strange to him, yet he knew somehow that they were true. The fear he saw in his enemy's eyes confirmed it.

"No!" Ratcatcher shrieked, his blows wild and unfocused. Around him a nimbus of dark energy swirled up from the sand, but it was ragged at the edges and the sun burned holes in it like a man pushing a knife through a sheet of parchment. "Who are you?"

"I am not who I used to be," said Yushuv, and thrust the blade into Ratcatcher's belly.

The man's body went rigid, as did the anima of shadow around him. His back arched and from his throat came a tortured shriek that was inhuman in its intensity. Dispassionately, Yushuv twisted the blade. Ratcatcher howled again, and the daiklave fell to the black sand. He looked down at Yushuv with an expression of shock and betrayal, and then sank to his knees.

With neither a smile nor a frown, Yushuv pulled the dagger out of Ratcatcher's gut. "Thank you," the man whispered, and fell forward onto the sand. Where his blood touched it, it turned white.

Yushuv wiped the blood from his dagger reverently. It came away clean and shining. The daiklave lay on the ground before him, and he knelt to lift it. The sword, too, was light in his hands, but something told him that it would not be proper to bear it.

"Not yet," he murmured to himself. "Not my time yet." Behind him, he could feel something folding into himself, a warmth and a power, and he guessed that he was cloaked in light the same way Ratcatcher had been. The man's body was still on the ground, but as Yushuv watched, it crumbled to dust. Soon all that was left was armor, and in seconds that crumbled, too. Again he was alone, save for the watching crow and the sun.

Abruptly the bird landed on the archway above the gate. Its gaze met his own, and it did an intricate little dance that could only be described as a bow. Yushuv inclined his head, and then turned. He raised his face and arms to the sun, and called out.

"What do you want from me?"

The words echoed, and hung there in stillness. Then, with a sound like the whispering of ghosts, the sun came and stood upon the sands. In form much like the radiant dead man who had led Yushuv through the tunnels, it placed its hand on Yushuv's brow in benediction.

"I am well pleased in you, Yushuv-who-was-once-another. You are worthy."

"I thank you." Yushuv fought the urge to kneel, certain that it would be the wrong thing to do. "What is this place? Why have you brought me here?"

"This place is nowhere, and you are here so that you might know yourself and return to the world more able than once you were. You have been Exalted, raised above mortals, Yushuv. Power is yours, and a great destiny if you choose to take it up."

"And if I don't?"

The glowing being before him smiled, or at least gave the impression of doing so. "Then it will take you up, and carry you along with it. The choice is yours."

Yushuv found his voice growing plaintive. "But what should I do? I've never even been outside my village."

"Travel," the voice said with gentle irony, "will be the least of your worries. Companions will find you, of that you can rest assured. Now you should sleep. Seek the blade you have given away when you awaken. It is more a key than a weapon, and it will unlock many doorways for you." Abruptly the man-form began to lose cohesion, and the glow rose once again toward the sky.

"What I ask of you is not easy, Yushuv. I know this, and it would not be asked were you not able to carry this burden. Remember, you are Exalted in my eyes, and my fire is your strength." With that, the light blazed more brightly, swallowing up everything else until there was only heat and brightness and Yushuv could feel himself falling....

In the catacombs, all was dark and still. Yushuv slept, quietly, curled up in the arms of a fleshless skeleton. Around him, the rats kept a wide berth, and the dead men stayed with them.

Chapter Ten

The Prince of Shadows awoke with a start. Around him, the room lay cloaked in perfect darkness. Nothing moved, nothing breathed, nothing stirred. Yet his heart was filled with unease, and his brow was furrowed as he arose from his bed.

Naked, he flung open the doors to his chamber. A scattering of torches lit the hallway dimly, reflecting off black stone and showing plainly the low silhouette huddled against the floor. No breeze stirred the torches and no shadows danced. There was merely light, and darkness, and the faint rasping of labored breath on the cold stone floor.

With a frown, the Prince strode forward to the huddled shape and prodded it with his foot.

It was, as he suspected, a rat. At his touch, it rolled over to display a gaping wound in its belly. Its eyes were feverish and bright, and its muzzle was wet with blood. It looked up at him, and he down at it, and their eyes met.

Without warning, the rat gave an ear-rending shriek. Arching its back, it thrashed about violently on the floor. The Prince watched, bemused, as the rat's death throes spattered blood across the floor. Then, deliberately, he raised one foot and brought it down on the animal's neck. It thrashed once, and was still.

"I see it is time to find Ratcatcher. And so soon, too."

Without another word, the Prince turned and returned to the blessed dark of his chamber. The corpse of the rat lay behind him, forgotten.

Chapter Eleven

It was morning when Yushuv awoke, though he had no idea how he knew this. The center of his forehead burned as if he had been branded, though when he rubbed his fingers across his brow he detected no mark there. Otherwise, he felt astonishingly good. His ribs no longer ached, and the myriad scrapes and bruises he'd incurred in his flight from the stranger had healed.

With a yawn, he climbed to his feet. The tomb no longer felt oppressive to him, but rather a place of reverence. Carefully, and without knowing quite why, he bowed to the armored skeleton in the middle of the floor. Around him, all was still, and he could sense that the dead men had gone back to wherever they'd come from. He was alone.

The exit to the chamber lay to the south, and Yushuv walked through it with quick strides. He hesitated for a second, then turned and rummaged among the bones. Quickly he found what he was looking for: a long, wicked knife with a serrated edge. It had lain, forgotten, among the skeletons since its owner had fallen here centuries ago. The blade was still sharp, though— miraculously untouched by time. Yushuv contemplated it for a moment, then stuck it through his belt. Its mere presence was comforting.

Finding the stairs to the temple took little more than an hour, as Yushuv had only a vague sense of where he stood. At each intersection he took his knife, knelt, and carved a rayed half-circle into the floor, to indicate the direction from which he'd come. The process was laborious, but Yushuv was quite certain he'd need to return to this place, and as such was diligent about marking his trail, at least until he found himself in familiar tunnels. From there, memory and the buzzing of flies guided his footsteps.

The stairs that led up to the temple cellar had been carved from black stone, and had been worn smooth with time. Empty sconces for torches marked every fifth step, and a charnel stench wafted down from the top of the stairwell. It spiraled upwards in slow turnings, each step broad and flat. Yushuv ascended at a steady pace, never once looking back. The sound of insects grew louder, and then Yushuv reached the final stair.

The massive doors to the temple had been torn from their hinges, and the hinges themselves were nearly ripped from the walls with the strain. One door lay on the floor in front of him, splintered wood marking its edges. The other was nowhere to be seen. The room ahead was only slightly less dim than the tunnels from which Yushuv had emerged, and the humming of insect wings was omnipresent. A sniff told Yushuv that blood was omnipresent as well, and taking the knife from his belt, he strode forward into the slaughterhouse.

The room had once been an antechamber to the tunnels and nothing more. Now it was an abattoir. The wooden benches that had lined the walls were smashed, and the rows of pikes and poleaxes that had rested neatly in niches had been systematically splintered. The temple door lay broken on the floor, its wood stained dark with blood. Beyond it lay the bodies of the temple guards, guileless in death. Blood pooled everywhere on the floor, and even from the chamber entrance Yushuv could see that few of the bodies were intact. He shuddered, and stepped forward.

Up close, the carnage was worse. At least four men in temple livery lay dead on the ground, though the tangle of limbs made an exact count difficult. Their hands still held weapons, and it was clear they had died fighting; no cowards lay here. They had died just the same, however. Throats were slashed, bellies ripped open and limbs mangled with monstrous efficiency, and Yushuv suddenly pictured with alarming clarity the dance of death that must have taken place here. The guards rushing to their posts, the elegant stranger bringing his serpent-headed blade to bear, the terrible artistry of strokes that severed limbs and ended lives, and the screaming as men died in vain. For a second he could almost hear the cries, and then reality intruded as the swarming insects rose up, annoyed at his presence.

Ignoring them, he stepped through the archway that served for an entrance at the far end of the room and out into a wide corridor. Wan sunlight filtered through the hallway, and half-seen murals of religious scenes covered the walls. The corridor was wide, with a sandstone floor and dimensions that would have been pleasantly airy under normal circumstances. Now it simply felt empty and hollow, more so when Yushuv noticed the huddled shapes on the floor.

Yushuv looked left, then right. He knew he'd been taken to the temple for consecration when he was very small, but never since then. The priests were bogeymen of a sort, aloof from the town and deliberately terrifying to small boys with quick fingers. Their rites were hidden behind veils of secrecy, and while they dwelt in the town, they most assuredly were not of it. As such, Yushuv had stayed clear of the temple, and had no notion of how to escape it.

He looked left again, and then right. Neither choice seemed appetizing, but the cool breeze from the catacombs flowed to the left. Shrugging, he followed it.

The rest of the temple held tableaux much like the first one. Here and there bloody bootprints indicated that the stranger had passed this way, but most were lost beneath pooling blood or buried beneath corpses. Priests, soldiers and servants; all had fallen to his wrath. The slaughter was ruthless and all-encompassing. Cadavers lay strewn in bedchambers, in hallways, in corridors and, on one memorable occasion, strewn across three rooms. Nor was the devastation limited to the living inhabitants of the temple. Tapestries were pulled down, urns smashed and murals defaced. Sacred incense had been stuffed in corpses' mouths and then set alight, the sweetness of the scent mingling horribly with the stench of offal. But through it all, there was no sign of the stranger's continued presence. Yushuv was alone. He knew this just as surely as he knew his name or the sound of his own voice, and so he walked unafraid through the temple, which had seemingly been reconsecrated as a shrine to death.

Eventually, inevitably, his wanderings led him to the

sanctuary. Here, as elsewhere, the destruction was complete. The prayer mats were torn with a malicious deliberation that Yushuv found chilling. Not a single one had been missed, and Yushuv could again imagine the stranger at work, checking with calm precision that every last implement and artifact had been desecrated. Blood and other, less identifiable substances had been smeared on the murals of the five dragons that hung around the room's edges. Yushuv wandered from each to each, dispassionately noting smaller details of destruction as he went. Here a brazier had been knocked over, spilling its coals to peter out on the ground; there a scroll had been unwound and casually trod upon. And at the front of the room stood the altar, which Yushuv approached last.

The altar was of white stone inlaid with gems, an odd burst of ostentatiousness in the generally austere temple. At its feet lay a priest, his eyes closed and his hands clutching his belly to keep his guts in. Stains on the altar vestments showed where the stranger had wiped his sword clean, and bloody handprints showed where he'd tried to cast the altar down. It still stood, though, silent witness to the horror around it.

Yushuv stared at it. In a way, this was all his fault. It was he who'd shown the stranger the way, and thus it was he who'd brought this death down upon them. He felt oddly hollow inside. He was no stranger to death; no one in the village was. Children died from fever and women died bloodily in childbirth and cows were slaughtered for festivals, and even the children knew what it was like to get blood on their hands in the course of a day's work. But butchery like this was beyond comprehension. Distantly, Yushuv felt that he should be feeling something: sadness or guilt or disgust. There was only quiet acceptance, and the nagging of the burning at his brow. "I'm sorry," he whispered to the dead priest◦a priestess, he saw now, ancient and wizened and clearly in terrible pain when she died◦and turned to go. There was nothing more for him here.

He wended his way back out, hurrying his way past more of the stranger's handiwork. Once or twice he passed scorpions in the halls. It was clear that the flies were merely the harbingers of invasion, and that all the town's vermin would be here soon. He walked faster. Ahead, the main temple doors stood open, though wrenched badly. The stranger had failed here, or perhaps he had been at the end of his rage and not felt the need to exert himself any further. In either case, they hung at sad angles, and with a turn Yushuv could slide between them.

What he saw outside was smoke and desolation, and one last priest holding his guts in on the steps.

The village had been put to the torch. Livestock roamed free in the streets, walking unconcernedly over huddled shapes that had once been Yushuv's neighbors and kin. Huts and lodges were reduced to smoldering ruins, though here and there a rare building still stood, forlorn amidst the ashes. In the distance a lone dog yowled, mournful for its master. The town square housed a hasty barricade that had done no good. Corpses lay strewn across it, arrayed with unconcern. Blood showed dark in spots against the ground and, as Yushuv watched, the hot wind tried to bury the dead with a handful of dust.

"No," he murmured, not believing. "Not the whole village. He couldn't have killed everyone. Not everyone, and left me alive." His eyes filling with tears, he took a step forward, then another. A handful of clouds scudded along, low against the horizon, and trails of smoke wafted up in a vain attempt to join them.

And the priest on the stairs reached out and clutched at Yushuv's ankle.

He screamed and fell backwards, landing painfully against the stone. His wrist hit the edge of a step and the knife flew from his grip. Desperately he kicked at the grip that held him, which loosened and then slipped. Panting, Yushuv scrambled back up a few stairs and waited. His forehead burned painfully, and he stared fearfully at the figure below.

It turned and looked at him, and Yushuv shrieked again. The priest was a man, perhaps as old as Yushuv's father. His head was clean-shaven, as was his chin, and his lips and teeth were crusted in dried blood. "Boy," he said. "Come closer, boy."

Yushuv shook his head violently, and backed away another step. The priest coughed, a rough, painful hacking sound, and looked up, imploringly. "Please, boy. I just want some water. Just some water."

Yushuv scrambled to his feet and ran back into the temple. "Water," he said, and ran.

Miraculously, there was an unslashed skin of water in one of the priests' quarters. Yushuv gingerly stepped over a corpse to get it, then walked back more slowly. Part of him hoped the priest would be dead by the time he returned; another part of him felt distantly ashamed for that feeling. He quickened his pace and re-emerged into the sunlight, blinking.

The priest was still alive, and had half propped himself up. One arm was wrapped tightly around his belly, though blood showed all around it. The other beckoned Yushuv closer.

"Thank you, boy. You're a kind one. Just bring it to me, and I'll stop bothering you soon enough." He coughed, raggedly.

Yushuv extended his arm, edging forward a step at a time. The waterskin dangled as he edged it into the priest's hand, then let go and stepped back. It fell to the stone with a slapping sound, and the priest fumbled for it.

"Damn you, boy, I won't bite. Where is it...ahh, there." He lifted the skin and pulled the stopper weakly, then poured a gout into his mouth. Pink-tinged water ran down his chin and onto his robes. Yushuv just sat on the top step and watched.

When he had finished, the priest laid the half-empty skin on the stone. "Come here, boy. Let me give you a blessing."

Yushuv stood and swayed uncertainly. "You don't want to bless me."

The priest spat, bloodily. "It's a dying man's gift, boy. You don't want to refuse it. Come here."

Yushuv bowed his head, bowed to the inevitable, and walked forward. "Heh. That's a good lad," the priest said, and propped himself up further. Then, abruptly, his eyes widened in fear.

"You..." he said. "What are you?"

"I don't know," Yushuv said. "But I don't think you want to bless me."

"Anathema," the man breathed, his eyes darting to the knife at Yushuv's waist and then back to his brow. "You're Anathema. This is your work, boy."

Yushuv took a step forward. "Stay back," the priest warned. "Stay away from me."

The boy raised his hands in the air. "I brought you water. I have not harmed you."

"You are a monster," the priest replied venomously, and wriggled backwards. "You're not human. You're in league with the man who did this."

"He left me for dead. In the catacombs. He's no friend of mine. And I gave you water." Relentlessly, Yushuv advanced down the steps.

"Lies! All lies!" He slid down another step, leaving a smear on the stone behind him. "I'll take no water from you." He spat vainly, his eyes fixed on the boy in front of him.

"You have no idea what you're talking about." Yushuv knelt down, his face close to the man's. "You think I'm a monster. I'm not. Yet. But people like you will do their best to make me one." Abruptly he stood and kicked the waterskin over to the priest. "Take the rest. It's a gift to a dying man."

"I refuse it."

"Then die thirsty."

Yushuv walked down the steps and into the remains of the village. Behind him the priest howled, but Yushuv ignored him. He strode quickly, following well-remembered turns to the hut where he once dwelt. Once or twice he saw playmates dead in the street, but he passed them without slowing down. His sandaled feet raised clouds of dust which the wind picked up and carried away. Overhead, vultures and their courtiers circled, lazily waiting for Yushuv to stop disturbing their feast. He ignored them as well, and pressed onwards.

Miraculously, his home still stood, though cinders drifting on the breeze made it an open question how much longer that would be the case. Steeling himself, he ducked inside.

Mercifully, no one was there. The hut was empty, his mother's cooking fire still smoldering in the hearth and his father's tools gone from their accustomed place by the wall. The sleeping mats lay on the floor, neatly made up. A foul smell drifted up from the kettle that swung over the flames; dinner had long ago burned and crusted over. Gagging, Yushuv fled from the smell and went deeper into the hut. Quickly, he took a few things—a satchel, some food, another waterskin, a blanket, a rag to tie around his brow and hide whatever had frightened the priest so—and headed for the door.

Emerging into the sunlight, he stopped. It was clear that he could no longer stay here. The bodies would attract wolves, and worse, and when they ran out of dead food they'd go looking for something live. Besides, he had no desire to live in this place; the ghost of the priests would no doubt haunt him after all.

That left him with a single choice: leaving. The supplies he'd taken from his home would serve him for a few days; long enough for him to reach another town and hopefully find shelter. Belatedly, he remembered the glowing man's injunction to find the dagger, and decided that doing so might not be such a bad thing.

The sun was still in the east, so he chose to follow it. Mentally he noted houses that had burned down—this one belonging to Shalak Grey, the blacksmith, that one once the property of Aliana, who served as physicker to the people and beasts of the town. His life lay in ashes; it was time to move on. His pace quickened, and he hurried toward the rough track that served as a road elsewhere. He'd never followed it, of course. His whole life had been spent in the confines of the village. He'd never even heard the town named. It was simply home. But home was dead, and so was everyone in it.

Yushuv found his father at the last turning before he left the village. He lay, face down in the road, his body contorted as if in great pain. His bow, strung, was still in his hand, and a half-full quiver of arrows rested on his back.

He took a halting step forward, then another one, then stopped. Until now he'd hoped, somehow, that his family had escaped. Here was proof they had not. He opened his mouth as if to speak; nothing came out. Tears stung at the corners of his eyes, but would not flow. His father was dead in the dust, and the vultures were waiting.

Feverishly, Yushuv knelt in the dust beside his father's corpse and worked at it, trying to turn it over. *He should at least face the sun,* he found himself thinking, and with a heave flipped the body. With a thump it settled back into the dirt, and the dead fingers relaxed their grip on the bow. Yushuv pulled it aside, then stared in disbelief.

His father had never been a handsome man—his face too narrow, his nose too sharp—but in death he was hideous. He was drawn and pale, his face set in the grimace of a man who's dying just fast enough to feel it. All the color had been leached from him, and his mouth was bloody from where he'd bitten through his tongue. There were no wounds on him, though—no bloody gouges or slashes like Yushuv had seen with the priests. He was simply dead, and there was nothing more to say.

Clearly, the stranger had done this. But how? Yushuv pondered for a moment, then decided he really did not want to know. However, the sight was enough to steel his resolve to leave. If the stranger could do this, it would be best to leave quickly, lest he return to check up on his handiwork. It pained Yushuv to leave his father's body there, but burying him would take time, time Yushuv did not have. He considered for a moment longer, then set to work.

Carefully, Yushuv sat his father's corpse up long enough to loop the quiver from its back. After a moment's consideration, he took the charm around his father's neck as well. Grey stone on a leather thong, it had been given to him by a spirit, his father had said. As such, he'd hidden it from the priests. They tended to take such things poorly. He had no further use for it now, though, and Yushuv took it as a remembrance. If a spirit had given it to his father and still remembered, all the better. If not, it was still better that he had it than the wolves.

Gently, he lowered the body back to earth. Sprinkling a handful of dirt on its chest, he leaned over and kissed his father's brow. It was icy cold, and a faint twinge reminded him of the mark on his own forehead. It was over here. It was time to go.

Scooping up the quiver and his father's bow, Yushuv set out at a trot. Behind him, a dying priest howled to the heavens for vengeance. As the boy vanished in the distance, the heavens kept their own counsel.

Chapter Twelve

Ratcatcher dreamed. The Prince of Shadows commanded it, and he dreamed.

In his dream, he saw the Prince, terrible and beautiful. Behind the Prince were the ramparts and crags of his citadel, and beyond them a low and threatening sky. The gates of the castle stood open, and the road before them rose up from a cavern. It was paved in skulls, and mice scurried from eye socket to eye socket.

From the depths of the earth, Ratcatcher heard a sound. It was the noise of hooves on stone, or perhaps on something stone-like. In the distance, the sound of claws on stone could be heard, thousands of them scrabbling for purchase. And in the road before the Prince was a single dead rat with a golden blade through its belly. It opened its eyes and stood on its hind legs. With its forepaws, it drew forth the dagger from its gut, and presented it to the Prince, who took it gravely. Then the rat turned to him, Ratcatcher, and *hissed.*

"Hurry," it said. "Bring your tidings and hurry. The Prince has no patience for you."

Ratcatcher awoke. The Prince of Shadows commanded that he dream no longer, and so his sleep was disturbed.

"I am summoned," he said, and wearily crawled out of bed to prepare for the journey home.

Chapter Thirteen

It was in the town of Stonebreak that the Guild finally found Eliezer Wren. Stonebreak itself was a poor shadow of Nexus, a trade town established by merchants upstream toward Sijan in hopes of siphoning off some of the traffic along the River of Tears. It had a council of syndics, who ruled in imitation of Nexus's rulers but less effectively, and a market that was legendary for being a haven of cheats, swindlers and lesser specimens of humanity. Still, the town did a remarkable business, in large part because most of those who traveled here felt certain that they would be the swindler and not the swindled. Approximately nine-tenths of them were incorrect in this assumption, but hope springs eternal, and so Stonebreak's market and docks bustled.

The town's architecture was mostly dull gray stone, constructed hastily from the great boulders dredged from the river, and then patched again and again when roofs sagged or walls crumbled. The entire city had an air of impermanence. Wren had once heard it described as "a place waiting to be told to move along," and found little in that statement to disagree with.

That may well have been why he liked the place, and why he inevitably drifted there. Everywhere he looked in Stonebreak, there were third-rate cheats and transparent agendas, and it was something of a relief to him to once again be embroiled in the schemes of the petty, instead of those of the great. To cheat the cheaters, to unmask the swindlers; this was surely part of his task as much as hauling his weary bones across the Realm at Kejak's whim.

In truth, his plans were uncertain. While he was sure of a summons from his master at some point, in the interim he was very much at loose ends. In truth, he'd been so long in the harness that he was no longer quite sure what to do with himself without a task set before him.

And so he came to Stonebreak, intent on doing little deeds while waiting for the larger ones to find him. There was an Immaculate sanctuary there as well, where he could study and fast and meditate, and hopefully make atonement for his shortcomings in the field. Wren was painfully aware that he was not a particularly good initiate, and on occasion found himself wishing he could be more devout, more studious, more...everything except what he was.

However, he knew that wishing for that was like wishing for the rivers to turn to wine, not that he'd touched wine since he'd shaved his head and joined the Order. He was Kejak's creature, and had been groomed to be such since long before he'd known it. Often he wondered how far back Kejak's hand had touched him. His childhood? The night he'd decided to run away and join the Guild? He'd certainly had some sort of influence on the day Wren turned his back on that life, and had no doubt crafted the events that led Wren to the Order seeking refuge.

Sometimes, Wren reflected, *the cage is more comfortable if one closes the door oneself.*

Not entirely satisfied with that thought, he walked the streets of Stonebreak, and waited for purpose to find him.

Chapter Fourteen

He'd waited until evening. Such was the best time for what he was going to attempt, and if it failed, he'd want the cover of darkness under which to make his escape.

Ratcatcher looked around. He'd ridden out of town and now found himself standing, a very bemused horse next to him, in the middle of some peasant's field. A quick glance showed that the farmer was apparently cultivating a healthy crop of weeds, but that was the peasant's problem. If he'd had enough time, Ratcatcher reflected, he'd have poisoned the well just to show his irritation with fools like this one, but time, it seemed, was of the essence.

The Prince had summoned him. The Prince was untold miles distant. The Prince was not a patient man. Ratcatcher knew all these things to be true, and he knew also that no matter how quickly he rode to the Prince's citadel, no matter how many horses he rode to death underneath him, it would still not allow him to arrive before the Prince grew angry at the delay.

It was entirely possible that the Prince was already angry at the delay, but there was nothing that could be done about that. Still, the best thing Ratcatcher could do would be to return to his liege lord's presence as quickly as he could, regardless of the potential risk.

That meant walking the Labyrinth.

Ratcatcher hated entering the Labyrinth. While one could save a tremendous amount of travel time by dropping beneath the skin of the world and into the great maze that underlay all things, doing so was not without risks. Getting into the Labyrinth was easy enough for an adept of Ratcatcher's skill, but getting out was another thing entirely. Stable paths through the maze were few, and the landscape constantly changed. Stone tunnels could suddenly become deadly swamps, and rains of glass and blades were common. Mindless, ravening things stalked the halls, as did servants of the dead gods and other things that dwelt within. One had to know one's route very well indeed, or risk either straying into the domain of a hungry power with a taste for trespassers, or getting lost and wandering the maze for all eternity. Nor was this last worry an exaggeration; he had seen Lost Ones on prior trips through the Labyrinth, but never dared speak with them. One had met his eyes, once. That had been enough.

In the east, the moon peeked over the horizon. It was fat and bloated, and stained the color of old blood. "As auspicious an omen as I am likely to find," Ratcatcher said, and then began chanting. The words were nonsense, intended not to be understood but rather to thrum out of tune with the fabric of reality. Beneath his feet Ratcatcher felt trembling, and smiled. It was working.

He redoubled the pace of his chanting, and drew his sword from his back. Reddish-black sparks, fragments of his anima, danced along its length. The pounding beneath the ground grew stronger, as if something were about to burst forth. In the farmer's distant cottage, a child was crying, and his dog was whining to the uncaring sky. There was power here, and it was making its presence felt.

Ratcatcher reached the end of his chant. For an instant he held the blade aloft, then drew it through the air in a vertical slash. There was a horrific, tearing sound, and the tear he'd cut in the fabric of things simply hung there. A cold wind blew forth from it, heavy with the breath of the grave. Occasionally it shimmered, and faint cries could be heard beyond it.

Ratcatcher sheathed his sword and examined his creation. It was perhaps six feet tall, too short for him to ride through. He'd have to lead the horse.

Grumbling, he did so. It shied away from the rift once, but he yanked savagely on the reins until it stepped forward. Boldly, he walked through the rift and vanished. Tentatively, the horse followed him.

Behind them, the doorway closed with the sound of the

tide coming in through a narrow channel. The child, however, continued crying long into the night.

Chapter Fifteen

The first night was warm, and for that Yushuv was grateful. He'd gone as far as he could along the dusty track that served as a road, though every time he looked back it seemed that the village had receded just a little. Even after heat and distance allowed the ruins to vanish in the haze, there remained the telltale pillars of smoke straying up to the heavens. It was hours before these blended, mercifully, into the dusk.

The first day's journeying was easy enough, though the bow grew heavy after an hour's walking. Yushuv had heard tales of far-off cities where the streets were paved in silver bricks, but here travelers had to make do with a dirt track, beaten down by countless caravans, riders and wanderers. Still, the walk was more pleasant than it might have been. The land through which the road traveled was best described as "civilized": long meadows marked on occasion by farms and homesteaders' huts. Sheep grazed in fields, occasionally watching his progress with passive interest before returning to their repast. There were no inns and no towns, but Yushuv had not expected any. The Threshold was not as well populated as once it had been, and he knew that the nearest village was a full day's ride away. How much further, then, for a boy on foot?

Occasionally small streams ran parallel to the road before snaking off lazily. Sturdy wooden footbridges forded these, and willow trees dotted the streams' banks. These were the only trees Yushuv saw, and they nodded sadly toward the waters that nourished them. As he walked, Yushuv tried to imagine this land as the site of ancient battles, but the image would not come. He could not see the green fields dotted with corpses, or the slow streams thick with blood. Yet he knew that that had once been the case, and for a second he wondered if the dead here slept peacefully, or hungered for a return to war. Not liking the answer that seemed most logical, he hurried on, and tried to put as many paces as he could between himself and his former home before nightfall.

The rag Yushuv had tied over his forehead did little to soothe the burning he felt beneath it, though he soaked it in the cool water of each stream he came across. Each time, his reflection showed him that his brow was marked with a sigil he'd seen here and there in the catacombs. It bore a resemblance, if he squinted hard enough, to the rising sun, and it shone gold against the dark tan of his skin. As the day faded, it troubled him less and less, and by nightfall, a dull ache was his only reminder that it was still there.

As the evening closed in, Yushuv pondered the question of shelter. While the rag hid the mark on his brow from casual passersby, he suspected that it would not hold up under close scrutiny. The reaction of the priest to his appearance, not to mention the word "Anathema," gave him a clear idea of what his reception would be were his new nature to be discovered.

As such, he resolved to spend the night under the shelter of a willow tree. As the western sky dimmed from red to purple behind him, Yushuv found a stream and traced its course a few hundred paces off from the road. Finding a suitable tree, he examined the trunk and frowned, then shimmied up it with skill that would have done a squirrel proud. He wedged himself between two branches, then tore carefully rationed chunks from the supplies he'd taken from home. These wouldn't last more than another day or two, he knew, and he'd have to augment them one way or another before long.

That, however, was the next day's problem. He took the quiver and bow and set them firmly in another notch, then wrapped himself in the thin blanket he carried and settled in for a night's sleep.

In the morning, he climbed down from the tree, dropping lightly onto the balls of his feet and then splashing down into the creek to wash his face and refill his waterskin. The evening had been restful, though his dreams had been odd, and marked by the sound of the beating of heavy wings. But the dead of his village had not visited him even in dreams, and he felt refreshed. The mark on his brow now felt warm, rather than burning, and Yushuv marveled at how limber he felt. He'd gone to sleep expecting a morning's full of aches and cramps from sleeping in the fork of a tree, yet the only pain he felt was a dull rumble in his stomach that reminded him that he needed to eat. A glance at his reflection in the water made him marvel further; the shape he saw there moved effortlessly and smoothly, so unlike the clumsiness for which the other children had taunted him.

Feeling quite pleased for no reason he could define, Yushuv set off. Birds exploded from the trees as he passed, and he could see fish swimming in the shallows. Algae waved lazily in the brook's slow current, and he imagined he could see each frond and shape on it. Already the sun was well above the horizon, and the night's pleasant warmth was beginning to dissolve into the kettle of the day's heat. Spotting the road ahead, Yushuv hurried forward.

The second day's travel passed much as the first had, though there was slightly more traffic along the road. Whenever a telltale dust cloud appeared in the distance, Yushuv would bolt from the road for whatever shelter he could find. Often he took refuge in pastures, or behind abandoned houses. When possible he kept to creekbeds, to avoid leaving tracks, and he'd wait patiently until he was alone again on the road before venturing forth. While he was fairly certain the stranger had forgotten all about him, he still dreaded the possibility of the man's return. Yushuv was quite certain that his continued survival was an error his father's killer would gladly rectify, and while he had no idea what direction the stranger had taken after finishing the slaughter at the village, prudence dictated that he treat every approaching cloud of dust as if it harbored death.

When evening came, he killed a rabbit, wasting a pair of arrows in the process. He found one, broken, and managed to kindle a small fire with its pieces. Well back from the road, in the shelter of another willow tree, he spitted the carcass and roasted it as best he could. The result was half scorched, half nearly raw, but it tasted delicious. As night fell, once again he climbed a tree and made his camp there, pausing only to pour water on his fire lest the smoke betray his position.

And again, he dreamed of the sound of wings.

The third day passed much as the second had, as did the fourth and those thereafter. Yushuv grew more adept with the bow at a frightening pace, and now evenings found him carving from willow branches rough arrows which nevertheless flew straight and true. Travelers were more frequent, and on occasion Yushuv found himself skirting small towns. While days had passed since he'd spoken to another human being, Yushuv nevertheless shied from the possibility of meeting others. At best he'd be a penniless stranger, another beggar boy on the streets. At worst, he'd encounter someone working for the stranger, or have the Wyld Hunt called on him. None of those possibilities appealed to him, and so he kept to the shadows whenever he could. The land here was better, supporting more trees and brush, and as such there were more places for him to hide when other travelers approached. At times he wondered why he continued to do so, since each man or woman passing along the road seemed to do so with a studied indifference to anyone else who might share the way with them.

Chapter Sixteen

The ghost that accosted Ratcatcher as he rode through the Labyrinth was a thing of shreds and tatters, a memory of a woman that could scarcely remember itself.

"Master," she said, and prostrated herself in front of him.

Ratcatcher regarded the ghost for a moment, then said, "Get up. Do I know you?"

The ghost scrambled to her feet, awkwardly. She wore ragged leather armor and a torn helm, and her feet were bare. Something had slashed deep into her belly, and so her torn guts were on constant display. "I have news for you," she said, and waited.

Ratcatcher looked around. The cavern he was in was relatively sedate, as far as the Labyrinth went. Twitching corpses dangled soundlessly from nooses hanging from the arched ceiling high above, but the floor was nothing more than cobblestones, and the walls were made of smooth marble. A sound like a geyser's bellow echoed from one of the chamber's many entrances, but other than that, the room was quiet. That could change at any second, but in the Labyrinth one seized the moment when one could.

"Yes?" Ratcatcher's voice was full of exasperation. "You have news, you say? And stop calling me 'master.' It's a dangerous thing to say here."

"Yes, master," the ghost answered, her voice a soldier's. Ratcatcher winced, but before he could speak, the ghost continued. "You called me to service in the tomb beneath Qut Toloc. You called others to service, but they did not heed you, or deceived you. They knew of what you spoke, but lied to you. They serve another power now. I do not. I am loyal."

"If you are loyal, would you please stop speaking in riddles? I've no time for this."

The ghost started to say something, stopped, then began again. "The others found the boy. They showed him Toloc's resting place, and spoke of a blade the boy had taken from among the bones and sold to a man named Malaky."

"A resting place?" Ratcatcher leaned forward in the saddle. "Could you lead me back there?"

She shook her head. "Only a few know where that chamber is, master. I have been barred from it. But I thought you should know of the weapon, and journeyed here in hopes of finding you."

"Does everyone know my comings and goings? Am I a trade caravan, that children wait for me at the side of the road?" Ratcatcher complained loudly. The ghost stood silent, not sure if she should answer. The laughter of the hanged men drifted down from above.

"Never mind. I don't even want to know why you chose to look for me here. Go back. Find your way into that burial chamber. I'll return and find you. Do you understand me?"

The ghost nodded, once, and then turned and walked off. She had a limp, which struck Ratcatcher as curious. With no real flesh to be torn, no scars to bear, there was no reason for a ghost to limp, or stagger, or favor one arm. Yet they did, they always did. It was a mystery of the ages, and not one he could solve now. There were other matters to attend to.

His mood much improved by the news, Ratcatcher peered ahead at the various exits from the cave. All were dark, and none were inviting. Memory told him that he should choose the one on the left, as the one in the center led to the realm of Rabark the Blossoming Contagion, and the one on the right led to pits of green flame that burned endlessly. The one on the left, however, led to a relatively safe path through unclaimed territories, and a quick route to the Shadowlands near Thorn.

So memory told him, at least. Trusting that memory, he urged the horse onward, and passed into the shadows.

Behind him the hanged men tittered and laughed until their nooses tightened and they choked in silence. Ratcatcher, had he known, would not have smiled.

Chapter Seventeen

It was the twelfth night after Yushuv left the village when the dreams finally awakened him. He opened his eyes with a start and looked up through the canopy of leaves overhead. A swift glance up told him the moon still rode high in the night sky, while overhead he could hear—no dream now—the sound of slow, heavy wings. A raiton's harsh croak cut the night, louder than any he had ever heard, and then the sounds of the wings faded into the distance.

Carefully he reached for the bow and nocked an arrow, but did not draw. Instead, he willed himself to silence and immobility, listening for something that he could not name, but which he somehow knew was out there. Beneath his perch, the brook chuckled nervously to itself, and a thousand insects sawed the dark with their songs. For a long moment there was no other sound, and nothing moved. Even the night air was calm, the breeze slumbering as heavily as Yushuv had been. A moment longer, and then even the distant sound of wings faded away.

Yushuv relaxed. It was only a bird, one whose flight had somehow merged with his dreams. Satisfied, he lowered the bow and settled back into his perch. It was still several hours before dawn, time for any traveler with sense to sleep and gather his resources for the coming day's journey.

And then came the howl.

Yushuv sat bolt upright, his hand reaching instinctively for the bow he'd just set aside. The sound that had just cut the night was no wolf's cry, though it was kin to a wolf's howl in the same way a wolf was kin to a dog. The sound was long and low and lonely, and it spoke of the sort of hunger which decent and sane men would never want sated.

Yushuv barely dared breathe. The sound had come from the north, not far away, and he was suddenly struck by the certainty that whatever beast might be hunting in the dark, it was most certainly hunting him. He drew back the arrow and waited, eyes straining the dark for he knew not what.

Another howl came, closer this time, and then another, mixed with an odd snuffling sound. The insects had fallen silent; only the creature's voice could be heard. Yushuv clutched the bow tightly, willing his heart to beat more quietly so that the beast would not hear its pounding. Again there was silence, undercut only by a sort of deep whine of the sort made by hounds tired of looking for the kill.

Suddenly a series of splashes erupted from the stream, moving steadily closer. The beast was trotting upstream, steadily closer to where Yushuv perched. He held his breath as the sound of its footfalls reached the tree where he sat, paused for a moment, and then moved on.

Yushuv exhaled, trembling. It had missed him. He did not release his grip on the bow, however, even as the heavy splashes faded into the distance.

In the distance, the raiton screamed again. The beast lifted up its head and howled in answer, a note of warning in its voice. The raiton croaked once more, defiantly, then wheeled off, and the creature splashed its way up out of the stream and Yushuv could hear it no more.

Nevertheless, he did not relax. It was still out there, somewhere. The continuing silence of the insects was proof enough of that. If it had left the stream, it would have done so to find the road, and if it had found the road, it would find his scent there.

And if it found his scent there, it would be able to follow it back to him.

A howl of triumph confirmed this train of thought, and the sound of something large crashing quickly through the creekside underbrush filled Yushuv with fear. His grip on the bow slick with sweat, his stomach knotted in terror, he waited. In the darkness, the creature's pace slowed, the sound of its heavy breath louder with each step.

Just outside the curtain of leaves surrounding the tree, it halted. Yushuv shifted fractionally in his perch, and then with a snarl it appeared.

To say that it had the shape of a wolf would be accurate enough, though no wolf was ever that broad or that tall. Its fur was black, frosted with silver, and its eyes were huge and red. The beast's long tongue lolled over its jagged yellow teeth, and the foul stench of its breath wafted up to where Yushuv was perched. A detached part of Yushuv's mind wondered how he could see it so well, and he realized that it was glowing ever so slightly. He gasped at the realization, and it looked up at him, eyes bright.

Yushuv steeled himself and sighted along the shaft of his arrow. "Begone, spirit," he said, sounding braver than he felt. "I'll put an arrow into you before you can blink."

The beast made a sound that could only be a chuckle. "Will you, little man?" it said in a voice like a rusty blade being sharpened. "And what then?"

"You can talk," Yushuv said, not daring to let it become a question.

"I can speak man-tongue when I need. Can you?" It laughed again, and circled slowly around the base of the tree. Yushuv's aim followed it.

"Well enough. I told you, begone. Leave me be. I have no quarrel with you."

The beast yawned, deliberately opening its maw wide and daring Yushuv to shoot. "You speak well for a village boy. If you were still a village boy, I'd have no quarrel with you either." Suddenly, the beast leaped, throwing itself against the tree's trunk. It hit with a hollow thud, its jaws snapping at air inches from Yushuv's foot. He scrambled for a higher perch as the tree shook, and the beast brayed with laughter.

"They call me Bonecrack, boy. How do they call you? I like knowing the names of my suppers."

"You seem to know enough about me; you should know my name," Yushuv retorted. "As I now know yours, spirit."

"You know what men-folk call me, village boy, not my name. Only Raiton knows that, and he's not telling. And even without your name, I can still take your throat in my jaws and drink your life's blood." Again Bonecrack pounced, and again Yushuv scrambled back, nearly overbalancing and falling to earth in the process.

Bonecrack's maw split in a wolfish grin. "I'm just playing with you, village boy. You'll not escape."

Yushuv's response was to send an arrow into the ground hard by Bonecrack's left front paw. It stuck there, quivering, and the beast looked at it curiously.

"The next one finds your heart," Yushuv said calmly. "Leave now."

"I don't think so, village boy," it growled. "There's a price being whispered about for your eyes, and no child's bow is going to keep me from them."

"This was my father's bow, Bonecrack. It's no toy." He fired, and Bonecrack swiped the arrow out of the air with a massive paw.

"Without a man to bend it, it's a toy. A sword in a child's hand won't cut, either. Go ahead. Bend your bow. Empty your quiver. I'll gnaw your bones when you're done."

In the dark, Yushuv smiled. "You will? Then is it a bargain?"

Bonecrack growled. "A bargain? What are you talking about, man-child?"

"Your offer. If you let me fire my arrows at you, I'll sit here and not struggle when you come for me. After I finish, of course." Yushuv's voice was all brave innocence, the sound of the fool who rushes to accept the merchant's bargain that's too good to be true.

Bonecrack threw back his head and laughed. "You can't hurt me with your sticks, child. It's a bargain; I'll even make it easier for you, so you'll end this foolishness quickly." It sat back on its haunches and panted, looking for all the world like a household dog eager for its master's attentions. "You may proceed, boy. I'll sit here until your quiver's empty," it said, and its voice was filled with boredom.

Yushuv nodded. "You will, too, won't you?" he said, and hopped down from the tree. "Of course, my father taught me always to save one arrow. This quiver will never be empty,

Bonecrack. You'll squat here forever and wait for me, and mountains will turn to dust before you're free."

Bonecrack howled then, a sound that slashed the night and shook leaves from the tree. In the distance it echoed, and dogs at distant homesteads carried the cry. "Damn you! I'll break this chain if it takes a hundred years, and I'll dig your bones from your grave to crack them in front of your ghost. You won't escape me!"

"You forged the chain, Bonecrack. It was none of my doing." Yushuv walked up to where the spirit sat. "But I'll give you the satisfaction of knowing that your freedom's closer than it was." Carefully, he drew the bow and sighted. "I wonder if this will hurt you. I hope so," he added conversationally, and then released.

The arrow pierced Bonecrack's paw, and punched deep into the earth beneath it. Thick blood gouted from the wound, the same red as the spirit's gaze. It roared in agony, and Yushuv quickly drew and fired again. The shaft took the spirit in the eye, and a third went down its gullet. Bonecrack's cry became a strangled thing, and it thrashed in its agony as best it could.

"These...won't...kill me, boy," it choked out. "I'll...come for you."

"I doubt it. And if I can't kill you, I'd better not waste any more arrows on you. Remember me, Bonecrack. Remember the village boy." On a whim, he pulled the rag from his forehead and smiled grimly. "Better yet, remember me as I am now."

With that, he strode off into the night in search of a more congenial tree in which to sleep for the remaining hours before sunrise, and of Bonecrack he thought no more.

Chapter Eighteen

"Whose are you?"

Ratcatcher stopped his progress and looked up to see who spoke. Hanging from the ceiling by a whiplike prehensile tail was a creature akin to a monkey, but hairless and wizened. Its arms and legs were so long as to remind him of some sort of spider, and the smile it bore on its lopsided head was not a kind one.

He looked around. The corridor itself was one of the plainer ones he'd passed through, being covered in smooth green tile the color of jade. The stones were warm, but not uncomfortably so, and he'd seen no other travelers along his route.

Until now.

"I am called Ratcatcher," he said. "Now stand aside and let me pass." He made no move to advance, but for the moment he refrained from having his hand stray to his sword. While the shriveled thing guarding the way didn't look dangerous, appearances could be deceiving in the Labyrinth. This watcher might be more dangerous than it seemed, and that was before one considered the possibility that the floor itself might swallow an intruder, or the walls split open and disgorge a horde of foes.

"I said *whose* are you, not who. I have no interest in who you are, only the name of the one you serve." The creature dropped to the floor, somersaulting in midair and landing squarely on its feet. It rocked back and forth and spoke in a singsong pattern, as if to a child. Closer now, Ratcatcher could see that its skin was a mottled gray, and that it barely came up to his chest. Its fingers and toes sported wicked claws, and it stank like old, stagnant water. Ratcatcher wrinkled his nose in disgust, and the creature caught his reaction and grinned like a clever ape.

"Tell me first whom you serve, and I'll tell you whom I serve. Fair enough?" He took what he hoped was a subtle step backwards, which would ideally mitigate the stench that flowed from the creature in waves. It didn't, and behind him his horse whinnied nervously.

The watch-beast scratched its chin with its long fingers. "There's no harm in that, I suppose, even if you live to carry the name with you. I am called Crothos, and I serve Rhuxus the Devouring One, She Who Bears Many Names In Darkness. You have been leading your beast through Her domain for many hours now without Her leave, and She does not bear any love for those who intrude on Her lands uninvited. Now, your master's name, quickly, lest She grow impatient." It leaned forward and stage-whispered, "She is known as the Devouring One for a reason, you know."

Inwardly, Ratcatcher cursed. Either his memory of the safe pathways through the Labyrinth was faulty, or Rhuxus had expanded Her realm since the last time he'd traveled this way. The latter seemed likely, as the monstrous beings that ruled here were in a constant state of war with one another, each struggling to subsume its neighbors before being devoured itself. Rhuxus, though, had a particularly unpleasant reputation. It was said that She manifested as a vast lake of boiling pitch, which flowed hither and yon through the caverns and passageways She ruled, devouring everything in its path. It was also said that she had no love for the Prince of Shadows, as she made war on the dead gods he served.

All in all, Ratcatcher decided that his chances of returning to the lands of the living were not very good at all.

To cover his discomfort, he bowed from the neck, not daring to meet the watchman's eyes. "I serve the Prince of Shadows, and travel on his business. I had no intention of straying into the Devouring One's domain, and I do humbly apologize for distressing Her with my presence. Indeed, it would seem best that I hasten on my way, so as to remove myself from Her realm and thus disturb Her no longer."

The watcher blinked its huge eyes, but did not remove itself from his path. "A pretty plan, yes, but a better one would have been to choose a different path. Where do you go, servant of Shadows?"

"To wait upon my master's pleasure..." Ratcatcher began, but his voice trailed off as the beast loped past him.

"Pretty horse," it said, stroking the stallion's muzzle with long fingers. "So very pretty to bring to such a dark place." The horse rolled its eyes in terror and stamped, but did not bolt. For that, at least, Ratcatcher was thankful.

"The steed was loaned to me by my master so that I might labor on his behalf, and is not mine to give. Were circumstances otherwise, I would gladly make a gift of it to the Devouring One, so that Her hunger might be sated."

The watcher whirled to face him. "Her hunger will *never* be sated, cur, until She has devoured all of Creation. Were you schooled in the paths you tread, you would know this. Does the Prince keep you for your wit and counsel, or merely to beat you upon his whim?"

Ratcatcher felt his face flushing, and willed himself to be calm. "The Prince values my services, and I render them gladly, as you render yours to your mistress."

"Oh, does he?" Crothos was all sly malice and wicked grin, its fingers trailing along the horse's flank. "Then why did he bid you come this way? Did you not know that he is wroth with thee, and gave you as a gift to my mistress, in hopes of winning peace with Her?"

"You are mistaken," Ratcatcher said evenly. "My master did not bid me come this way. I chose the path of my own accord, so that I might return to his place of power more quickly." He fought to keep his voice steady. Could the Prince have betrayed him? It was possible. His master had been less than pleased with him when they had parted company, and he held no illusions as to his ultimate value. If the Prince decided that there was more gain to be had by sacrificing Ratcatcher than by retaining him, then sacrificed he would be. It was one of the many bargains each Deathknight in the Prince's service made, understood, and accepted. Serving the Prince brought with it power, instruction in matters arcane, and many other benefits. It also brought with it a demand for absolute loyalty and a need to submit to the Prince's will in all things.

And if the Prince's will was your death, so be it.

Still, Ratcatcher could not believe that the Prince meant to sacrifice him like this. The dream-sending had merely called him back to the citadel. The decision to walk the Labyrinth had been his own, or at least he thought it was, and surely the Prince would not have promised him to the Devouring One had he not been certain that Ratcatcher would take this route.

"Confused, poor little cur? You say nothing." Crothos drifted back behind the horse, which kicked at it. Laughing, the watcher stepped neatly aside as the horse's hoof whistled through air. "It has spirit, it does. Unlike you. Simply going to stand there? Let yourself be led away meekly? I had thought more of the Prince's servants, 'til I met you."

"If my prince wishes it, I will give myself up gladly," he replied, mind racing. Running was an option, though he suspected that Crothos had friends hidden in the near vicinity. Even worse, the tunnel was too low for him to mount up, which meant either leading the horse or leaving it behind. He did not relish the latter possibility, but the former would be difficult at best. The other option would be to attack Crothos and take things from there. All of this depended, of course, on the notion that the beast had been lying, and that no bargain had been made. Rhuxus might be willing to overlook his unpleasant dealings with a servant who had put words in Her mouth. If Crothos was merely carrying out Her orders, then Ratcatcher was doomed regardless, and killing Crothos would simply make his torments that much more intense.

"Why don't I believe you? Such long pauses. You are plotting your escape, are you not? Silly dog. There is no escape, not from Her hunger." Crothos made its way up along the horse's opposite flank, shaking its head gently. "It was too late when you first set foot here."

"Perhaps," Ratcatcher said, and struck him. The blow was all power and no finesse, a simple punch from a mailed fist that sent Crothos spinning. It squealed and bounced up on all fours, but in that instant Ratcatcher struck the horse's flank. "Go!" he shouted, and off it went, galloping down the tunnel as fast as it dared on the slick tiles.

Before Ratcatcher could finish turning to face his enemy, Crothos was on him. "You will die!" it hissed as its claws tore his cheek, narrowly missing his eye. It clung to him with animal strength, both legs wrapped around him while one hand clutched at his throat. "You are Hers, and you will die."

Ratcatcher grunted and caught Crothos's questing hand at the wrist. He squeezed, and felt bones crack in his grip. Crothos shrieked and strove to claw out his throat, but succeeded only in drawing furrows in the metal of his gorget.

"Not today, I think," was all he said, and wrapped his arms across Crothos's back. Briefly, Ratcatcher wished his armor bore as many spikes and excrescences as did his master's, but he might as well wish to be in a tavern in Lord's Crossing for all the good it did him. Instead, he merely tightened his grip, and squeezed.

Crothos flailed in his grip. It loosened its grip around Ratcatcher's waist and twisted this way and that, but the Deathknight's hold was relentless. "She will not forgive," it howled, and clawed repeatedly at his face. Again and again it struck, each time drawing blood.

Grimacing, Ratcatcher squeezed. Crothos was tough, far tougher than a creature of flesh and blood would be, but the strength Ratcatcher poured into his grip was inhuman. Closing his eyes to protect them from the beast's questing fingers, he poured his very Essence into the act of crushing the life from the thing besetting him. "You...won't...find out...if She does," he growled, and redoubled his efforts.

Suddenly, like a bubble bursting on the surface of a pond, Crothos's back snapped. The yellow light went out of its eyes and it sagged against Ratcatcher's chest. "You were to be my gift to Her," it said, faintly, and then slithered to the ground in a heap. Ratcatcher kicked it once. It did not move.

"Marvelous," he said bitterly. "Now to find my horse."

"RATCATCHER." The voice came from behind him, from the corridor down which the horse had fled. He turned, slowly.

She was there. Where once there had been a corridor paved

in sullen green, now there was only Rhuxus. Her bulk filled the corridor and, Ratcatcher suspected, stretched endlessly beyond. The stench of pitch boiled off Her, and a rough shape rose from Her depths to face Ratcatcher where he stood.

"Devouring One," he said simply, and bowed his head. There was no point in running. Either Rhuxus was pleased with him, or She was not. Nothing he did would make a difference either way.

"YOU HAVE SLAIN MY SERVANT." It was a statement, not an accusation.

"It claimed it spoke Your mind, Devouring One, when clearly You would not stoop to having one so lowly as Your agent. Such arrogance should be punished."

"DO NOT PRESUME TO SUCH THINGS. IT IS ABOVE YOUR STATION."

"Yes, Devouring One," he replied, instantly humbled.

A pseudopod of pitch reached out from the vast mass of Rhuxus, reached past him but came so close he could feel the torn skin of his cheek blistering. It found Crothos's body on the floor, flowed over it, enveloped it. "HE IS MINE, AS HE ALWAYS WAS." There was a pause as the tentacle withdrew. Where Crothos had been, there was a yellow stain on the floor. Nothing else gave evidence that it had ever existed. "YOU, TOO, ARE MINE IF I WISH. YOUR PRINCE CANNOT HELP YOU HERE." Another pseudopod reached out and danced in the air before him. It flickered forward and back like a snake, scenting the air before it struck.

Ratcatcher closed his eyes and bowed his head, waiting for the inevitable. "I know this, Devouring One."

Abruptly, the tentacle withdrew. "I DO NOT WISH WAR WITH YOUR PRINCE OR HIS MASTERS AT THIS TIME. YOUR LIFE IS MY GIFT TO HIM. TELL HIM THAT, AND WHEN YOU RETURN, BRING ME RICH SACRIFICES. YOUR WAY IS CLEAR FROM HERE TO THE SHADOWLANDS THAT WILL BRING YOU HOME, FOR I SO WILL IT."

Ratcatcher started to sink to his knees, caught himself and turned it into a bow. "Thank You, O Devouring One. I shall bear Your message." He paused, as a thought struck him. "But what if I do not pass this way again? I would not see You await your sacrifices in vain."

Rhuxus laughed, a deep, bubbling sound that filled Ratcatcher with fear. "HAVE NO FEAR," She said. "YOU WILL RETURN TO ME. ALL THINGS DO."

With that, Rhuxus withdrew down the tunnel with astonishing speed. Within seconds, She had vanished, and even the tiles of the corridor had cooled sufficiently that he could walk upon them without fear of injury.

Resolute and relieved, and not a little weak in the knees, he assessed his situation. The Shadowlands were not far away, and once he reached them, it was not far to the Prince's citadel—assuming he could find his horse.

That, however, was a secondary worry. It was more important to leave the Labyrinth before Rhuxus changed Her mind.

Humming to himself, he started walking.

Quickly.

Chapter Nineteen

The citadel was not large, as far as such things went, but the dead men who dwelt there did not complain. Hewed from obsidian, it had five towers, each with a broken crown. This was deliberate, as it gave the building the appearance of a jagged claw raised against the heavens. The towers had no windows, nor did the main keep, and arrow slits and murder holes were few and far between. The single gate was wood treated with pitch, and black iron studs had been driven into it with blows from a titanic hammer. The land surrounding the citadel was ashen gray, but the fortress itself was so black that it seemed to drink in whatever light was unfortunate enough to fall upon it. It was a blight upon the land and a monument to death, and its master, the Prince of Shadows, was well pleased with it.

Now its gate stood open, and a man on a black horse rode through into the expanse of the courtyard. Grey dust caked both horse and rider, and the beast's eyes were wild. Its flanks were scabbed from where its rider had used his spurs mercilessly, and it shuddered as he leapt from the saddle. He turned and, without hesitation, took a knife from his belt and slashed its throat. The horse collapsed, blood fountaining from its neck. The rider strode off toward the ebon doors of the main keep, not sparing a single look behind him.

Around the stricken stallion, the ghosts gathered, waiting for it to cease its struggles. It tried to rise once, screamed, and fell in a pool of gore. Once more it shuddered, and then lay still. The ghosts in unison turned toward the place where their master dwelt and then, as if they had received some sort of silent benediction, began to lap softly at the spilled blood.

Inside the citadel, the man who called himself Ratcatcher took off his helmet and tucked it under his arm. Shaking himself slightly to free himself of road dust, he oriented himself, then strode down a long corridor carpeted in scarlet. Candles guttered in sconces every twenty or so paces, shedding just enough light to emphasize how pitiful their efforts were. Ghosts bustled silently around him on their own business. He ignored them, and they him. They all served the same master, after all.

In his travels, Ratcatcher had heard all sorts of whispered stories about what the inside of a Deathknight's citadel was like. Most of the tales were lurid ones, told in hushed tones around low fires late at night. They spoke of torture pits and groaning souls, of walls that dripped blood and vivisection tables manned by grinning cannibals. It was all that Ratcatcher could do to keep from laughing aloud. The Prince of Shadows' home held none of these things. All it housed was dim lights and the silence of death, which was precisely what its master desired.

At a pair of massive double doors bound in iron bands, Ratcatcher stopped. This was his master's throne room, and while he had been bidden to report as soon as he returned, still he hesitated. The Prince of Shadows' moods were occasionally mercurial, and the fact that the doors were closed was not a good sign. No sound came from within⊙not that this was a surprise⊙and Ratcatcher found himself turning on his heel rather than tugging at the massive doors. Perhaps he'd come back later, when the signs pointed to a more welcoming reception.

Of their own volition, and with the faintest whine of their hinges, the doors opened. "Welcome home, Ratcatcher," came a languid voice. "I thought I recalled commanding you to hurry home to see me. I trust you didn't misunderstand me."

Ratcatcher turned and dropped to one knee, his head bowed. "My prince, I had thought that since the doors were shut, you did not wish to be disturbed. I see I was in error, and humbly request that I be allowed to make amends." He kept his eyes resolutely on the floor. To meet his master's eyes now could be seen as a sign of defiance, and defiance would mean death.

The Prince of Shadows sighed. "You thought wrong, and I see you still choose to speak when I had suggested rather strongly that you not. Still, it means nothing, however, in these times. Just be certain not to think next time the opportunity arises."

"Yes, my prince," Ratcatcher breathed, his head still bowed.

"Very well. You may approach, and you may speak as well."

"Thank you, my prince." Humbly, Ratcatcher stood and strode into the throne room. It was bare, with a floor of polished black marble and a high, vaulted ceiling. No tapestries hung on the walls, and the only furniture was the massive, ominous throne of the Prince of Shadows himself. It rose straight from the stone of the floor and had been carved into the shape of a huge, crashing wave. Looking up at it, Ratcatcher could not shake the impression that he was about to be overwhelmed by a tide of darkness, which was no doubt why the Prince had ordered it crafted thus. Overhead, a massive chandelier crafted from the bones of creatures long dead and monstrous swung slowly to and fro. A fistful of candles guttered in places, creating shadows which danced around the room fitfully. Ratcatcher had long ago learned not to follow the motions of those shadows; they did things that he was quite certain shadows should not do.

And in the center of the silence sat the Prince of Shadows. He looked young, surprisingly so, and it was a constant surprise to Ratcatcher how delicate his master seemed. His face was boyish and his frame was slender, and he wore a single circlet of black metal around his brow. His garb was silk; black, of course, shot through with threads of red and gold and bone-white. His feet were small and bare, and they rested on a cushion of black silk at the base of the throne. Across his lap lay a heavy black mace, and in his right hand was a wine cup that had clearly once been a man's skull.

"You've got blood on your knife still," the Prince said, and Ratcatcher looked down, embarrassed. "Why?"

"A thousand apologies, my master. I gave my horse to the ghosts in the courtyard." He paused. "It was of no further use to me. I was forced to take it through the Labyrinth, and it... suffered there."

"Hmm. Bring the blade to me." Ratcatcher nodded assent and extended his blade hilt-first. The Prince set down his wine and took it. He turned it over in his hands once, then brought the knife to his mouth and licked it clean. A frown crossed his face. "You rode this one hard, yes. I am glad to see you heed my sendings so well. There may be hope for you yet."

"I would hope so, my prince. I bear news, and I felt it was best to return with it as quickly as possible when you commanded me."

The Prince reclined on his throne. "Tell us."

"I think I've found the grave of another Solar. If not, I've found something very much like it."

The Prince leaned forward, his eyes intent. "Interesting. Give me the details."

Ratcatcher took a deep breath. "I was riding through some of the border towns at the Realm's northwest edges while hunting that priest for you. You know the sort of place I'm talking about—a collection of huts that might still be in the Empire because no one's mentioned that it's not, but the peasants will hoe the dirt no matter who's in charge. The biggest town in the region is called Boneford for no reason that anyone can fathom because the nearest river is three days' walk. There's a temple there, though, stocked with too many priests. At least, there used to be." He paused, and looked up for a sign that he should continue. Almost imperceptibly, the Prince nodded.

"I headed towards this batch of hovels because I thought the temple—Earth aspect, of course—might provide me with some amusement, as well as a good place to find some information on this priest of yours. I never got that far, though, at least not at first."

"What happened?"

"I found a sinkhole when I went to ground for the day. I could hear dead men's whispers down in it, so I thought it best to explore. That's when I found out why they call the nearest town Boneford."

"And why is that?" The Prince's tone showed a dangerous level of boredom. Ratcatcher swallowed hard, and continued.

"My prince, the master undertakers of Sijan could labor in the catacombs under that temple for a decade and not clear away a tenth part of the bones that rest there. I talked to many of the dead men there, though most fled from me. One told me that a battle had been fought there eight centuries ago, and that an entire army had made war on a single woman."

"Woman?"

"Solar, one would think. Another ghost later told me that woman was named Toloc."

"Mmm." Suddenly the Prince was very attentive. "Indeed. You may continue."

"Thank you, my prince. The ghosts in the tunnels told me that the priests have been carefully sorting the bones, looking for the body of the Anathema so they can destroy it and all its accoutrements. Apparently the battle was fought in the dungeons and chambers beneath the Solar's citadel, and there were so many bodies that they collapsed the palace on top of it rather than bring the corpses out. Then someone realized that there still might be a rather dangerous collection of artifacts and gewgaws buried down there, so the Immaculates set up a temple and began burrowing through the mess they'd made. However, being priests, they haven't gotten very far. But to be fair, it's only been centuries. Perhaps they haven't had enough time."

"Just the story, please, Ratcatcher. Your feelings on the Immaculate are well known to me. I have no wish to hear them again." The Prince yawned, and stretched, and utterly failed to smile.

Ratcatcher blinked, as if a bullwhip had been cracked an inch in front of his eyes. "Of course, my prince. I most humbly beseech your pardon for my digression."

"Do not digress further by continuing to apologize. It grows tiresome."

"Certainly. As you wish." Ratcatcher could feel the Prince's eyes on him, could feel himself losing composure. Stammering, he hurried on with his tale. "While I was down there, I spotted a child, spying on me. As by then I was quite lost, and the ghost was quite unwilling to show me the way out, I simply let the boy lead me to the stairs to the surface. These, happily, led me to the interior of the temple, where a veritable herd of priests attempted to stop me. I showed them the folly of their ways, and attempted to discuss with them the whereabouts of their missing Anathema. Unfortunately, most either would not speak with me or shortly lost the ability to do so. I left the temple and sacrificed the village, and proceeded thence to my horse. It seemed more sensible to return here when you summoned me and bring you the news than to try to search the catacombs myself.

"Along the way, a shade I had spoken with in those catacombs found me again, and told me more. I learned the name of the one who is interred there, and that a blade of hers was stolen. The boy sold it to a man named Malaky, it would seem, so this artifact is loose in the wide world."

The Prince yawned. "Is there anything else?"

"Merely that my loyal little ghost is barred from the burial chamber, but will seek it if she ever returns home. I also have tidings for you from Rhuxus the Devouring One, who bids me tell you that She gives you my life as a gift, and that She seeks no quarrel with you or the ones you serve at this time." Ratcatcher coughed, nervously. "It would seem Her domains have expanded lately, and the route that I chose took me through them. One of Her servants was unruly, and I was forced to deal with it." He paused, suddenly uncertain. "Have I erred?"

"No more than usual, Ratcatcher. I will send embassy to Rhuxus and see what She really wants. The fact that you stumbled into Her lap is merely a happy accident for Her. You should, however, devote some time to choosing a better course for your next journey. Now, let us discuss the tidings you bring." Abruptly the Prince was standing, striding across the floor of his throne room and bristling with nervous energy. "You have done well," he said, "and perhaps better than well. I am just curious about the loose ends that remain, and how they tie to strands from my own loom."

"My lord?"

"The boy. You interrogated the priests, but you forgot to put the child to the question, even though he was the one you found actually amongst the bones, yes? And now we find that he has laid his hands on a Solar's blade, and has seen a Solar's grave. But you let him escape."

"My prince, I thought I had wounded him mortally. Besides,

he was just a boy, and the Immaculates awaited."

The Prince of Shadows frowned, and began pacing around Ratcatcher in a slow circle. His feet slapped on the floor, loudly, and Ratcatcher winced at each footfall. "As a matter of fact, it is entirely possible that this boy might have seen the Solar's grave even before the dead men showed him. Boys are clever that way, you know. They're good at finding things they're not supposed to."

"My prince, he was just a bone rat!"

"A bone rat, you say?" The Prince glided closer. "And what do you mean by that?"

Too late Ratcatcher remembered the stories about where the Prince had been born, and of his early service in Sijan. "My prince, I just meant to say that the boy was of the sort that robs graves for a living, and nothing more. He hardly seemed capable of solving a puzzle that had defeated the Immaculate for centuries."

"Ah." The Prince stood directly in front of Ratcatcher now, tendrils of black wisping out behind him. "Even so, he lives, and with knowledge that many, many folk would gladly kill for. If I did not know better, I'd swear you were growing soft on me, my servant."

Ratcatcher stood stiffly, not daring to move. "He told me the way out, and that I'd find priests waiting for me. It seemed more fitting to let him live, and to have the dead men follow him."

"Ah." The Prince reached out and with one finger traced the line of crimson tear tattoos that wended their way down Ratcatcher's torn and scabbed cheek. The finger came away wet with blood. "I applaud the artistry of it, but I find the practical side somewhat lacking."

Ratcatcher felt the blood running down his cheek, and he trembled with the effort to control himself. The Prince of Shadows had obtained a mastery of power that he could barely dream of; if he raised his hand to his lord, it would be the last action he ever took. "I fail to see what you mean, my prince," was all he said, and he struggled to keep his voice level. One of the tendrils of the Prince's anima wrapped around his ankles; he did not dare look down at it.

"My servant, must I tell you everything? You will rest here tonight. Tomorrow, you will set forth and find the boy. I do not think it is a coincidence that you stumbled onto Toloc's grave just as my astrologer is telling me to beware Qut Toloc. No, find the boy. Find the blade he took. Find the grave he took it from, and if that is not enough for you to do, find me Wren. Pelesh the Exchequer will give you all the jade you could possibly need before you go. I'll send others toward Qut Toloc and its secrets as well. My servants are more efficient than priests, don't you think?"

"Yes, my prince."

The Prince smiled. "Good. I'm glad you agree. Now go to your room and rest. Tomorrow, find a new horse and see Pelesh, then go." Very slowly and very deliberately, the Prince traced his finger down Ratcatcher's other cheek. It left a bloody trail. "You are dismissed."

Ratcatcher bowed. "Thank you, my prince." He turned, and at a pace that was not quite a run, left the room. The doors closed behind him, and in his empty throne room, the Prince of Shadows sat and listened to the silence.

Chapter Twenty

Pelesh the Exchequer was not a generous man. He was small and stooped, and his skin was pale and fine as parchment. He wore a black robe with a silver medallion on it, and his fingers were crabbed and ink-stained. He hated Ratcatcher, and Ratcatcher hated him right back.

At the moment he sat behind his desk, which was covered in neat stacks of coins of every description. Before him was a small pouch, also dyed black, and embroidered with the Prince's seal. He was, unsurprisingly, frowning.

"That's not half enough, Pelesh," Ratcatcher said with the tone a man might use to explain to a small child precisely why the minnow he'd caught would not serve as dinner. "I'm going to go hunt down a dagger the size of your greedy little fist. It could be anywhere in the Realm or beyond by now, the only clue I have to its location is the name of a pissant Guild factor from the frayed ends of civilization, and you want to send me forth with a handful of spare change? The coins aren't going to breed if you leave them alone in the dark, you know. Pfah!"

He spat on the floor and, slowly, Pelesh peered over his desk at the mark on the tiles, then just as slowly looked up at Ratcatcher. "I give you what I deem prudent," he said, in a voice like cracked leather.

"Prudent? Prudent!" Ratcatcher sat back, his face a mask of amazement. "There's prudence, and then there's penury. And for another thing, find me another pouch, one without the Prince's crest on it. This is going to be difficult enough without letting every Dragon-Blooded halfwit from here to Crystal know whose errands I'm bound on."

"There are no Dragon-Blooded in Crystal." Pelesh's tone was smug.

"There will be, if I carry this thing and head north. What do you know of Crystal, anyway? You haven't left this chamber in ten years, except to eat or piss."

"Vulgarity will get you nowhere, Ratcatcher," Pelesh said evenly. "I have been instructed by His Majesty to give you what I feel you will need for your journey. A new horse has been chosen for you, and its saddlebags have been packed. They will be waiting for you. You'll have the hounds as well, I think. As for financial resources, you will receive precisely what I have assigned to you and not a splinter of jade more. I think you are right about the pouch, however. I'll have another one found for you and it will be placed with your things. Clever of you to notice, really." He looked up and saw Ratcatcher's face pale with fury. "Now, really, if you're that upset over not having enough money, I'm sure you can discover ways to find some on your own. The Prince keeps on telling me how clever you are, after all."

With that he turned back to his accounts, leaving Ratcatcher to loom over his desk, trembling with rage. After a few seconds, Pelesh looked up again, making a great show of seeming to be surprised by Ratcatcher's continued presence. "Still here? What do you want now?"

"I want," Ratcatcher said in a tightly controlled voice, "enough in my purse to do this thing properly. Is that too much to ask?"

Pelesh considered. "For you? Mmmm, yes, actually it is. Though Shamblemerry will be very amused to hear of this encounter."

"Shamblemerry? You favor her over me?" Ratcatcher drew back in astonishment, nearly tipping over a low table covered in scrolls.

"My loyalty, as always, is to the Prince, Ratcatcher. This is something you would do well to remember. But it is no secret that you do not rank high among our Prince's servants, and that others are better loved than you. Many would be happy to see you fall, and their favor is more worth cultivating than yours. Succeed at these tasks the Prince has set before you and this may yet change. In the meantime, try me no further. Leave my chambers. You'll have nothing more from me." With that he turned, presenting his back to Ratcatcher.

"If the Prince did not favor you..." Ratcatcher breathed.

"But he does," came the words over Pelesh's shoulder. "Good day."

Still fuming, Ratcatcher left. Pelesh permitted himself a small chuckle, then bent to his work and thought on the matter no more. Come morning, the man would be on the road and out of Pelesh's thinning hair, and hopefully the universe itself would take care of him.

And if not? Then Pelesh would deal with him when he returned. He doubted Ratcatcher would, however. In truth, he wasn't even sure the man was supposed to.

Chapter Twenty-One

Ratcatcher loved the docks of Nexus. They were dirty and mean, and constantly buzzing with activity. Trade was the blood that pumped through the city's veins, and as such the docks were busy day and night. Cargoes of jade, of spices, of silks, of lumber and of a hundred other things passed across the docks each day, and when the sun went down, huge bowls of oil were set ablaze so that the labor might continue by night. Massive, brooding custom-houses overlooked the docks, and stern-faced city watchmen shepherded each cargo to make certain that smugglers would at least have to work hard to import their wares. Sweating gangs of longshoremen hauled on lines to bring fat junks laden with goods into their berths, while others loaded wagons or herded coffles of slaves into holding pens so that they did not interfere with the work, or seek to drown themselves in the river. Smoke was everywhere, and there was a constant traffic of small children running messages to and fro for whatever they could beg.

Most of the cargoes bore the chop of the Guild, which surprised Ratcatcher not at all. Guild ships carried Guild goods to Guild warehouses, where they were handed off to Guild merchants in Guild caravans to carry them into the wide world beyond. Independent traders were forced to the older, run-down piers at the end of the waterfront, and often their cargoes met with "accidents" unless the Guild-backed labor gangs that unloaded those ships were paid off. Smaller trade associations were less lucky. Their ships often foundered mysteriously—not near Nexus itself, where trade was sacred, and interference with it brought death—but upriver, or off the coast, or anywhere a Guild-bought man might see an opportunity to put an auger to work or drop a careless spark.

It was late afternoon when Ratcatcher came to the docks. He'd stabled his armor, horse and hounds upstream on the Yanaze, with a woman who thought herself akin to darkness and whom the Prince of Shadows owned, body and soul. She'd been happy to help Ratcatcher once he revealed what he was, promising him the best care for his animals, the safest shelter and the most discreet confidence. She'd offered him her body as well, but he'd spurned her. She was not uncomely, but his thoughts were all for the hunt, and willing prey did not appeal to him.

And so he had taken passage down the river on a barge loaded with great timbers of a reddish-hued wood that grew far to the east. The trip into Nexus was a brief one, and once the captain had been paid a few pieces of jade he was content to let Ratcatcher pace the decks, watching the lowlands roll by. Taking the horse would have been faster, but Ratcatcher was in no hurry to be recognized. The stallion was clearly not the sort one could buy at a village market, the hounds even more unusual, and his armor unique. To ride into the city thus would have been to alert every Dragon-Blooded warrior, devout Immaculate and lurking spirit that an agent of the Abyss had presented himself as a challenge. Therefore he traveled clad in simple black, his hair tied back with a length of silver wire and his torn face half-hidden by a scowling mask. Only his sword, with which he would not part, marked him for who he was, and there were enough barbarians, mercenaries, heavily armed madmen and would-be Wyld Huntsmen stalking the city streets to make one more unusual blade look like nothing more than eccentricity. The sailors on the barge were wise enough to ask no questions, and the ship's master had been paid not to, and so he came to the docks in relative anonymity.

The captain of the barge had not heard of Malaky, but recommended that Ratcatcher find a man named Greenstone, who could often be found by the docks. Greenstone was not a harbormaster, but he did a great deal of work for the Guild in matching ships and cargoes, and not a man or ship reached the docks without him knowing of it. The captain went on to describe him as short, with a scarred face and a bad ankle that made him slow to walk and quick to reach for the wine bowl. Ratcatcher thanked him with more jade, and strode off the barge cheerfully while the foreman of the labor gang on the docks shouted at him to get out of the way.

A wide alley choked with wagons, hustling workers, beggars and dirty children stretched behind the docks, running parallel to the riverfront and providing the main avenue by which cargoes were brought into the city. City watchmen moved back and forth through the chaos, checking wagons and shooing wharf rats, but as Ratcatcher bore no pack and no cargo, they ignored him.

Cries from behind alerted Ratcatcher that a wagon was coming up on his position, and rather than argue the point, he pressed himself against the stone wall that marked the landward side of the avenue. Pack animals straining, the cart rolled past at an agonizing pace while the drover cursed and cracked his whip. Behind it, men pushed and strained, and kept a sharp eye for any items that might fall from the load.

"You're new here, aren't you?" The speaker was a girl of perhaps eight, all huge eyes in a round and dirty face. She wore a man's tunic, belted at the waist with a length of thin cord, and her feet were bare. There was no fear in her gaze, only scorn.

Ratcatcher caught himself nodding. "I don't intend to be here very long, though."

"Looking for work with a caravan? I can take you to a hiring factor, for a price." Her voice was strong. No doubt she'd done this many times before.

"Looking for a man, actually. Two, if truth be told. Find me either one of them and I'll pay you." Ratcatcher attempted a winning smile, then realized what effect this might have in conjunction with his mask and settled for a carefully neutral expression.

"Wrong."

"Oh?" He drew back in surprise.

"First you'll pay me, then I'll find those men for you." Her tone was flat, brooking no argument.

Ratcatcher laughed. "The Guild doesn't know what it's missing without you, girl. Fair enough, a coin to you to find my men, and another to buy your silence. Do we have a bargain?"

The girl held out her hand. "Bargain. Now, let's see your coin."

Deliberately, Ratcatcher reached into his purse and brought out two pieces of jade. He held them between two fingers over the girl's outstretched palm and said, "First, your name. If you lie to me, I'll come looking for you."

The girl snorted derisively. "Any name I'd give you would be a lie, and if you can't find a man here, you can't find me."

"I won't be looking for you quietly," he replied, and dropped the jade into her hand. She shuddered minutely, and said, "They call me Shining Amber. Who do you want me to find?"

"Greenstone," Ratcatcher said, satisfied, "and a Guild factor named Malaky."

The wagon finally rolled past, and she laughed. "Greenstone? You *are* new here. That's him," she said, and pointed to a figure in the near distance, haranguing a dockside foreman. Still laughing, she fled, and vanished into the crowd.

Ratcatcher debated going after her, but decided against it. She'd given him what he'd paid for, after all, and trying to find her in the mob would be pointless. At best he'd make a laughingstock of himself, at worst he'd make an enemy of every guttersnipe in Nexus. While he seriously doubted that an army of street children could so much as scratch his much-abused cheek, dealing with them would no doubt attract attention, and that was something he could ill afford. He looked up the street again, saw that Greenstone was still arguing, and made his decision.

Greenstone had just finished his argument when Ratcatcher caught up with him. "Your pardon, sir, a moment of your time?"

Greenstone looked up and grunted. He was an ugly man, with a square face that someone had introduced to a knife a long time ago. His left ankle bulged in his boot, and Ratcatcher surmised that it had been broken and set poorly. His hair was raggedly cut, but rings of gold and jade gleamed on his fingers.

His clothes were fine, embroidered with gold thread and small gems, and he carried himself with an air that bordered on arrogance.

"Hiring fair's a day from now at the central market. Don't need mercs down on the docks anyhow. The labor gangs take care of themselves. Now move along." With a curt nod, he dismissed Ratcatcher and began limping up the shallow incline toward the custom-houses.

"You misunderstand me, sir," Ratcatcher continued, and reached out to catch the man's elbow. He whirled, and suddenly a dozen thugs with knives, wooden clubs and the odd belaying pin materialized out of the crowd. They formed a circle around Ratcatcher and Greenstone, and the rest of the traffic flowed around them.

"Don't touch me," Greenstone said quietly. "You *never* touch me."

"I most humbly apologize," Ratcatcher replied, releasing the man's garment and taking a step back. "I merely meant to ask you a question—one having nothing to do with hiring, I assure you—and clearly overstepped my bounds. I do beg your pardon."

"Heh." The Guildsman brushed at his sleeve, as if Ratcatcher's touch had left some sort of stain there. "Business questions cost. I'm a busy man."

"I'm sure you are." Ratcatcher reached into his purse, felt how few coins remained there, and again mentally cursed Pelesh. "Still, I give you my word that the asking of the question, and the answering of it, will take less time than we have spent already debating the nature of its asking. And I will, of course, pay for your time."

"Yes, yes, you will." At a gesture from Greenstone, the thugs stepped closer. Sighing, Ratcatcher reached into his pouch and brought forth half his remaining jade. A heavyset, pale-skinned man wearing little more than short trews and a series of intricate tattoos broke from the circle and took the money roughly from Ratcatcher's grasp. Grinning apishly, the thug brought the money to Greenstone and handed it to him, then took a place just behind his master.

Greenstone poured the money from hand to hand twice, then tucked it away in a belt pouch. "You've bought your question. Ask it."

"I'm looking for a man named Malaky. I'm told you know where to find him."

"What do you want with Malaky? There are better men to deal with in Nexus, I assure you."

"Perhaps. But he's the one I want to talk to."

Greenstone shrugged. "Suit yourself. He's unreliable. Drinks too much, spends too much time on the road, and sits in Shotan Fong's pocket like a child's pet toad." There was a round of low laughter from the bodyguards, and Ratcatcher wondered what it meant. "Still, he's in the city now, if you really need to find him. He's friends with a laborer named Stone Turtle, who works down at the Pier of the Stooped Crane. It's four from the end on the ocean end of the waterfront, and you'll find him resting his poor little feet at this time of day. You can tell him I sent you, if he proves stubborn. He always does, you know."

Ratcatcher bowed his head a fraction of an inch. "I thank you for your assistance—"

Greenstone waved him off. "You thank me for not having you dumped in the river. Now if you ever have another question for me, rethink it and find someone else to ask. We're done." He turned and walked off. Around him, the thugs melted back into the crowd, leaving Ratcatcher alone on the busy street.

"The Pier of the Stooped Crane. I'd forgotten how quaint Nexus was." And Ratcatcher, too, disappeared into the teeming throng.

His name was Stone Turtle, and it had not been given in love. He was heavy and slow and ponderous, and his neck was so short as to be invisible. Suspicious by nature and slow of wits, he worked the docks for the Guild and was perfectly happy to do so. He also performed other services when called upon to do so, such as dealing with thieves who tried to steal from Guild warehouses, and tying barrels full of rocks to the ankles of those who displeased his employers. He had a round face and a beak of a nose, and his hair was sandy and thin. Stone Turtle wore a brown tunic and brown trews, which he tied off with a belt of rope, and brown leather boots that had seen better days. His eyes were dark and sunken, and he looked as if he'd chewed and swallowed each word he heard as it came along.

Ratcatcher found Stone Turtle along the docks, his back to a mountain of lashed-down barrels and a half-empty wineskin in his hand. The day was almost done, and the last slivers of sun shone redly to the west. Even so, Stone Turtle shaded his eyes with his off hand and stared up at Ratcatcher with an expression that promised a thrashing if he even looked at Stone Turtle's wine.

"I'm told you're a man who knows things," Ratcatcher said, and squatted on his haunches in the barrels' shadow. "I'm a man interested in learning things."

"Hunh. Whoever told you that was having fun with you." Stone Turtle's voice was deep and slow, as if it came up from the bottom of the river itself. "I ain't interested in knowing a damn thing except which barge gets loaded next."

"Hmm. That's strange, a man who called himself Greenstone told me that you'd be the man to talk to for what I want to know."

Stone Turtle grunted. "Greenstone's a liar." There was a pause. "And a drunkard." Ratcatcher waited for the slow spark of curiosity to catch in Stone Turtle's mind. Inwardly he seethed, but trying to hurry this man would be like trying to hurry granite. Finally his patience was rewarded. Stone Turtle looked up from his wine and squinted. "What'd you ask him about?"

Ratcatcher was all breezy nonchalance. "Oh, nothing in particular. He just said you work with a man called Malaky sometimes, and I was wondering if you could tell me where to find him."

"That bastard!" Stone Turtle erupted to his feet. "Me'n Malaky work secret." With slow malevolence he turned his gaze on Ratcatcher. "Why'n you want to know? You from the Guild? You think I been stealing? Stone Turtle don't steal nothing!" He advanced, heavy-footed, on where Ratcatcher stood, his hands balled up into impressively large fists.

Ratcatcher smiled and put his hands up in a friendly gesture, palms out. "I'm not from the Guild, I swear to you, and I certainly don't want to get into a fight." The latter was most definitely true, he reflected. While dealing with this mud-colored buffoon in front of him would take no time at all, it would, however, be entirely too tempting to do so in a fashion that would draw unwanted attention down on him. And so he smiled, and he took a step back, and he smiled some more.

"Enh? Then who sent you? What d'you want with Stone Turtle?" The man stood there, clenching and unclenching his fists.

"My master did, and I can assure you he has no interest in anything except where to find Malaky." Slowly Ratcatcher reached to his belt and dipped into the bulging leather pouch he carried there. Just as slowly, he withdrew a handful of silver coins, and held them up in front of him. "Now, if you don't want to tell me where I can find your friend, I understand, but I'm simply looking to do some business with him, and you know, it's unfair that he should be the only one getting rich from it...." He let his voice trail off hopefully, and watched Stone Turtle's piggy little eyes focus in on the coins.

"Hunh. That's more'n Stone Turtle gets for workin' with Malaky." He put out one massive hand and opened it, and one by one Ratcatcher dropped the coins in. Then the thick fingers closed over the coins, and they vanished from sight. "You can find 'im at Threecreeks. It's a tavern couple blocks off'n the river by the custom-house with the silver balance painted on it. He'll be there t'night, t'morrow, then he's off on the five-town circuit 'gain, an' it'll be two weeks afore he's back. You jus' don' tell 'im that Stone Turtle's th'one who told ya how t'find 'im, y'hear? Don' want 'im mad at Stone Turtle!" Satisfied, the giant turned himself around and shambled off.

Ratcatcher blinked in amazement, twice, then went looking for Threecreeks. Hopefully Malaky the factor would be there, and he'd still have the dagger on him, and this little farce could be ended quickly.

And if he was really lucky, they'd have some decent wine as

well. His step quickened as, up above, the sky grew almost dark enough to be to his liking.

Threecreeks was the sort of place best described, if one were being gentle, as a dive. It was dirty, and the sign of three blue ribbons tied together that hung over the door was fire-scarred and worn. The door was heavy oak, permanently held open by an iron spike in the flagstone before the lintel, and the interior was dark, smoky and foul-smelling. A woman in a leather cuirass that had seen much ill-usage stood before the doorway, arms crossed and frowning. With a twitch of her head she motioned Ratcatcher inside, then turned back to patrolling the street with her eyes.

The promise of squalor made by the exterior was more than kept by the inside. Ratcatcher stooped to enter the main room, and immediately wished he hadn't. Flickering oil lamps hung from the ceiling on knotted chains, and Ratcatcher knew instantly that every time a fight broke out here, the lamps would come crashing down to set half the place ablaze. Rough-hewn wooden stools were set around rougher-hewn wooden tables, and a sickly fire sat in a central hearth under a fat black kettle. Swinging doors at the back marked the entrance to the kitchen, while stairs next to them led up to what Ratcatcher presumed were cheap lodgings. Behind the bar stood a woman who could have been twin to the one outside if she were thirty pounds lighter, drawing mugs of beer and bawling for the serving slave. Men and women sat in groups of two or three, muttering darkly amongst themselves and staring balefully at any newcomers who dared intrude on their haven. On the ceiling someone had painted the sign of Threecreeks, badly, and Ratcatcher found himself hoping the smoke would finish the job of obscuring the painting that darkness had begun.

Hostile stares met his eyes as he looked around the common room. He'd never actually had Malaky described to him, he realized, and as such his search was going to be more difficult. For an instant he pondered shouting "Is Malaky here?" and waiting for his target to flee in panic, but as amusing as the resultant brawl would no doubt be, there was no guarantee that his target would not wind up accidentally perforated in the fracas. Reluctantly, he abandoned the notion and instead waded through the human flotsam to the bar.

After several long minutes, the barkeeper noticed him and looked his way, disapprovingly. "What'll you have?" she asked, reaching for a damp rag with which to move a spill to a different spot along the countertop.

"I'm looking for a man," Ratcatcher began, tentatively.

"Hah. You look the type. Try the Distinctive Jade Garden, or if you're low on cash, the Turning Mirror down by the waterfront. If you're pretty enough under that mask, you might even make some coin there. But we don't deal in that here."

Ratcatcher gritted his teeth and smiled blandly. "I'm not looking for a man for that," he said, and resisted the urge to reach across the bar to do her an unpleasantness. "This is strictly business. Financial business," he added when he saw the sneer start to rise on her face.

"Lots of men come in here," she said noncommittally. "Lots of women, too. Even the occasional eunuch."

Ratcatcher shook his head in annoyance. "Yes, yes, I'm sure you get the occasional talking dog as well, and that he doesn't pay for his drinks. I'm looking for one man. His name is Malaky, and he's a buyer for the Guild."

The woman spat on the counter, stared at it briefly, then wiped it up with the rag. "You're doing business with Malaky? You'd do better at the Turning Mirror."

"And you're better off telling me what I want to know. There's profit in it for you if you do, less every time you try to be witty and half-accomplish it. The choice is yours." As he did this, Ratcatcher took her hand in his and *squeezed*. She was not a weak woman, and the calluses on her fingers spoke to many years of holding a sword, but her efforts were like that of a child trying to break free from his father's stern grip. She whimpered once, and looked up to meet Ratcatcher's eyes. He shook his head slightly, then raised his other hand to his lips. "Shhh," he said. "Say anything, and I'll squeeze tighter. Now, take your other hand and point out Malaky to me. When you do, I'll let you go and leave a very nice handful of money on the counter for your trouble. If you shout, scream, or try to stab me in the back, I'll kill you. If you tell anyone that I was here looking for Malaky, I'll come back and kill you. And if you serve me a mug of beer that you've spat in, just to prove how marvelously brave you really are, I'll burn this place down around your ears with you and all of your customers inside. Nod if we have an understanding."

Slowly, she nodded. Tears formed at the corners of her eyes.

"Excellent. Now, where is Malaky?" Slowly the bartender turned, then fixed her eyes on a rangy man slumped near the fire.

"That's him," she said through gritted teeth. "If you're going to kill him, his tab is yours, and it's not small."

Ratcatcher laughed daintily, and released her hand. "Oh, no worries on that score." He brought most of the remainder of his jade out of his pouch and laid it on the counter. "This should do for him, no matter how long he's been drinking. It should also buy your silence, and perhaps a favor should I ever return. Now, draw me two mugs of beer and go about your business before I decide to become less generous."

She snatched her hand back and immediately started trying to rub some feeling into it. "What are you?" she whispered, staring wide-eyed.

"A slave," he answered more or less truthfully. "And a man who is very impatient for his beer. If there are no further questions..." He let his voice trail off meaningfully. Still staring, the bartender drew a pair of ales in beaten leather mugs and placed them on the counter. Fearfully, she made a sign against evil and made her very deliberate way over to the other end of the bar.

Ratcatcher took the ales and maneuvered through the crowd to where Malaky sat. The man was tall and thin, a dejected tangle of arms and legs hunched over a low table. He looked as if some wasting disease had tried its hand with him and then decided not to bother, and an empty mug sat on the table next to him.

Carefully, Ratcatcher snagged a stool with his boot and dragged it to Malaky's table. "Mind if I join you?" he asked, and sat down without waiting for an answer. He set both mugs down, and shoved one over toward Malaky. "Go ahead. It's for you."

Blearily, the man unraveled himself and looked up. His eyes were bloodshot;that much Ratcatcher could tell even in the gloom of Threecreeks. "For me?" he said, in a voice that was thick and slurred. "Nobody ever buys a drink for me unless they want something. What do you want from me, eh? Ain't got nothing left to give!"

"Shhh." Ratcatcher spoke softly and calmly. "It's for you, and what I want from you won't cost anything. I just need to know if you still have the dagger."

"The dagger?" Abruptly, the man sat bolt upright. "Don't know what you're talking about. Now gimme that."

"Ah, ah, not so fast." Ratcatcher pulled the mug away, still smiling. "You're an important man, a Guild factor. I'm sure you deal with lots of knives. But this one was different. It was golden, about this long," he momentarily abandoned his grip on the beer to place his hands about six inches apart, and in that instant Malaky made a successful swipe for it. The factor guzzled greedily at it while Ratcatcher waited, then drew the back of his hand across his mouth. Ratcatcher smiled, thinly, and continued. "I understand you bought it from a small boy in a village called Qut Toloc. Is this true?"

Malaky belched, loudly. At another table, someone laughed, but when Ratcatcher turned the entire bar was a sea of studied indifference. When he turned back, Malaky made a great show of being deep in thought, stroking his chin and nodding up and down.

"That one, I remember it. Qut Toloc's not a town. It's a temple with some huts in its shadow, and children who steal from the bones underneath. Can buy some decent fabric there, sometimes. Not much else, except what the children find."

Ratcatcher nodded. "And one of them found a knife?"

Malaky took another long pull of his beer. "Dagger. Not a knife. Damned good one, too. Sold it when I met up with Fong's caravan a few weeks a-gone. He bought it himself, too. Paid good jade for it. Don't remember what happened to all the jade, though."

"Try not to worry about it. Where's Fong now?" Ratcatcher leaned forward, eagerly, and as an afterthought pushed his mug across the table as well. Wordlessly, Malaky cradled it, looking across the table at Ratcatcher as if daring him to take it back.

"Fong's on circuit. Fong is always on circuit. He was in Nexus nine days ago, though. If you ask at the Guildhouse, they'll tell you his route. Don't tell them I sent you, though. Big Guild secret and all. They can tell you where he is and you can catch up. The caravan's slow, slower with Fong in it. The fat man doesn't move too fast, you know."

Ratcatcher nodded. "I know. Drink the beer. It's a present. You've been wonderfully helpful."

"It's nothing," Malaky mumbled as Ratcatcher rose, already focused entirely on the mug in front of him. "Just keep my name out of it."

"Of course," Ratcatcher said as he left. "I've already forgotten it."

Early that morning, Ratcatcher left Nexus, headed upriver toward Lookshy. He left with knowledge of the route of the caravan housing Guildmaster Shotan Fong, and he left with a great deal more jade in his purse than he had possessed previously. Behind him were a series of mysterious disappearances along the dockside, none of which were ever traced to the stranger in the half-mask. Greenstone was left unscathed, but strode forth from his home in the morning to find a pouch of severed ears pinned to his door with his bodyguard's knife. Neither the bodyguard nor the owners of the other ears in the pouch were ever found.

Ratcatcher also left a small pouch of jade with a street runner with instructions to get it to Bright Amber by morning or else face the wrath of the river dead. Unsurprisingly, the jade was in the girl's hands by sunrise.

Unseen, he left a bottle of fine wine on a certain table by the fire at Threecreeks, which Malaky the factor passed around the house so that others might toast his generosity. Everyone who drank of it spent the next hour emptying their guts on the tavern floor, and word spread that Threecreeks' wine was not to be trusted. It closed a fortnight later.

The mask Ratcatcher threw in the river, and his journey to the homestead where his horse was stabled was swift. He paid the woman who had kept his horse and hounds in jade, and took passage over the river in the morning. The boatman was paid well for his silence, and with his pay took his own passage downriver so that he might never see that passenger again.

It had been, Ratcatcher decided as he headed northeast toward where he was told the caravan awaited, a most satisfactory visit to Nexus. Then he put spurs to his horse's flanks and rode forth. Behind him, his hounds bayed and followed.

Chapter Twenty-Two

"Fong wants to see you."

"I beg your pardon?" Wren turned as he felt a tug on his sleeve, and found himself face to face with a short, swarthy woman wearing the jerkin and baggy trews of a Guildsman. Her nose showed clear signs of having been broken ungently some time in the distant past, and her eyes were narrowed in a permanent squint.

Wren gracefully plucked his sleeve from her grasp and stepped away. "I'm sorry," he said. "I don't know anyone named Fong. Perhaps you should inquire at the Shrine of the Illuminated and Devout Hymn-singer. It's four streets up and two to the left. Just turn at the fishmonger's stand—but don't buy anything—and you'll see it. And now I bid you a good day."

"Shotan Fong wants to see you," she repeated, stubbornly. "He told me to find you, Eliezer Wren, and that he wants to see you. He said that he has 'a problem that can only be solved by your priestly expertise.'"

The foot traffic of a Stonebreak morning swirled about them, but to Wren it was as if he and this woman were the only two people in the city. He felt cold, and a hard knot formed in the pit of his stomach. "He said that? Those exact words?"

The woman nodded. "He also said that no harm would come to you. The past is the past, he said."

Wren snorted in disbelief. "The past is the past, which is why he keeps using it to draw me. What's your name?"

"My name?" She looked startled, as if she had been prepared to deliver her message and nothing more. "Gentle Alabaster."

"It would be," Wren murmured, then stepped forward and seized Alabaster's hair. She began to shriek, and he clapped a hand over her mouth. "Filthy whore!" he bellowed. "Plying your trade amongst honest tradesmen! By the lights of the heavens, I'll banish thee from their sight!"

So saying, he dragged her into an alley. Alabaster struggled, but Wren's grip on her was firm. Around them, passersby stared briefly, then continued on their way. No one made a move to help Alabaster; several pointed and laughed.

When they had ventured deep enough into the alley, he pinned her against the rough-hewn wall of a looming tenement. After a moment's consideration, he uncovered her mouth, but shifted his grip on her to a wrist, lest she try to run.

"Are you mad?" she asked, her voice almost a scream. "What did you think you were doing back there? I'm no whore!"

"No, but you're an idiot," Wren hissed savagely. "Speak quietly, even here. Do you want the whole city to know your business? Discuss such things with me in the middle of the street—you might as well hire minstrels to sing it in the taverns, and puppet shows to explain it to the children. There are ears listening, Stupid Alabaster, and eyes watching, and Fong's business is not the sort that he wishes others to see."

Sullenly she made a half-hearted attempt to set herself free. "Then why the performance? That will just make them remember us more."

Wren shook his head. "They'll remember a fanatic Immaculate screaming nonsense, nothing more. They got a good show, and that's all they'll mark. I'm astonished Fong sent someone as..." he caught himself in the instant before he said "naive," and instead said, "inexperienced as you to find me. How did you find me, for that matter?"

She smiled, but not prettily. "There are a dozen of us, all with a scroll bearing your likeness. It's not a good likeness, but you're not a handsome man."

Sighing, he let go of her. "Fine. He's getting sloppy in his old age. So, why does the illustrious master Shotan Fong want to see me?"

Gentle Alabaster shrugged, and began smoothing imaginary wrinkles in her jerkin. "I was not privy to that information. I will say, though, that he seemed most frantic that we find you soon. I've never seen him this anxious."

Wren snorted derisively. "You've never seen him when he's lost a half-sliver of jade, then. Fine. Where is he?"

"I'll take you to him," she said, too quickly. He quirked an eyebrow at her, and she half-blushed. "I don't know where the caravan is now, but I know its course. I can find it."

The Immaculate nodded, his arms folded across his chest. "Ah. That's better. We'll leave as soon as I hire a horse, then."

"There's one waiting for you at the stables of the Bronze Flame." Defiantly, she added, "It's not that bad, and it's near the Guild custom-house."

"It is, at that," Wren said distantly, wondering exactly how much effort had gone into herding him toward Fong. It was clearly a trap, and not a very good one. Fong's usual dealings were as subtle as spidersilk. The very clumsiness of the thing was what made Wren feel better about it. If Fong was making no effort to hide his hand, perhaps his need to see Wren was real and urgent after all.

And if he walked away, Wren reflected, he'd never know what had gotten the fat Guildsman into such a tizzy.

"Well then," he said with an effort. "The Bronze Flame it is. I trust you've already seen to provisions? Of course you have; you're Guild. How far do we have to travel, do you think? Never mind, I'm sure we'll have plenty to talk about along the way." He saw her blanch at the prospect, and mischievously added, "When I'm not chanting hymns, of course. They shouldn't take more than, oh, five or six hours each day."

"I'll...I'll meet you at the Bronze Flame. In an hour!" she said, and fled out of the alley. Wren laughed quietly. Her hasty departure would add a nice touch of verisimilitude to the lie he'd spun earlier.

Whistling, he walked out of the alley. The Bronze Flame lay close to the docks. He'd known it well in his younger days, and suspected this was why Fong had chosen it. The fat man forgot nothing, which was the reason he'd managed to survive for so long.

Reaching the inn would be a matter of minutes. In the meantime, he should at least pay his departing respects at the Shrine he'd mentioned to Alabaster. It was right and proper that he pay his respects to the Wise and Honorable Teachers who dwelt, studied and prayed within.

And if by doing so, he coincidentally left a trail that others could follow in case he disappeared, well, so much the better. Fong wasn't the only one who could be cautious, after all.

He wondered if Fong knew that. Wren certainly hoped he did.

Chapter Twenty-Three

Not for the first time, Holok wondered why they had bothered to wait for him.

He rode at the tail of a straggling column that should have been, by all rights, a Wyld Hunt. The road they followed had been marked only on the most ancient of maps found in the main shrine at Lookshy, and gazing at it Holok could feel the mapmaker's disdain. Qut Toloc, it seemed, had never been a popular destination.

The Hunt had been waiting for him when he'd stepped onto the cutter from the Imperial City. An escort had met him before he'd even reached the docks, and whisked him to the Temple of the Everchiming Bell, where the Hunt had been assembled. They assessed him coolly while a nervous astrologer by the name of Sheltered Stone raved about monstrous signs in the heavens.

After approximately three minutes of this, Holok had endured enough. He politely but firmly advised Sheltered Stone that he knew far more about the situation than any nervous astrologer might, that the circumstances were potentially dire, and that there was no time for sitting around and discussing interpretations of the position of the comet called Mirrin's Arrow. There had been silence, then grudging acquiescence, and the Hunt had been on the ship headed for Nexus an hour later.

The others seemed a fairly typical lot of Huntsmen, and as one they ignored him. His presence was one they could not explain and did not desire, and as such they avoided speaking to him whenever possible. While he was garbed in traveling robes such as any lower-level monk might wear, his command of the situation at the temple had indicated that he clearly was something more. He refused to enlighten them, however, as to what exactly that was. If they were clever, they would discover it, and in the meantime, he wore a band of red cloth tied across his brow.

The road itself was well enough kept, if narrow, and it alternated between mud and dust with charming regularity. In places, attempts had been made to pave it with huge blocks of stone, but these were rare and soon abandoned. There had been infrequent towns, and more infrequent attempts at ambushes, but the former held no interest and the latter held no challenge. Vultures feasted well on the corpses they left in their wake.

They rode when the lead Huntswoman said they rode, and stopped when she ordered they stop, and occasionally she asked Holok if they were still following the correct path. He answered her as she asked him, with as few words as possible, and they continued onwards. Such had been the nature of the journey this far, and thus it was likely to continue, albeit at as swift a pace as his horse could manage. There had been attempts to find him something swifter in several of the villages they'd passed, once it had become clear that they'd find nothing better. Even the pack animals and servants seemed to make better time than he did, though they were no doubt more used to this sort of thing than he was. It had been a long time, after all, since a Hunt had required his personal attention, and longer still since one had ridden so far into the Scavenger Lands.

Ahead of him, he could see a few of the members of the Hunt rein in with visible annoyance. Their horses were bred for the chase, lean stallions used to swift pursuit. Such steeds were not used to waiting while a man in Immaculate robes trotted behind them on a stolid riding mount, and neither were such steeds' riders. Sighing, he patted his horse's flank and suggested that it pick up its pace. Time was, after all, of the essence.

Miraculously, the horse obeyed, and Holok uttered a small prayer of thanks. With a shout, the Huntsmen wheeled their mounts and pressed onward. Servants called out direction and harness jingled. Implacably the procession moved forward, for somewhere in the distance, Qut Toloc was waiting for them.

Chapter Twenty-Four

"It's not gold, but you already knew that. For one thing, it's too damn heavy." Guildmaster Shotan Fong turned the dagger over in his hands, careful not to cut himself. The blade was about ten inches long, crafted with clean and simple lines, and to the untrained eye it would indeed appear to be made of gold. An intricate sunburst design had been hammered into the blade, and the handle was wrapped in a rotting piece of leather. It smelled faintly of mold, and Shotan Fong found his nose wrinkling involuntarily at the stench of it.

Shotan Fong was not a man used to dealing with unpleasant scents, or indeed anything unpleasant at all. Laying the dagger down on his desk with noticeable effort, he clapped his soft, pudgy hands. Immediately, a slave dressed in white linen entered the tent. The slave was tall and fair-skinned, and had the vacant look common to those who had once been sold to the Fair Folk. His head was shaved, and in his hands he held a delicate glass bottle.

"Perfume," Shotan Fong said to his guest by way of explanation, and took the bottle. "Would you care for some?"

Wren smiled gently and shook his head to indicate the negative. He was seated on black silk cushions, but otherwise had chosen the garb of the perfect ascetic, clad in gray robes and sandals. He steepled his fingers against his temples and looked after the departing slave. "That was always one aspect of the business I never could quite stomach."

"The slave trade?" Fong spread his hands in a gesture of dismissal, and the silk of his robe rippled on his short arms. He was a round little man, with a sweaty face and a bald pate, and his movements were short and sudden. He pulled the stopper from the perfume bottle, which had been made in the shape of a swan, and waved the dipper around dramatically. "Nonsense, Eliezer. You were marvelous at that sort of thing. You were never squeamish in the old days. Don't tell me the Immaculates have cut your balls off along with your hair."

The priest shrugged. "The trade itself never did. It's the way of things. Everything has a place and a price, after all. But selling slaves to the Fair Folk, then buying them back afterwards never sat well with me. That part got into my dreams and stayed there. It's why I left, you know."

Fong laughed without humor and leaned forward. "You mean, it's why you pinched a double fistful of jade from the Guild treasury and bought yourself a life in the Order. Let's not mince words. After all, we both consider ourselves far too clever for that. Don't think that your little trick has been forgotten, though. The Guild never forgets."

"I never thought of myself as clever," replied Wren quietly. "And the Guild's gotten more than its money's worth out of me. Don't try holding me up for more, Fong. You don't have enough water and salt to bully me. I'm here out of curiosity, not fear." He matched the merchant's glare with a calm stare of his own, and it was the fat man who flinched and looked away.

"I wouldn't dream of trying to get you to do something against your will, Most Immaculate One," said Fong. He accented the title slightly, making it almost a mockery. Then, with effort, the merchant restrained himself. "But that's neither here nor there. Something has dropped into my lap a while back, and I think that may interest the Order. I want your opinion on it before I proceed with trying to sell the unholy thing." He grabbed the dagger from where it sat on his desk, thought better of the weight, and then pushed it toward Wren with both hands. "What can you tell me?"

"As an initiate or as a former Guild member?"

Fong snorted his laughter. It was a fleshy, unpleasant sound. "Either. Whichever salves your precious conscience."

"Then I'll look at it as a priest. The merchant in me would have slit your throat for this thing already." Without a further word, Wren took up the blade and examined it, his breath coming in a hiss as the unexpected extra weight caught him off guard.

Outside the tent, the bustle of the camp continued unabated, the faint sounds of men dealing with unruly pack animals coming and going on the breeze. Already, chests full of trade goods were being loaded in preparation for the next morning's departure. The Guild caravans never stayed in one place too long, and that was one of the things Eliezer had loved about that life. Constantly being on the move had allowed him to leave his own demons behind, at least long enough for him to create new ones. But there were still times when he missed the road, missed the spectacle of the brightly colored market tents and the crowds of new customers whose faces lit up at the sight of exotic goods.

But there were other memories as well, ones which made him glad to have left this life behind. And so he resisted the urge to lose himself in the sound, and instead gave his full attention to the blade in his hands. Saying nothing, he held it up to the light, peering at it from this angle and then from that. Faintly, he could see animal designs etched into the blade above the sunburst. The detail of the work was astonishing, and Eliezer found himself suppressing a low whistle. Gingerly he peeled the rotting leather away from the blade's handle and let it fall to the rich carpet that covered the tent's floor. Horrified, Shotan clapped his hands for another slave. Wren studiously ignored him, for beneath the leather was another marvel. The blade's grip had been carved in the shape of a great serpent, engaged in battle with a lion. The snake's coils formed the actual grip of the dagger, while the lion's head formed the pommel. The expression of rage on the lion's face was so detailed, so true, that he half-expected it to snap at his fingers. "Magnificent," he breathed, and immediately wished he hadn't.

"What's magnificent?" Fong demanded, his pudgy fingers clenching and unclenching. "Let me see."

Wren shrugged. "Suit yourself," he said, and with effort, flipped the dagger across the desk. Fong shrieked and fell backwards onto his cushions as the blade came straight down in the middle of the desktop.

"You idiot," the fat man raged. "You could have killed me. If I'd tried to catch that, it would have taken off my hands, at the very least! What were you thinking?"

"I was thinking that since your best trick is keeping your overstuffed hide in one piece, Fong, you were in no danger." Wren's voice was calm, and only the faintest hint of a smile played at the corners of his mouth. "Now, take a look at that piece of work."

Fong snorted. "I don't have to look at it. It's sunk six inches deep in the top of my desk, and let me tell you, Eliezer Wren, this kind of wood doesn't come cheaply. It's going to cost dearly to repair this, dearly indeed. I hope you still have some of that Guild money of it, because you're going to need every penny—"

"Take another look." Abruptly Fong was silent and after a moment, the priest continued. "I gave it a light flip, and yet it carved itself that kind of a hole in your desktop. It's been buried for an age of the world, and yet it's still that sharp. No rust, no dulling, not even a notch in the blade after all that time and dragons know how much use. No, this is something very interesting, which you would have noticed if you hadn't been so intent on screwing your eyes shut so you could scream more loudly."

"I did notice," the merchant said acidly. "That's why I called for you. I'm beginning to wonder if doing so was a mistake." He propped himself back up and leaned on the desk, the better to examine the mysterious dagger. "What do the carvings on the blade mean, or don't you know?"

"Know? No. Have guesses?" Wren wrapped his hands around the blade's handle and, with a grunt, pulled it free. "I have a few."

"And?"

"It may be tied into the worship of the Hundred Gods. Or it might be something else. Hopefully, it's the former."

Fong's eyes narrowed in a suspicious squint. "And if it's not?"

Dramatically, he sighed. "If it's not, I'll make sure that the demons of the outermost dark devour your soul right after they eat mine because the world is coming to an end." Wren saw the startled look in the merchant's eye and almost laughed. "No, no, it's nothing like that, I promise." He hoped that he wasn't lying. "Now, tell me where you found this marvel."

"Hmm." The merchant pursed his lips disapprovingly. "It's no great story. The thing came up through channels. One of our factors, a greedy little bastard named Malaky, claimed to have found it. He thought it was gold, of course, and wanted gold prices for it. That's what he got, more or less, but I'm beginning to think it was a bargain. How much do you think this will fetch from a collector back in Nexus, Wren?"

Wren ignored him. "Where does this Malaky live, and where did he say he found it?"

"He didn't, which is why I thought he was lying about finding it in the first place. His circuit is north and west of here a bit. He stops in about a dozen little anthill towns on the edge of civilization. One is just large enough to have a temple in it. I'm surprised I have to tell a priest of your standing that tidbit. As for the rest, they're just piles of mud under piles of straw. You just need to find one of the villages and Malaky will be along soon enough. It's his circuit. We don't trust him with anything more. When he has anything good to sell, he meets a circuit rider at a hostel on the route between Great Fork and Rubylak."

"A name, Fong. I need a name. If I go looking for a village where the peasants have dung on their boots, I'll be wandering from now until the end of time."

"Boneford's one of them, I think. The name makes no sense—there's not a river that a child couldn't leap over up that way, so there's no need for a ford."

"And the bones?"

Fong shrugged, an effect not unlike a mountain enduring a landslide. "I'll be damned if I know. Take a spade when you go and you might discover something."

"Hardly," Wren drawled. "I prefer to leave the dead resting. Troubling them is a recipe for bad luck, and we've both had enough of that already."

"True, true." Fong's hands fluttered in front of him. "Now, if that's all you want, I'll take that dagger back."

"Mmm, I think not." Wren smiled softly and practiced lazy cuts in the air. "This sort of thing is not for you, Fong. How much do you want for it?"

"Eliezer, Eliezer..." Fong came around the desk, all smiles.

"I couldn't possibly take Immaculate jade for something like this. It just wouldn't be right." His pudgy hands reached out for the blade.

Wren took a step back and quirked an eyebrow. "So you're making a gift of it? I must say, Fong, that's very generous."

"No, no, you misunderstand me." Abruptly the civility left Fong's voice, and the shrill whining Wren knew so well had set in. "I mean that I have another buyer for it already, and you've told me enough to set a fair price on it. Now hand it to me gently, Wren, or the guards I've got stationed around the tent will turn you into a pincushion." The little man's eyes were cold and hard, and with a curious sideways shuffle he planted himself deliberately between the priest and the tent's entrance.

Wren glanced left and right, calculating his odds. He could see the rough shadows of archers against the tent's west wall, and assumed that as many were to the east. Experimentally, he hefted the dagger, but its weight was too great for knife fighting of the sort he was used to; it weighed more than he expected a longsword to Using it for anything other than straight thrusts would be awkward; his one advantage was that Fong didn't know that.

With a single stride, he closed with the merchant, his off hand grabbing the front of the fat man's tunic. In the same motion he yanked the man forward just far enough to press the tip of the blade against his breastbone, and smiled. "Think you can call them before I spit you, Fong? Are you willing to bet your life that you can?" He let the fat man stammer for a moment, then spun him around and wrapped his arm around Fong's windpipe. His other hand kept the dagger pointed at Fong's vitals, and he took a single step toward the exit.

"Do you think you're going to be able to walk all the way back to the temple with me like this, Wren?" Fong's face was bright red, and his voice was choked. "Don't be an idiot. My men will shoot you the second you walk out of the tent. Abyss knows half of them won't mind if I get killed in the process. You're a dead man if you do this, priest."

The priest shrugged, a motion which made Fong choke interestingly. "Possibly. I'm willing to take that chance."

Suddenly, he stopped. "But if you're not, we might have something to talk about. None of this makes sense, Shotan. Why call me here if you have a buyer, and why the archers?"

"Client...demanded it," the merchant gasped. "Said...your head...was part of what he was buying."

"Not *enough*, Fong." Wren jerked the fat man's neck savagely. "Why me?"

"Don't...know."

"Think harder," Wren hissed. "I find I'm *very* curious about this."

"Why ask him when you can ask the client himself?" Wren looked up. Standing just outside the tent, holding the flap open with his right hand, was a pale, smiling man. In his left hand he held a pitch-black sword hammered into the shape of a serpent, and behind him were a half-dozen bravos with short swords and parrying knives at the ready.

The priest swore, and brought up the dagger. "Take a step closer and your fat friend dies."

Chuckling, the stranger stepped into the tent. His hair was black and long, and it was held in a silver clasp shaped like a coiled snake. His face was long and thin, with a hawk nose and high, arrogant cheekbones. He was smiling, but it was the smile of the fisherman who enjoys the struggles of his catch on the line.

"Oh, he's no friend to either of us, Wren. Go ahead and kill him. It will make it easier for us to talk." Fong started sputtering, but the priest tightened his grip across the merchant's throat and he abruptly coughed to silence.

"And abandon my cover? No, thank you. Who are you, and what do you want with me?"

The stranger bowed extravagantly, mockingly. For the first time, Wren could see that the man had a row of tiny crimson tears tattooed down his left cheek, and for some reason the sight disturbed him. "I don't have a name anymore, though I've been called Ratcatcher. And to answer your second question, I don't want anything from you. I've already killed enough Immaculates this month. If I kill you, too, there might be a shortage." He straightened then, and yawned extravagantly.

"My master, on the other hand, has expressed something of an interest in you, and that is why I am here. How do you feel about travel?"

Wren took a step back, dragging the Guildsman with him. "I've no taste for it at the moment. Perhaps another time?"

The Ratcatcher tsked, but did not move. "That won't do. Now, let's see how this little drama might play itself out. I could simply stab both you and the fat man—I don't think my sword would much mind the extra work. Perhaps I could simply call for the archers outside the tent to fire, and take the secrets my master needs from your corpse after it had cooled sufficiently. Or, if you were wise, you could simply surrender, hand me the dagger, and live to see at least a dozen more dawns. The choice is, ultimately, yours."

"You make it all sound so appealing." Wren took another step back, and could feel the canvas wall of the tent behind him. "Do I get any other choices?"

"Not really, no." Ratcatcher brought his sword before him and settled into a guard position. "Don't try my patience, monk. I can get the answers I want from your ghost with no trouble at all."

"I'm sure you can," said Wren, and relaxed his grip on Fong's throat.

The fat man sucked in wind and began to shriek for his guards. Wren let him get a single syllable out, then caught him again and spun around with the fat man still in front of him. Reversing the dagger, he shoved Fong against the canvas of the tent wall, slicing through it and letting the merchant's body shield him. A series of shocks and a burbled scream told him that Fong had caught a series of arrows in the belly, and then the wall was tatters and Wren was outside.

Dropping Fong's body to the dust, he took in the situation. The archers were using short bows, which had saved him from getting skewered along with his erstwhile host. There were two to the left and three to the right, and already they had new shafts nocked. With a shout, he went left, diving between the two archers and ducking. One loosed as he came in, but the arrow sailed over his shoulder. The other dropped his bow and went for a belt knife, but as Wren went past he brought the dagger across the man's belly, and he doubled over. Ahead of Wren stretched rough avenues bounded by tents. Behind him he could hear a general alarm being raised, and men scrambling for weapons. He sprinted onwards.

The thrum of bows sounded, and an arrow went whizzing by his cheek. Cursing, he ducked to the right, into a narrow alley between two smaller tents. A heavyset man stitching a sole back onto a boot looked up in alarm as Wren sprinted past, then dove into his tent for cover. Another man piled out of the same tent, a curved sword in his hand, and took up pursuit. Wren slowed deliberately, then when the man got close, he turned and brought the dagger around in a wide sweep. The man staggered to a halt just in time to avoid being gutted, and struck wildly. Wren ducked, and the sword cut the air over his head. As his pursuer brought the sword around for another strike, Wren stepped inside the man's guard and caught his wrist at the top of his swing. The man's bearded face took on an expression of first surprise, and then pain as the priest twisted his grip. A soft crunching sound told Wren that the fellow's wrist was broken, and his sword dropped to the ground. The man drew breath as if to shout, and Wren dispassionately kneed him in the groin. The air knocked out of him, the Guildsman doubled over silently, and Wren brought the hilt of the dagger down on the back of his head.

The man collapsed to the dust, and Wren saw blood on the lion's mouth. Wordlessly, he turned and ran again. The whole camp seemed to be in a state of alarm, with merchants diving into and out of tents, children screaming, and teamsters trying to restrain rearing horses and camels. Metal rang on metal, and Wren grinned. Presumably some of his pursuers had stumbled onto one another and made the wrong assumption.

Against the sunset ahead, the tents thinned out and a line of wagons formed the edge of the camp. Beyond that was scrub and desert, and the narrow ribbon of road that led between cities. The stretch he'd taken to get here lay on the opposite side of the camp, as did his horse. There'd be no way for him to reach either without being spotted, and while his luck had been good so far, he had no intention of testing it further. If he kept to the road here, he'd be ridden down shortly, and so that was hardly an option either.

The desert it would be, then, he decided, and ran on. He dimly recalled that near here the ground was broken up by gullies and washes, and he prayed he'd find one to take cover in before the pursuit organized itself. The dagger still bloody in his hand, he ran on.

The Ratcatcher turned Fong's corpse over with the toe of his boot. The man's lips were caked with blood and dust, and there were five arrows firmly placed in his chest and gut. Most were broken off from where the fat man had hit the ground. Fong's eyes were open, wide with fear, and the Ratcatcher declined to close them. A few yards away, the archers were tending to their fallen comrade, and a single glance told Ratcatcher all he needed to know about how that particular story would end. Behind him he could hear the hired thugs Fong had provided stumbling through the tent. When they emerged, they gawked at the sight. One finally turned to him for an explanation.

"Fong's dead. The priest killed him." Ratcatcher said it simply, as if talking to a child. In a sense, no doubt, he was. "He ran off between those two tents. Raise the alarm and catch him!"

The men ran off. Ratcatcher had no faith whatsoever in their ability to actually catch Eliezer Wren, but their pursuit would no doubt cause him to waste his energy. When the hired knives and Guildsmen had worn him down, Ratcatcher would run him to ground. The priest might even have enough left in him to make the hunt interesting.

"And I love clever rats," he said to no one in particular, and walked off. Behind him, flies began buzzing around Shotan Fong's corpse, but not a single one dared to land. After all, no one had granted them permission.

Chapter Twenty-Five

The cry that rose over the scrublands behind Wren was not the baying of hounds. He looked over his shoulder and out of the gully, keeping his head low, and scanned the horizon for pursuit. There was no visible sign, and for that he was thankful.

Sound, however, was a different matter. From the west came a horrible howling, mixed with eager barking and occasional yelps of pain. The impression was that of hounds on the hunt, but something about the pitch and timbre of the calls didn't quite match his recollections of such. He'd been hunted before, more times than he cared to remember, and he knew what leashed hunting dogs were supposed to sound like. What he heard now was terrifyingly different.

Off in the distance, a slow-moving pillar of dust told him that the Guild caravan was moving again, which was a small comfort. Since the caravan itself was moving on, he wouldn't be hunted by the entire wagon-train's worth of men, women and bloodthirsty children. While he was quite certain that Fong had been no better liked now than he had been ten years previously, he was equally certain that the Guild had not gotten any more forgiving about visitors whose presence left senior Guild officials dead. The fact that members of the caravan were not engaged in actively hunting him down meant one of two things: Either they'd disliked Fong so much that they were perfectly happy to let his killer go; or they'd already set something far worse on his trail.

Another howl ended that debate decisively. He scrambled back into the refuge of the gully and began moving, keeping his head down and the dagger out. He had perhaps an hour's start on his pursuer, and from the sound of things that wouldn't be nearly enough. While the dry ground didn't take footprints well in most places, he was quite certain that whatever was behind him would have no trouble picking up his scent. Furthermore, he was heading west, so any time he showed above the gully mouth he'd be silhouetted against the last embers of sunset, while his pursuer moved out of the gathering dusk.

It was, Wren decided, an Imperial crock of shit. However, he was fairly certain he'd been in worse situations and survived, and he was quite certain that waiting around for the not-quite-hounds behind him wasn't helping his chances any. Cursing under his breath, he picked up his pace.

The gully itself was only four feet deep and twice that in width, but it gave promise of greater things. Occasional scrub plants lined the gully's walls, grayish-green in the fading light and pressed close against the reddish soil. The gully floor was bare and cracked, letting him pick up the pace. Unfortunately, it would also do the same for his pursuers. Anyone finding the gully would also find him in short order, particularly if they were running on four legs instead of two. Head down, he ran.

From behind came a fresh chorus of the hideous baying, much closer this time. Whoever held their leash, he realized, must be letting them go all-out. That also meant that the unseen huntsman was probably on horseback, and Wren found himself wishing heartily that the man's horse would find an ankle-breaking crevice in the dark. With luck, the resultant spill would be fatal.

Ahead on the left, a dark space indicated where another gully met this one. Getting closer, Wren saw that this one's bottom was covered in smooth, round stones, which would do a much better job of covering his track than the sand he was currently running on.

He paused at the gully mouth. What he had in mind was risky, but at the rate the hounds were gaining, they'd be on him in a matter of minutes. He liked his chances against one hound, but not against a pack—and less against whatever it was that was coming.

Steeling his determination, Wren sprinted past the gully entrance and ran another hundred strides. Then, breathing out a prayer, he reached up and grabbed the gully lip, swinging himself up and out. Keeping as low as possible, he scuttled back in the direction of the second gully. Hopefully the hounds would follow his track and keep going down the original gully, at least long enough to buy him some additional time.

A few hundred anxious steps in the dark were all it took for Wren to find the side gully, and he dropped into it as noiselessly as he could. He'd made certain he'd returned to it well up from the gully mouth, the better to hide his scent, though he couldn't be sure it would work. The still night air wouldn't betray him with a stray breeze, but even so, better safe than sorry.

The gully itself was beyond his expectations. While not nearly as wide as the one he had left, it was almost as deep, and had precious little sand at the bottom to show his footfalls. Tough, wiry roots stretched across the top of the gully at intervals, making it impossible for a rider to maintain his seat if he tried moving at any rate of speed. If he hadn't been seen, Wren decided, he just might be home free.

Moving up the gully, he pondered what his next step might be. Obviously, heading back to Kejak would be a good idea, though the walk would be long and unpleasant. He had a sneaking suspicion of what the dagger might be and why someone like Ratcatcher might be interested in it, and the sooner he got it into the appropriate hands, the better.

That still left the question, however, of why this Ratcatcher and his mysterious liege were interested in him, Eliezer Wren, personally. He'd certainly made his share of enemies over the years, but couldn't think of one, under the circumstances, who'd be likely to have the fealty of a creature like the Ratcatcher.

Unless, he realized with a chill, Ratcatcher and his master had been following his track to Talat's Howe. If that were the case, he was in a great deal of trouble indeed.

Down the gully, he heard the almost-barking of the hounds. Hopefully it was just a trick of the night air that made them sound as close as they did. The dim clatter of hooves on dried earth rang up the gully as well. The sound faded as the rider slowed, and then a peal of laughter rang out into the night.

Wren knew that laugh. It was Ratcatcher.

He swore, and scrabbled forward. If Ratcatcher and whatever

he was leading were that close, then getting out of the gully onto flat ground was suicide. His only hope was following the gully to its end, and hoping the obstacles he'd already passed would slow Ratcatcher enough to give him time to find more shelter. It was a slim hope, but slim was better than none. Already he could hear paws on stone, and a crashing sound told him that Ratcatcher had taken a sword to the roots that blocked his way.

Ahead, the gully petered out into nothing. Wren sprinted forward. He was at the top of a low rise, with nothing around but dust and hard-packed earth. A fast glance behind him was enough to tell him that he didn't have much time to think about his decision. Without another thought, he went straight forwards and down the other side of the rise. The sky was dark, illuminated only by those stars not masked by clouds rolling in from the west. A few low scrub plants broke up the landscape, but they were sparse enough that Wren could run without fear of stumbling across one.

Over his shoulder, triumphant barking told him that the hounds had broken from the gully and were close at hand. An instant behind that, hoofbeats on dry earth followed.

Halfway down the long slope, Wren stopped. There was no more sense in running; Ratcatcher's pack would bring him to ground sooner or later. Flight was just tiring him out, and if he was going to make a stand, he might as well make a fight of it as well. Pulling the dagger from his belt, he dropped into a fighting crouch and waited. For a moment he wished he'd thought to bring a staff with him to Fong's, but that was wine on the table now. The dagger was all he had, and the dagger would have to do.

The pack came over the top of the hill, howling, and Wren's eyes widened in shock. They had the bodies of hounds, at least— long and muscular, and their fur was as gray as slow sickness. Their legs were long and their paws wide, and they ran like the wind. But their heads were not the heads of hounds. Instead, their faces were the faces of men. They ran with their tongues lolling out, calling back and forth to one another as dogs would, but from human throats. Their eyes were mad, and their skin was the same plaguey gray as their fur. Their nostrils flared wide, and foam flecked their lips as they saw their prey in front of them. As one beast, they howled, and the sound froze Wren's blood.

The first of them reached the priest an instant later, and he caught it across the throat with his dagger as it leapt for him. The howl faded abruptly to a hideous shriek, and the dog's black blood fountained into the night air.

The hound collapsed to the ground, and Wren took the momentum of his slash into a roll to the left. Another beast dove at where he had been a second before. He threw a kick at it as he came out of his roll, felt it connect, kept moving. More hounds arrived and encircled him, moving as he moved to keep him penned. Wren feinted left and threw himself to the right, but a grinning hound was there, waiting for him. He smashed its face with his heel, but the moment he took to do so let the pack draw close once again.

A yelp behind him made Wren turn as another hound leapt for his throat. Wren brought the blade up to impale it, but even as he did so, a second sank its teeth into his ankle. Reflexively he kicked and felt the grip loosen, but that meant that his swipe at the first hound missed. It hit his chest and bowled him over. He hit the ground hard, but the shock of the impact let him shove the dog away from him with his off hand. It whined as he threw it aside, even as one of its brethren went for the monk's face. There was just enough time to bring up the dagger again, and the beast's howl of triumph trailed off suddenly into a whine of pain. With an effort, he pulled the blade out of the dog's belly, and hot blood gushed out after it. The sound of baying was deafening now, and as he staggered to his feet he knew that it was only a matter of time.

The circling hounds seemed to sense this as well. Again and again they made feints at his hamstrings, forcing him to turn constantly and put weight on his injured ankle. One leapt for his dagger hand. He spun and tagged its ear as it went past, but stumbled as he did so, his wounded ankle giving out and pitching him forward. Somehow he half-caught himself, left palm flat on the ground. The dagger in his right hand was red with blood and so was he, and for a long instant nothing moved or spoke.

Then suddenly the rest of the pack was on him all at once. Mouths with human teeth tore at him. He slashed wildly and felt the dagger thud into flesh again and again, but the wave of enemies seemed endless. Howls of pain cut the night, but for every hound he slew, another leapt upon him.

Finally a pair of jaws seized his wrist and clamped down with a sickening crunch. Wren felt his grip go slack, saw the dagger tumble to the ground. Unbelieving, he watched as a hound calmly picked the blade up in its mouth, then trotted off. The other beasts held him, one on his chest to weigh him down and others clamping fast to wrists and ankles to make sure he could not move. The one on his chest leaned toward him and panted, its breath rotten with the stench of raw meat. Wren gagged, and looked into its eyes.

There was madness there, and something that might have been intelligence, and most of all a terrible hunger. Whatever had bred these things, it had done a marvelous job of stripping anything remotely human from them. "You're not a man any more, are you?" Wren ventured. He expected no response.

Slowly and deliberately, the thing extended its tongue and licked his face. The expression it wore could only be termed a smile.

Wren thought seriously about vomiting, then the beast licked him again and it was no longer something he had any control over. The beasts lifted their muzzles to heaven and bayed, and Wren was sure that they were laughing.

And then, over the crest of the rise, Ratcatcher came trotting.

He rode a black horse that was eighteen hands high, with red nostrils and red eyes. All its tack was black as well, and it made no sound as it picked its way down the slope. Ratcatcher held the reins in one hand and the dagger in the other, and on his head was a helmet shaped like a hooded serpent's cowl. His hands were encased in black riding gloves, and a torn and tattered cape flowed behind him.

Wren spat feebly, to clear his mouth of vomit, and stared up at him. There seemed little else he could do.

Slowly, Ratcatcher rode in a circle around the priest. His look was frankly appraising, and his expression clearly said that he was unimpressed with the chase he'd been led. Behind him trailed the other hounds, now silent as they followed in their master's wake.

"Kill me, then," croaked Wren. "You have the dagger. You've won. Get it over with."

"Oh no, my dear priest," said his pursuer, smiling. "I couldn't do that. As Fong told you, Eliezer Wren, the Prince of Shadows wants to see you."

Chapter Twenty-Six

The third night after Bonecrack, Yushuv decided not to sleep. He'd been left alone by the raiton-dreams since his encounter with the spirit, and that was enough to make him suspicious. He'd walked all night that night, and stayed awake to greet the dawn. The experience had calmed him, and somehow he felt stronger than if he had slept.

He'd meant to press on then, but without warning a voice called his name.

"Yushuv," he heard, and then more softly, "Listen to me. Your life depends on it."

"Who's there?" He spun around, looking for the source of the words. No one was there. The sky was blue and empty of all save the sun, and the few trees by the roadside held only birds.

"A friend. Leave the road."

"I won't leave until you show yourself to me!" he shouted. "Why should I believe you?"

"Perhaps you shouldn't. But what do you lose by listening to me? A few minutes' walking? And you might gain your life."

"That's not a good answer!" No reply came, and Yushuv suddenly felt very naked and very vulnerable. He looked left and saw nothing, looked right and saw even less. He was alone.

"I'm probably going to get myself bitten by a snake doing this," he grumbled to himself, and choosing randomly, went off the road to the left. Behind him, a single raiton's croak was heard, and then silence.

The land was wetter here, and marshy in places, so he had carefully picked his way to a grove of thick-trunked, sad-leafed trees that provided shelter. A snake that crawled among the trees' massive roots provided his breakfast, though he doused his small fire as soon as the meat had finished roasting.

Even as he did so, a clatter from the road attracted his attention. Climbing up one of the thick, black-barked trunks, Yushuv perched in a branch to get a view of the commotion.

Riding past was a party of mounted warriors, clad in ornate armor and flying banners from their saddles that proclaimed their allegiance to the various Great Houses of the Realm. They moved at a brisk trot, and a terrible purpose radiated from them. Some shone and crackled with cloaks of reddish light; others merely bent low in their saddles and urged their horses onward. In their midst was a bearded and husky Immaculate priest, his scarlet robes dusty from the road and his face implacable.

"The Wyld Hunt," he whispered to himself, and with a shock he realized that it was him that they were after. Surely they were bound for his home village, and when they did not find him there, they'd come looking along the road. An unreasoning urge to flee back into the depths of the woods gripped him, mixed with a smoldering fury that told him to advance on the road and show them what they were trifling with. Unconscious of doing so, he reached back to his quiver and pulled an arrow from it, sighting along its length to target the priest. His forehead burned, and his limbs trembled. *Do it*, a voice in his head whispered. *Make them pay!*

Abruptly, the procession passed out of sight. Behind them trailed servants and pack animals, the former grumbling about the pace that was set and the latter merely complaining as best they could. Yushuv felt the strength and anger draining out of him. He took the arrow off the string and hugged the bow to himself, willing himself to be small and still lest they come back. Firing at the priest would have been foolish. There were many hunters, and their powers were unknown to him. A few arrows would have done nothing. Instead, it was best that he sit here and wait, at least until night. When nightfall came, he'd have more cover, and perhaps a better idea what to do.

So counseling himself, he slept.

Night came, and with it the flapping of wings.

Yushuv awoke. He did not dare rekindle his fire, but instead huddled in the tree branches. The memory of the riders was still with him, and he felt cold panic claw at his stomach when he thought about them.

Overhead, a raiton croaked something unspeakable into the night. He could see its outline clearly against the moon, and then it flapped its wings and soared more widely.

"I know what you are," Yushuv shouted up at it. " At least, I think I do. You've been following me. Why?"

The great raiton spread its wings and slowly descended in circles. It came to rest on a branch just above Yushuv's head, and for the first time he realized how large it was. The bird easily dwarfed any bird Yushuv had ever seen. Its wings were longer than his arms, and it looked as if it could carry off a small child with neither fuss nor inconvenience. It cocked its head and looked at him, and Yushuv saw the unmistakable gleam of intelligence in its bright eyes.

"You can talk," he said accusingly. "You're the one who warned me to leave the road, aren't you?"

"Would you have listened if I'd used raiton-speech? Or simply flapped my wings over you? That was good enough to rouse you from dreams, but stronger wine is needed when you are waking." It shook itself curiously, like a dog shivering itself when wet, and then hopped down a branch. "You are stubborn."

Yushuv had nothing to say to that, so he said nothing. Instead he reached into his pack and pulled out a strip of jerky, nearly the last he had. Wordlessly, he offered it to the raiton, which snatched it from his fingers and wolfed it down. It swallowed the jerky and stared at him.

"You show respect, Yushuv, even when you don't know that you are. You have honor. In this, you are much like your father."

"My father..." Yushuv reached inside his tunic and pulled out the charm he'd taken from his father's corpse. "Did you give this to him?"

The raiton's head bobbed up and down. "Bone wrapped in a dead man's sinews, yes, I gave him that. After he gave it to me, of course, though he did not know he gave it at the time."

"You're speaking in riddles."

The raiton threw back its head and laughed, letting out harsh, deep croaks that scattered birds from nearby trees. "I am *Raiton*, Yushuv. How can I not?" Seeing Yushuv's expression, it sobered a bit. "To all things there is a purpose and there is a nature. It is my nature to tell true things as if they were lies, and to make rich presents of riddles. I can no more change it than you can change what you are, though you are indeed changed. More than that, I cannot say."

Yushuv frowned. "You're being confusing again. I suppose that's the point, though, isn't it?"

"Clever boy." The raiton hopped closer. "Your father was a heretic, you know. He worshipped the Hundred Gods more devoutly than the Immaculates would like, though the Immaculates themselves know we're not gods at all. Riddle me that, boy—an Order founded to preserve order by lying about the order of things. It exalts those whose Exaltation is lesser, and casts down in the dirt those called to the heavens. On the whole, a most curious way of striving for perfection, do you not think?"

"I don't know." Yushuv's brow furrowed with thought. "There was just always the temple, with the monks, and underneath it the bones. Everyone acted like it had always been there, the same way the fields or the stream had been. I wonder why we never wondered about it."

"You weren't supposed to, that's why. Wondering makes a man question. Questioning leads a man to answers, and answers, once found, can never be lost again."

"That doesn't explain anything," Yushuv said accusingly. Again, the bird croaked laughter.

"It's not supposed to. Dear Yushuv, you are important, far more important than you know, but not every word uttered, not every thought guessed at, is intended for your benefit." The bird cocked its head. "I am old, and I have earned the right to complain about something that has vexed me for more centuries than you have years. I have even earned the right to do so in front of a well-meaning but ill-informed young man who's too quick with his bow and not quick enough with his ears. A teacher will come for you, Yushuv. Save your questions for him."

Yushuv crossed his arms. "I don't even know what questions to ask," he said sulkily. "How am I supposed to know what I should be doing or where I should be going if I don't know anything?"

"Ah, but you do know where you're going, or at least where you think you are. Yes?"

"I...I thought that I did. I was following the dagger," he ended, somewhat lamely. "But I don't know where to look for it."

"Then why did you choose this path? Every road, even the one leading to Qut Toloc, has two directions to it. Why this one?"

"I don't know." In genuine puzzlement, he added, "It just felt right."

"Ah. Then it was the right choice. You've made many choices, though you did not know you made them. You chose to bring water to the Immaculate, and to leave your home. You chose the path you took, and the manner in which you trod it, and you choose how you would make your parley with Bonecrack."

"But I didn't choose anything," Yushuv cried. "I just did what felt right."

Again, the raiton laughed. "And is that not making a choice? It is rather that you did not deliberate. You did not sit in counsel and stroke your beard and say great things of ponderous wisdom before coming to the conclusion you could have reached in an instant. Your purpose is clear, Yushuv. Hold fast to that."

"I'll try. I just wish I knew what I was choosing."

The raiton made a sound halfway between a whistle and a sigh. "Then listen to me, Yushuv. I will tell you what I may, as best as I may tell it. I do this not for your sake, but for your father's, as he honored me." The raiton settled onto a branch, and its voice took on the singsong tone of chanting. Fascinated, Yushuv listened.

"The world was not always as it is now. This is the Second

Age of Man. The First was a time now long forgotten, when those whom the gods had blessed fought with the enemies of the gods and the fate of the world lay in the balance. The warriors doing the bidding of the gods were called Exalted, and they wielded mighty powers in their cause. Some were Exalted by the heavens, and some by the dragons of the elements, and such was their might that they cast down the enemies of the gods themselves. They laid waste to their enemies' dwelling places and cast down their citadels, so that they might oppose heaven no longer.

"So pleased were the gods that they granted the Exalted dominion over the earth. The Celestial Exalted were the greater in power, and it was they who ruled, while the Terrestrial Exalted were weaker, but more numerous. Between them they made a golden age in which there was neither disease nor privation. The Unconquered Sun smiled down by day, and His sister Luna by night, and all was well.

"Alas, then, that the enemies of the gods had pronounced a curse on the Exalted before their final defeat. They cursed the heavens' chosen to grow corrupt and wicked, and so the Celestial Exalted became. Their just rule turned to tyranny, and their peaceful realm was wracked with civil war.

"Among the Exalted were oracles and seers who cast auguries for the fate of the realm. They saw that, if the Dragon-Blooded rose up against the Exalted and slew them, then a sort of peace would come to the world."

"And if they didn't?"

The raiton's voice was grim. "They saw nothing."

"Nothing bad happening?"

"No. They saw *nothing*."

"Oh."

"Exactly." The raiton harrumped, and began again. "So dissent was fomented among the Dragon-Blooded, who rose up and slew the other Exalted—all save the Sidereal prophets, who wisely absented themselves from the scene. The battles raged for many years, but when they ended, the world was remade. The Dragon-Blooded now ruled a military empire, sending forth Wyld Hunts to strike down the other Exalted when they were reborn into the world. To keep themselves occupied, the Sidereals crafted for themselves a faith, which they called the Immaculate Order. It taught obedience to the Dragon-Blooded, revulsion for the so-called Anathema, and the merits of keeping quietly to one's station. They thought that this was the best method for keeping peace, for preserving order, and for preventing that which they had so fearfully prophesied. Perhaps they were right."

"But they killed so many people!" Yushuv cried.

"And many of those people killed many other people, or might have, or might one day have been tempted to. Such judgments are difficult to make. And yet, when you are the hunted one, they become not so difficult at all."

"Me? Hunted?"

"You. Hunted." the raiton said flatly. "Or did you think the monk to whom you brought water was delirious? You are Anathema, Yushuv. Chosen of the Unconquered Sun, heir to the power of the ages, and possibly to the curse as well. It's too late for you to hide. You've made friends and foes of spirits, been touched by the Sun and beheld the face of your enemy."

"The stranger in the tunnels…"

"…has given himself over to darker powers. He may wish you to do the same. Or he may try to kill you. He may even do both. You benefit from having a nemesis who is somewhat muddled in his thinking."

"He didn't seem very muddled when I met him." Yushuv's tone was defensive.

"May I remind you that he let you live? A purer evil would not have done so. That makes him quite interesting, but less dangerous than he might be. Then again, his hatred might yet be forged pure. It remains to be seen. Now, shall I finish my tale, or do you have more questions?"

"I'm sorry."

"Curiosity is never something to be regretted. Curiosity indulged foolishly is. 'Ware that you know the difference between the two. It is a difficult lesson to learn, as I myself discovered in another age of the world." The bird looked at Yushuv, daring him to ask. Yushuv, for his part, held his tongue.

After a quick nod, the raiton continued.

"Once the Solar Exalted and their allies were destroyed, the land was at peace for centuries. Centuries, however, are not really a very long time in the grand scheme of things, and before long the Great Contagion struck. It was a plague the likes of which the world had never seen before or since, and it struck down young and old, the powerful and the slave alike. There was no cure, and its victims died in agony. Whole nations were laid low, and on the plague's heels came a more terrible enemy. The Fair Folk rode behind the Contagion, bringing with them wild magics and ancient chaos. Those few survivors of the sickness were no match for this new foe, and they were cut down like wheat before the scythe."

"So what happened?"

"A very young officer, one of the Dragon-Blooded, did something very clever. The Realm of the Exalted had long guarded its borders against the Fair Folk, and mighty engines of defense had been set up, ages ago, to stand watch against just such an eventuality. This brave young officer evaded the safeguards that the Solar Exalted had set upon their work, and found the key to those engines. These she turned on the foes of the Realm, harrying them back to the places outside of the world. There they wait, still, and some of their brethren still lurk inside the Realm, hoping to open once again the gates to the outside. Beware the places where chaos is still strong, Yushuv. It can twist even one such as you."

"But what about the Dragon-Blooded who saved the Realm?"

"Ah. Her. The young officer, who was not so much older than you are right now. She did indeed save the Realm, and with those powers at her disposal, she declared herself Empress. Having seen what havoc she had unleashed on the Fair Folk, the other nobles of the Realm declared their fealty, and so was the world you know made."

"Oh." Yushuv let his legs dangle and sat for a moment in silence. "But now the Empress is gone, right? The priests said that she was in seclusion, but she's really gone."

"You're clever, boy. She is gone, and her Empire slowly crumbles without her. It is a dangerous time, particularly for a boy bearing the powers you do. Even without her, the Wyld Hunt still rides and the Sidereal priests scan the heavens for signs of your Exaltation. I have hidden as many of the signs of your coming as I could, but you shine too brightly to be hidden forever. You are on your own, lad, at least until you find another guardian—or until the guardian the Sun has appointed finds you. I bid you remember the bargains you've struck and the promises you've made, and to choose as well as you may when different paths open in front of you. Beyond that, there is nothing more I can say. My help to you has come at a great price, though you'll not know it until after it's been paid."

"But why help me at all?"

"Because your father left out part of his kills, when he hunted, for me. And because your mother honored me as well in her own way. And because those who would hunt you are humorless old men, and aiding you, regardless of what it costs, is as magnificent a jape as any I have imagined. Is that enough, Yushuv, or should I perch on your shoulder like a tame magpie and whistle when you offer me a crust?"

"I'm sorry. And thank you, for everything you've done. I think I'll miss you."

The raiton threw back its head and cawed, loudly. "You think you'll miss me? Oh, Yushuv, you are what the world has been waiting for all these years. Beloved of the Sun, and yet humble! You'll miss an eater of carrion on your journeys! Yushuv, Yushuv, there may yet be cause for hope, if hope is still allowed to us!"

With that, the great raiton rose and flew off into the night, still laughing. Yushuv listened until the sound of its wings had vanished beneath cricketsong. Then, mercifully, he fell into a dreamless sleep.

Chapter Twenty-Seven

Evening had come, and with it Wren had been unceremoniously kicked awake. There was a second's hesitation, and then the merciless iron boot found his ribs again.

"Wake, wake, slugabed" Ratcatcher called, mockingly. "Your noble steed awaits."

Wren groaned and rolled over, and the pain in his ankle made him immediately wish he hadn't. The wound where the hound had bitten him had begun bleeding again during the night, and it had caked to the thin blanket that Ratcatcher had provided for him. Pulling the blanket away tore the wound open once more, and did so in agonizing fashion. Gritting his teeth against the pain, he staggered to his feet.

Ratcatcher had already folded away the tent he'd slept in; Wren had been left to sleep outside. Nothing showed against the horizon to east or west except more flat plains and the occasional low hill, and a faint light in the western sky showed that Ratcatcher was intent on using every single hour of night. Two steeds waited at the far end of camp, one the coal-black monstrosity, seventeen hands high at the shoulder. The other was a dappled gray with a slight swayback; Wren had spent the last two nights tied securely to its saddle.

His capture had been brutally simple. Ratcatcher had simply peeled the dogs off him, then lifted him bodily with his off hand. Wren had been too tired and too weak to resist when the man had hoisted him, and then Ratcatcher had slung him across his back like a sack of meal. "Behave yourself and you'll live to the end of the journey," the man had said, and from his flat tones it was obvious that he was through with whatever game he'd been playing. Secure in the man's grip, Wren had temporarily abandoned any thought of escape and instead concentrated on avoiding as much additional pain as possible.

They'd made good time that night. Ratcatcher had slung him over the neck of his horse and ridden back to the site where the Guild camp had rested, and where a single horse now waited. Behind them, the hounds trailed along, conversing in almost-human voices and staying just clear of Ratcatcher's steed's iron-shod hooves.

With the horse were several packs' worth of provisions. Ratcatcher left Wren slung over his horse's neck while he loaded up both mounts. Then, with brutal efficiency, he hefted the priest and dropped him in front of the horse that had been left behind. "Get on," were his only words, and Wren had no choice but to obey. He slipped and fell once, and then felt Ratcatcher's hand at the back of his collar, lifting him into the saddle. From nowhere Ratcatcher had produced a length of black cord, and proceeded to tie his hands firmly to the pommel. The cord was not quite so tight as to cut off circulation, but it was tight enough to be painful with each jolting stride the horse might take. Wren winced in anticipation, and his captor chuckled.

Satisfied with his handiwork, Ratcatcher remounted his own steed and clucked to it. It sprang forward at a trot, with Wren's horse close behind and the hounds swarming around them like the many arms of a single beast.

They'd gone southeast that night, a trail of dust marking the straight line they'd cut on the plains. The moon was bright enough for Wren to half-see where he was going, but the ground was still treacherous with animal burrows and narrow washes. Often their pace slowed as they picked their way down a ravine or forded a narrow stream, but never did they deviate more than briefly from their course.

Wren had tried to escape once, with predictable results. Ratcatcher had preceded him down into a shallow gully awash with muddy water, and his horse had sunk deeply into the mire. Knowing he only had seconds, Wren had dug his heels into his horse's flank and turned it toward the mouth of the gully, praying that the mud would hold fast to Ratcatcher's steed for a minute longer. A shout of rage behind him let him know that his maneuver had not gone unnoticed, and then the hounds joined the chase with a mighty clamor of baying.

Knowing there was little he could do, Wren simply crouched down against his horse's neck and whispered encouragement. The howling at its heels probably had more to do with the unholy burst of speed it put on, thundering atop the gully wall. Each stride brought new agony to his wrists, but he closed his eyes against the pain, and the horse rumbled onward. Clods of earth fell into the water as they skirted the edge of the ravine, and a strangled yelp cut off by a splash told Wren that one of his pursuers had been unlucky in its footing.

In the distance, a muffled thundering told him that Ratcatcher had managed to free himself, but hopefully there was enough distance between them that the rider in black would be unable to close it. Bound though he was, he had a horse this time, and that might make all the difference. Behind him, the splashing of hooves in water grew steadily fainter, and up ahead were low shapes that looked likely to be shrubs. With luck, they'd be high enough to provide him with some cover, and if they were thick enough he might actually be able to shake off his pursuit.

He'd forgotten about the dogs, though. A half-dozen boiled up out of the gully in front of his horse, barking and howling. Clearly, nothing in its life had prepared the animal for anything like this; it reared and whinnied in terror. Only the cord kept Wren from falling, barely, and it dug deeply enough into his wrists that he felt the blood begin to flow. Then, from behind, the rest of the pack made its presence felt, snarling and nipping at the horse's heels. It reared again, looking for a break in the ring of its tormentors, all the while trying to dislodge Wren.

The priest, for his part, would have been happy to be dislodged, but the cords binding him held him fast, and it was all he could do to keep from having his wrists snapped like twigs. As the horse bucked underneath him, he grabbed fistfuls of mane and held on for dear life. Around him, the hounds continued their infernal baying, and Wren was sure that some of the beasts actually grinned up at him like naughty children.

He closed his eyes, held on as best he could, and waited.

A short eternity later, Ratcatcher arrived, dripping wet and furious. "That," he snarled as he improvised a lasso that hung loosely around Wren's neck, "was extremely stupid. Try it again and I'll have that bone factory you're riding drag you behind it for the next hundred miles." With a savage jerk, he pulled the noose tight, then strode over to his own steed and tied the cord to his reins. Experimentally, he gave a tug, and Wren fell forward, gagging.

"Excellent." Ratcatcher smiled thinly. "If you're foolish enough to try to run again, the rest of you is welcome to go. I'll still have your voicebox here. Think about that before you pretend to be a hero, priest." Empty-handed, he stomped back over to where Wren sat quietly. The blood from the priest's wrists had caked his hands, and the scent nauseated him.

Savagely, Ratcatcher took Wren's face in his left hand and twisted it to face him. "One more thing. You really must understand this," he hissed. "You're alive only because I can make a gift of you at the end of this ride. Your corpse will make a lovely present as well, and your ghost an even better one than that. So don't give me any more reasons to leave pieces of you out here, and you'll reach our destination with the same number of fingers you started with. Do you understand me, priest?"

Wren nodded. "May I have some water?" he asked.

Ratcatcher grinned. It was not a pleasant sight. "No," he said, and walked away.

They'd made camp in the lee of what passed for a hill, near some muddy silt that passed for a stream. Ratcatcher had driven them hard to make up for the time lost in the escape attempt, and several times Wren had nearly strangled before Ratcatcher had eased the pace slightly. Mocking stares let Wren know that the incidents had most assuredly not been accidents.

A bare half-hour before dawn they stopped, and Ratcatcher paused to drive an iron stake into the ground. This he used to tether the horses, and then he lifted Wren from his mount and bound his ankles. A grunt of disdain was the only recognition Wren had gotten from his captor; that and a rude shove into the dust. Edging back, he watched Ratcatcher at work.

If nothing else, the man was efficient. Without doffing his armor or breaking a sweat, he expertly set up a small campfire and pitched a tent. Unsurprisingly, it was big enough for one. A moment later, Wren's captor rummaged through a pack and brought forth a thin blanket of undyed wool. He tossed it to Wren, along with some hard bread and a canteen full of muddy water.

"This is for you," was Ratcatcher's comment, and then he went off to water the horses. The rest of the day passed in silence. Wren tried to sleep, uncomfortably, but the sun's glare and the constant panting presence of Ratcatcher's hounds did little to assist his efforts. It was almost a relief when sundown came and Ratcatcher roughly kicked him awake.

"It's time to ride," he said, and pulled the golden dagger from his belt. He saw Wren's eyes widen involuntarily in fear and shook his head. "This should be the least of your worries. We both know that it would be particularly pointless for me to kill you now. You've been too damn much trouble to throw away." With practiced ease, he sliced the bonds that held Wren's ankles. "Rub some feeling into your feet, then go down to the stream and get yourself some water. The hounds will be with you, so I trust you're clever enough not to run away. Am I correct?"

Wren nodded. "I'm not going anywhere."

"Wrong, you're just not going anywhere you want to be." Ratcatcher patted his cheek in a mockery of affection, stood, and strode off to strike the rest of the camp. Shaking his head, Wren chafed his ankles until they started hurting again, then gingerly struggled to his feet. His gait an imitation of an old man's, he shuffled down to the water. Slowly he bent down so as to splash some of the liquid on his face, and he winced as the movement brought fresh pain to his ankle. The dogs splashed around him, a constant reminder that he was a prisoner.

Best as he could, he put it out of his mind. The dogs' passage stirred up the water until it was a reddish brown; still, he carefully washed his wounds and then, making sure the dogs were all downstream, drank. The streamwater had a bitter taste of rust to it, and he felt the grit on his teeth, but after the day he'd endured it tasted like it had come from the uttermost west. Although hampered by his bound wrists, he rinsed the blood from his hands and soaked his tattered garments as well, in hopes of washing away some of the sticky dog's blood that marred them. Thin streamers of red trailed down into the creek. It wasn't enough, but it would do for now. Perhaps some of the flies would stay away if he were less obviously bedecked in gore. One could hope, at least.

Refreshed, he paused and watched the spirals the mud formed in the water. His eyes caught the way the quartz and mica in the silt reflected the last of the light, and for a moment he could ignore his captivity. Even here, in these desolate circumstances, there was some beauty.

Mordant applause broke his concentration and he turned to find Ratcatcher at the banks of the stream. "Is this your evening adoration, priest? Some kind of religious ritual?"

Wren straightened and shook his head. "Not at all. Just watching the water go past. The patterns can sometimes be fascinating."

"Oh, can they?" Ratcatcher stepped closer, patrolling the water's edge. Stooping, he picked up a pebble and flipped it into the water by Wren's feet. "How fascinating is that? Old mud returns to new mud, to be worn down into sand."

Wren knelt and retrieved the pebble. It was gray and nondescript, half-caked in reddish mud and vaguely egg-shaped. "And the sand becomes new stone, which men will build high into castles and towers that pierce the heavens. Or it washes out to sea and travels to places neither of us will ever see. There's something in that, I think."

Ratcatcher spat into the water. "I've seen places you can't imagine, Wren. I've no wish to see where this bit of stone will go. Take it with you; I'll toss it into the Abyss in front of you some day, and all your fanciful talk will mean nothing."

Wren's response was simply to cast the stone, two-handed, downstream. It hit the surface of the water with a small splash and a loud thunk, then sank from view. "I'd rather let it find its own path," he said, and turned toward shore.

"Suit yourself. The Abyss will swallow everything, sooner

or later. That's one of the things they teach you down in the dark, Wren. You'll learn the rest soon enough."

"I'm a poor student," Wren said, and splashed out of the water. His sandals squelched in the mud. Ratcatcher chuckled nastily.

"The schoolmasters I had don't much care what sort of student you are. You find yourself wishing you'd remember less of their teaching, Wren, because every word of it rings true. You have no idea what it's like to stand in the dark and have the dead gods whisper you their secrets. Your dragons are like the boys and old men who guard the gates when the soldiers have gone off to war. When the dead gods come home, they'll be swept away like chaff." Ratcatcher's voice was quiet, full of certainty rather than bravado. For a moment Wren even thought he sounded sad. Then Ratcatcher shook his head. "Come along. We've got a ways to go tonight, and the hounds are restless."

Wren looked at Ratcatcher quizzically. "What did they do to you?"

"They made me theirs, priest." His voice was pitying as he led Wren up the slope to where the horses waited. "You really know nothing, and the ones who pull your strings to make you dance are very happy to keep it that way. Once men like you would have hunted me as Anathema, or called out the Wyld Hunt to do the deed for them. But that was a long time ago, back when traders knew the way to the city of Thorns and the ancient bitch on the throne still had years and a thousand murders in her." As they approached the horses, he lifted Wren into the saddle and grimly lashed his hands to the pommel once again. Then the familiar cord looped itself around the priest's neck, dry and caked with dust.

"You know what it's like to be hunted like a dog, Wren, even if it was just for those few hours when I made you my rat. Now imagine feeling that way every damned day, with fat priests reading your death sentence out of a book they don't understand. A man gets tired of it, even a man who's been told he's not a man anymore." He whistled, and the dogs came pounding up from creekside, shaking themselves the way any dogs might.

"That's when you start looking for alternatives, my little friend. Even when you've got the sun shouting at you in your dreams, you start looking for other friends, ones who don't care so much about your precious book. I found my friends in the Underworld, priest, and I found my master there, too. I'm bringing you home to him. I have no idea why he wants you alive, but he does, and that's good enough for me. You'll envy the dead men when my prince is through with you, Wren. You'll envy them, and for a heartbeat, I might even envy you."

With that, he nudged his horse into a trot, up over the crest of the hill. Wren had no choice but to follow. The hounds did have a choice, but followed anyway.

Chapter Twenty-Eight

There wasn't much left of Qut Toloc for the Wyld Hunt to descend upon.

That was Holok's first thought as he rode through the village. Around him the riders of the Hunt whooped and roared, tearing apart the wrecks of houses looking for Anathema. One look told Holok that they needn't bother.

Fire had claimed most of the village. Most houses were burned-out shells, half-collapsed from the heat and scorched black by the flames. Some few had clearly been nothing but thatch; nothing remained of them but scorched patches of earth. Scavengers had been at the corpses in the streets. Most were picked to the bone, or near to it. Holok could identify a man's body here, a woman's there, but nothing more. One of the cleaner houses had been claimed by the Hunt's servants, and they had a cookfire going within, but the rest of the village had been gratefully left to the dead.

At some point in the past the livestock had managed to burst the gates of their corrals, and now the survivors wandered the streets. Most had wandered off or fallen prey to predators, but still a few sheep and cows trotted past the collapsed houses, blithely awaiting shepherds who would never call them again. One ram stared stupidly up into Holok's eyes, then ran off, bleating. A Huntswoman chased after it, curved sword glinting in the sunlight. She struck it repeatedly on the flanks with the flat of her blade, driving it first this way and then that until it was mad with terror. Others gathered around, laughing, as she continued with her sport, but Holok turned away in disgust. The Wyld Hunt had never been intended for such things.

Tying his horse to a surviving railing, Holok walked toward the temple. Unlike the other buildings, it still stood unscathed and unmarked by fire, but a terrible carrion stench rode on the breeze that wafted past it. Grimacing, he steeled himself and strode up the steps.

On the top step rested a corpse, one which the crows and wolves had miraculously left alone. It was a monk, a man whose face Holok vaguely recollected. His robes were stiff with blood, and on his face was an expression of agony. A smeared trail of dried blood on the steps showed that he'd crawled up several after being stabbed, and a full waterskin sat next to him, untouched. Holok frowned at the mystery, then proceeded into the temple proper.

It was, as he expected, a slaughterhouse. The bodies of monks lay everywhere, hacked and slashed with an animal savagery. Several of the corpses bore signs of having been hewn after they were already dead, and one was decapitated. The floors were covered in dried blood, and the walls were flecked with it. Flies buzzed everywhere, as thick as smoke, and rats and lesser vermin scuttled along the floors as if they resented Holok's intrusion.

"It's ghastly."

Holok turned. The leader of the Hunters, a woman named Neleh, had materialized behind him. She was tall and handsome, with features too strong to be called beautiful, and she wore little armor over a red peasant blouse and auburn leggings. Her hair was cropped close to her head. Holok had some vague intimation that she was related to House Cathak. She seemed quiet and competent, and she held a pair of slender, short swords before her in a guard position. "Whoever did this needs to be put down like a dog," she added, and gracefully stepped in front of Holok as he strode farther inside.

"Yes," he grunted, mildly annoyed that she'd taken point. "I was hoping we'd reach this place before something like this," he waved aimlessly at the carnage, "happened. I never imagined we'd see a slaughter like the one we see here. The thing we hunt must be unimaginably powerful, and well trained to boot. The monks who dwelt here knew their duty, and they were highly skilled."

"Not skilled enough, I think," said Neleh, and walked on.

Holok shook his head at her miscomprehension, and after a moment, followed.

"What rested down there?" Neleh pointed at the shattered doors, and the blackness of the stairwell beyond.

"Bones, mostly." Holok stepped neatly over the bodies of slain guards and looked down into the dark. "That was the reason for this temple being raised here, not that such things matter anymore. The thing that did this must have come up out of the dark. I don't understand how the guards were overwhelmed so easily, though. The doors were supposed to be barred."

"They were," said Neleh, prodding a shattered beam with the sword in her left hand. "I do not like this at all."

"Neither do I." Holok closed his left fist and concentrated. When he opened it, a ball of bluish light sat on his palm. He gestured to the gaping space beyond the doors. "Shall we see what's down there?"

Neleh laughed humorlessly. "Why not? Shall I alert the others?"

Holok shook his head. "They're having too much fun playing with the livestock. I shudder to think about the sort of trouble they could get into in the catacombs. No, leave them. There shouldn't be anything left here to trouble us, in any case."

Nodding, Neleh walked through the doorway, Holok following a step behind. The steps echoed under their footsteps as they descended, the wispfire in Holok's hand shedding just enough light to keep them from stumbling. They descended in silence, then ventured forward into the catacombs proper.

Two steps in, Neleh stopped.

"Yes," Holok asked. "What is it?"

"This…this place. How many men are buried here?"

Holok shrugged delicately, the light bobbing in his hand. "No one knows. They died putting down the abomination known as Toloc, who is also buried here…somewhere. The monks at this particular temple have been searching for her bones for centuries, with no luck. My suspicion is that the ghosts themselves are moving the bones, so that we'll never find them."

"Why would they do that?" Neleh was incredulous.

"There's precious little in the Immaculate Texts concerning the motivations of dead men, Neleh," he answered testily. "Now, shall we proceed?"

"I can't see anything down here," she said, a trifle too quickly. "Let's go."

"I'm not so sure of that, but I don't see the benefit of getting lost right now. As you wish." Holok turned and gestured, and Neleh walked toward the stairs. Holok followed, and they ascended in silence.

Halfway up, Neleh stopped again. "Did you hear that?" she whispered.

"Hear what?"

"Something down there is moving."

Holok snorted. "Rats, doubtless."

"Do rats click?"

"They do when they're walking on bones. Now, if you're in such a hurry to ascend, let us proceed."

"I'm no coward," Neleh warned, but took the steps two at a time just the same.

They were at the top step when Holok heard the click of bone on metal. He looked back, and cursed at what he saw.

The dead had risen, and they were coming for him. A half-dozen patchwork skeletons strode jerkily onto the stair. Pale green fire lit the empty sockets of their skulls and broken swords were clutched in their hands. They moved awkwardly but with surprising speed, clattering up the stairs with single-minded intent.

With an instinctive shout, Holok flung the ball of blue light at the first monstrosity. Trailing sparks, it caught the skeleton square in the chest and shattered it to flinders. Pieces of bone fell to the ground, coated in blue flames. The others stepped over the twitching fragments, never slowing their pace.

Neleh stepped forward to engage the skeletons, but Holok caught her arm. "Not here," he said. "We stand a better chance at the top of the stairs, in the light!" With that, he sprang up the stairwell, his feet barely touching the metal as he went. Behind him Neleh followed, thin ribbons of lightning arcing up and down her blades as she prepared herself for battle.

Holok went through the open door and turned, dropping into a ready stance. Beside him, Neleh did the same. "Watch my back," she grunted to him, unnecessarily, and then there was no more time for talk. The skeletons boiled through the doorway, and the battle was joined.

Holok heard Neleh's battle cry beside him and ignored it as he flowed into the first stance of Flame Serpent form. Blue fire hung in the air where his hands had passed, tracing an intricate web of flame. Where the skeletons touched it they crumbled to ash.

An open-fist punch to the face of the first creature turned its skull to ash. Its body staggered onwards for two steps, made a half-hearted swing and collapsed. Holok stepped over it, ducking under a thrust from another skeleton and then extending his leg in a sweep that brought his attacker stumbling into a palisade of eldritch flame. With an unholy howl, it pitched forward and scattered its remains on the floor.

To his left, Neleh battled two skeletons at once. Even as he spared her a moment's glance, Holok saw her take an opponent's arm at the elbow, leaving its sword to skitter harmlessly across the floor. It struck at her with its remaining fist and she leapt straight up, twisting in midair to come down squarely on its bony shoulders. It crumpled under her weight, and as her other foe struck, Neleh rolled forward underneath its blow. She came out of the tumble in a crouch with both swords extended straight forward, the blades between the skeleton's legs. It stopped its advance, but too late; with a shout, she struck up with her left hand and out with her right. The sharp crack of breaking bones mixed with the clatter of falling ones, and the skeleton's remains abruptly ceased moving.

The last creature faced Holok cautiously, holding its sword

in a low guard position to keep him at range. They circled left, until Holok's foot landed on the scorched shinbone of a previous opponent. He slipped slightly, just enough for the skeleton to see an opening for a thrust.

Holok drew his foot back, hooked it under the offending bone, and kicked it into the air. Seizing it in his right hand, he brought it across the skeleton's outstretched blade. Such was the force of the blow that it knocked the sword and the hand that gripped it loose, bones scattering as it spun through the air.

Mindless, it reached for his throat with its remaining hand. He spun to the left to avoid it, striking the skeleton's other wrist such a blow with the bone that both shattered. The skeleton paused for a moment, holding its ruined arms up before its eyes, then advanced.

Suddenly tired of the dance, Holok struck brutally and first. His fist moved though the skeleton's rib cage, fragments of bone flying as he did. His fingers closed on its spine, even as the ravaged arms came down upon his shoulders in a drummer's tattoo. Ignoring the blows, Holok tightened his grip and twisted. There was an instant of strain, then a sharp popping sound. The light went out of the skeleton's eyes, and Holok found himself holding a misshapen collection of bones, one that he had snapped in half. Disgusted, he let it fall to the floor in a jumble.

"Not a bad fight," said Neleh, sheathing her swords. "Do you think there are more?"

"This is the work of the Abyss, Neleh, though these," he paused to nudge a few bones with his foot, "were hardly worth the effort of dispatching. Not true walking dead, just bone oddments given some measure of a Deathknight's power."

"The bones don't match," she said, nodding.

"No. These were things of the moment, not warriors returned from the grave. Poor craftsmanship, as well."

Neleh snorted. "Fine enough work for a fight. I wonder what other surprises are waiting for us."

"I don't know. If these were left behind simply to serve as an unpleasant surprise for anyone exploring the temple, then there may not be any more. If the one who made them is still about, then you might yet get another fight." Holok knelt to the floor and began tidying the rough collection of bones. "It's a shame that the warriors whose bones these were have been abused thus."

The Huntswoman's expression was one of mild disgust. "You play with the dead, priest. I'll go back to warn the others."

"An excellent idea," Holok replied. "I'll join you when I finish."

Shaking her head in disbelief, Neleh trotted off. Holok waited until her footsteps had faded, then rose and strode over to the broken doors. "I believe it is time," he said into the dark. "She's gone."

Before him, a figure floated into view, rising from the depths of the catacombs and wrapped in a cloak of ashen gray. As the figure landed effortlessly on the top step of the landing, Holok saw that it was a woman. She was tall but slender, wearing form-fitting armor that gleamed as if it were carved from the heart of a monstrous seashell. She wore a helm that bore a hideous, grinning caricature of a woman's face, twisted in some dire amusement, and her hands both held short, wicked-looking sickles.

"You sent her away. Why?" The woman's voice was musical, her tone amused. "One would think you'd want allies."

Holok took a step back and settled into a guard stance. "Insufficiently skilled allies are more of a hindrance than a help. I'd spend more of my time protecting her than killing you. The Dragon-Blooded's strength is in their numbers."

"True," she purred, "but that has never prevented your kind from using one of them as a shield before. Why stop now?" She took two steps forward, knelt, and hooked a burned skull by an eye socket. It dangled precariously from a sickle for a moment, then fell to the ground.

"The past has nothing to do with this, servant of darkness. Is this your work?"

She laughed. "The skeletons? Yes. A trifle. The things currently besetting your lackeys? Mine as well. The slaughter in the village? Hardly. If it had been me, I'd have eaten the bodies." A flicker of revulsion crossed Holok's face, and she bowed, elegantly, when she saw it. "I am Shamblemerry, and

I am here, as are you, to see what has transpired in this place. The author of this travesty is named Ratcatcher, and I've as little love for him as you do. His Majesty the Prince of Shadows bid me abide him, however, and so I am here to cast my eye upon his handiwork, and to see what he left undone, and to fetch the boy that Ratcatcher left behind."

"The boy? I've seen none here. Perhaps we should exchange our observations?" They circled each other warily, Holok holding to his stance while Shamblemerry cut idle, intricate patterns in the air with her blades. Her gray cloak had vanished, and Holok realized that it had been the expression of her anima. Grey was an unusual color for such, and Holok caught himself wondering at the strangeness of it.

Shamblemerry feinted with her left hand, but Holok refused to flinch. She smiled, as if to let the priest know she was testing him, and continued the dance. "I've seen enough to learn why you put this temple here, and to understand why you've been sent. The Huntsmen are nothing. Your presence speaks volumes."

Holok shook his head imperceptibly, sadly. "Then you've learned enough that you're going to have to die. There are things here that your master should never learn."

"I'm not the one who'll be dying, monk. Kejak will need another set of errand boys." She feinted high with her left hand, then aimed a vicious swipe at Holok's belly. He dropped to his knees, and the cut whistled harmlessly overhead, but already her left-handed blade was descending in a wicked arc towards his head. Throwing himself to the right, he came to his feet in time to dodge a pair of uppercut slashes. Spinning, he launched a series of kicks at her side, but she parried each blow with the flat of one sickle or another, then launched a kick of her own at his groin.

Holok saw it coming and pivoted on his left foot. Shamblemerry's toe missed him by inches, and he brought his elbow down just behind her knee. Her leg snapped down, though without the crunch of bone that Holok had been hoping for. Shamblemerry dropped to the ground, slightly off balance, and cut awkwardly at Holok's ankles. He leapt over the blows and aimed another kick at her head, but she had recovered her balance and evaded it easily.

"You're slow, old man," she taunted as she came effortlessly to her feet. Behind her, the gray cloak flared out again, and Holok felt his own anima flare into life behind him. "I'll start cutting you soon."

"The wise mind does not make promises the unskilled hand cannot keep," he replied, and feinted a leg sweep before throwing a solid punch at Shamblemerry's belly. Falling for the feint, she leapt, and caught Holok's fist on her left ankle. Off-balance, she fell to the floor roughly, then rolled to her right as Holok's foot came down with enough force to pulverize a stray fingerbone that remained from the battle with the skeletons. He tried the same maneuver again, but she dropped the sickles and caught his foot in her hands. There was a moment's struggle, then she heaved with all her might and Holok went over backwards, spinning in midair so as to land on his feet. Shamblemerry reclaimed her weapons and sprang to a fighting stance as well, a speculative look on her face. "Is that bit of pap from the Immaculate Texts?" she asked disinterestedly.

Holok shook his head. "Actually, I made it up three hundred years ago, but it seemed appropriate. You're not ready for this, Shamblemerry. I wish, for your sake, that you hadn't been sent here."

"Keep your wishes to yourself, priest," she snarled. "I'll be making a toy of your shade soon enough."

"I doubt that very much," Holok replied, and his anima flared white behind him.

She attacked then, her strokes driven by pure savagery. Holok was forced back, step by step. Each blow fell so close on the heels of the last that there was no room for a counterstroke, and soon the monk felt the cool stone of the chamber wall against his shoulder blades. Still she attacked, and Holok found himself desperately parrying the sickles with his bare hands, striking their flats with enough force to divert them away from his body. Shamblemerry's battle cry was a wordless howl of triumph, her blows coming wilder and faster with each instant.

Suddenly, Holok threw himself forward. Both of

Shamblemerry's slashes passed behind him, and his weight bore her to the ground. In the instant before she could redirect her attacks, he sprang forward and turned, ready for another ferocious assault.

Instead, she half-turned and flung one of the sickles at him. The move took Holok completely by surprise, and the blade buried itself in his palm. Such was the force with which it was thrown that it carried him back to the wall and pinned his hand to it. Involuntarily he cried out, and then the warm blood began rushing over his fingers. He tried to step forward, but the sickle held him fast. Pain surged through him, and though he blocked it as best he could, it still tore at the edges of his concentration. Behind him, his anima cloak flickered and sparked, guttering now like old flame.

Lazily, Shamblemerry arose. "It ends here," she said, cutting experimental shavings from the air with her remaining blade. "You fought well for an old man. But now I will cut your throat, and then harvest those who rode with you. I'll drink your blood first, I think. Consider it an honor."

She removed her helm then and cast it aside; it fell to the floor, forgotten. She was astonishingly beautiful, with lustrous black hair and skin the color of alabaster, but her lips were set in a sadist's smile, and her eyes were cold and mad.

Holok said nothing, tensing himself for the blow. Slowly, Shamblemerry drew back the sickle, then brought it around in a horizontal stroke meant to tear open his throat.

Summoning all of his will, Holok raised his good hand and caught the blade. His anima flared with power, and as he closed his fist, the sickle crumpled. "I think I'll have to decline," he said as calmly as if he were addressing a new acolyte. "Your life is forfeit. You may wish to take the next few seconds to contemplate your crimes."

With a wrench, he tore his other hand loose from the wall, the sickle that had pinned it clattering to the floor. Shamblemerry sought to escape now, but her hand still clutched the broken blade, and that was held firmly in Holok's grasp.

"No!" she shrieked, as he brought his bloody hand to her throat. She dropped the sickle and tried to flee, but Holok caught her wrist and held her.

"Your breath is better used for other things," he continued dispassionately. "Prayer, perhaps, or cries for help. But I am Shajah Holok, and I have served the heavens for twelve centuries. You are as a child to me, Shamblemerry, and children who do not know their place should be punished."

With a hollow sound, her windpipe collapsed under the pressure of his grip. Her eyes caught his, full of disbelief and pain, and then the light left them. She sagged forward, and after a moment, he let her drop to the floor.

Holok regarded her for a moment, then took the remaining sickle and cut a strip of cloth from the hem of his robe. This he wound around his palm, awkwardly, as a bandage. Then he strode forth to see if the noble Huntsmen needed the assistance of a simple priest. The sickle he left behind.

Chapter Twenty-Nine

The second night with Ratcatcher passed much like the first, though Wren made no move to escape. While the landscape was now broken up here and there with low scrub, no good opportunities presented themselves for Wren to make another attempt. Even if one had come along, the rope around his neck served as sufficient discouragement to the idea. When the moon reached its height they stopped for a brief meal, then continued. After his uncharacteristic outburst, Ratcatcher was mostly silent, and Wren's attempts at conversation fell flat. A few awkward hours later, the monk gave up trying and instead watched the terrain fade by in the dark. Again they stopped in a sufficiently shady place, and again Ratcatcher took great care to hobble him lest he escape. Aching and feverish, Wren crept under his blanket and found himself praying, perversely, for night to come again. Too soon, he got his wish.

"We've got three nights' riding left to us before we reach our destination, so try not to die in the meanwhile," Ratcatcher said affably as he lifted Wren into the saddle. He patted Wren almost gently on his wounded ankle, and cracked a wicked grin as the priest cried out. "That'll teach you to play with strange dogs. They bite, you know."

"Now," he said as he tied Wren's hands fast to the saddle once again, "am I going to have to wrap a noose around your neck again, or are you going to behave yourself tonight?"

"I'm not going anywhere, Ratcatcher." Wren's voice was tired, defeated. "Just lead the way."

"An excellent choice." Ratcatcher sounded rather pleased with himself, and mounted up. "I trust you won't make me regret it." With a shout to the hounds, Ratcatcher started off. Obediently, Wren's horse followed.

A few hours before dawn one of the dogs pulled up lame. Its whimpering was almost human, so much so that Wren had to fight down the urge to call out and comfort it. Ratcatcher looked back at it every few hundred strides, his face showing an ever-increasing annoyance. Once he caught Wren's eye, and laughed at the concern he saw there.

Still chortling, he called a halt and leapt down from his horse. Wren sat stock-still in the saddle.

Ratcatcher's footsteps crunched on the ground as he walked over to the wounded hound. It sat on its hind legs, its tongue hanging out, and the expression on its face one of mixed devotion and fear. The others hung back in a rough circle, keening softly. Silently, Ratcatcher knelt.

"There's a good boy," he said softly, stroking the dog's head. "That's a good, good boy. You've run a long way, haven't you?" The hound whimpered, and lowered its head gratefully to Ratcatcher's attentions.

"Do you think you can run all the way home, boy? I don't think you can. You're hurt, aren't you, my good boy?" Again the hound whimpered, and Wren felt a sudden cold stab of trepidation in the pit of his stomach.

Ratcatcher looked up at him, a cold light in his eyes. Wren tried to look away and found that he couldn't. The howling of the beasts around him grew louder and more frantic, and his horse added panicked whinnying to the cacophony.

Still murmuring to the hound, Ratcatcher put its head in his lap. It whined softly and closed its eyes, and a second later Ratcatcher snapped its neck.

The howl from the others rose to a deafening crescendo. Wren's horse stamped its hooves nervously but held its ground, and Ratcatcher merely sat in the center of the circle holding the dying hound until its struggles finally ceased. Then he stood, still holding the corpse, and casually took the dagger from his belt. With a look of intense concentration, he selected the dog's right forepaw, and hacked it off with a single blow. The body tumbled to the ground, leaking blood.

There was a second of silence, and then the rest of the pack exploded into a frenzy. They fell on the dead dog ravenously, while a bemused Ratcatcher strolled around the carnage to join Wren, who sat stock still.

"Why?" the priest asked. It was a simple question, but it encompassed volumes.

Ratcatcher leaned on the horse's neck, casually. It whickered nervously, but did not move. "Why what, priest? Why the dead dog? Because it was never going to make it home, and this was a kindness. That's the sort of thing you approve of, yes? Mercy to the sick and the lame?" He strolled around the horse to the other side, waving the bloody paw. "Or perhaps you want to know why I fed him to the other dogs. That's easy; to keep up their strength. They're still a long way from home, and the longer they're out here, the weaker they get. Battening on one of their own gives them a little more sustenance than a rabbit might." His eyes glittered mischievously. "Of course, if you take issue with it, you're free to try to pull them off the carcass and give it a decent burial. Eh, priest? Feel like seeing to a dog's soul? I thought not."

Wren began to reply, then thought better of it. "Explain the paw, then."

"I saw your eyes following it. Curiosity is a lovely thing in a condemned man." Ratcatcher turned and walked out into the night, his voice trailing over his shoulder. "It's a gift, an offering to a spirit that dwells near this place. Otherwise it might decide to try to take you, and none of us would like that." With that, he strode off into the darkness a dozen strides, and called out wordlessly. There was a rush of wind, and then a single far-off cry. Ratcatcher answered it, then stood, expectant and silent.

Wren felt, rather than saw, something huge and spiderlike scuttle up out of the dark. It stopped where Ratcatcher stood, and its voice scratched at the edge of his hearing like a bow on a poorly tuned fiddle. Ratcatcher replied to it, holding up the bloody paw. It blustered for a minute, then Ratcatcher laid the paw down on the ground and backed away. The shape paused, and Wren could feel its eyes on him. The creature's gaze was hungry, and irrationally Wren felt the urge to prostrate himself.

Mine someday, whispered a voice inside his mind. *Remember me.*

Wren shivered. The beast gave another cry, then turned and passed back into shadow.

Looking immensely pleased with himself, Ratcatcher strolled up to Wren's horse and ruffled its mane with a bloody hand. "That went faster than I thought."

"What was that thing?" Wren looked, not at Ratcatcher, but rather out into the darkness. "I've never felt..." His voice trailed off. "I've never seen anything like that."

"And aren't you thankful. That was the manifested spirit of this place. It's not native, but it's found a home here, and it's quite happy as long as it's well-fed. I'll spare your delicate sensibilities the rest of the gory details." He strode up to the hound's corpse, which by this time had mostly been reduced to bones. A single dog worried at scraps of flesh on a mutilated leg, and Ratcatcher drove it off with a kick. Growling, it slunk off to join its fellows, and cast a hungry eye at Wren. He averted his gaze, and looked straight ahead.

With the dull clank of metal on metal, Ratcatcher hoisted himself back into his saddle. "We've still got traveling to do tonight, priest. Just remember old Kidercherlee out there in the dark and stay close. You're better off with my company than with its." He started forward, and obediently, Wren's horse followed.

The hounds, however, stood their ground. One by one they lifted their voices in a dirge, and Wren was surprised to see Ratcatcher join in the chorus. The sound faded behind them as they rode off, but always in the distance there was howling.

It was long hours before the dogs rejoined them along their path, and their muzzles were still bloody.

Chapter Thirty

Neleh kicked a corpse. It didn't move, so she kicked it again and moved on.

Walking down the dirty rut that served as the central avenue of Qut Toloc, she could see the others, at least those who had survived. Shiresh and Pelap were dragging bodies onto a pyre, while Holok stood by them, grim-faced and angry. A stained bandage on his left hand was the most prominent sign of the wound he had taken, and his robes were much the worse for wear.

A whinny from beyond a row of burned-out houses told her that Taenat had finished rounding up the last of the horses, and a minute later the woman strode into view with a half-dozen mounts on a tether. Taenat's armor was bundled neatly on the lead horse, though her quiver of javelins was still strapped across her back. "Damaged. Half the straps were chewed through. I'll need to get it remade when we get home," she said, and walked on. The horses followed obediently, and Neleh let them pass.

Out of the corner of her eye, she saw Holok motion her over. He was using a bloodstained hoe to tend the flames, seemingly oblivious to the pillar of greasy black smoke rising from the pile of bodies. Occasionally one of the Huntsmen would return with another cadaver to throw on the flames.

"I was astonished we could find enough wood to build this," he said when she got close enough to hear. "The fires have had their way with this town for days."

"Closer to weeks," she replied, wrinkling her nose at the stench. "Was this really necessary?"

Holok nodded. "We don't want them rising again."

Neleh shuddered slightly at the memory. She'd burst from the temple after the encounter with the skeletons only to find the town overwhelmed by chaos. Dozens of bodies had lurched to their feet and hurled themselves at the Huntsmen, slow but relentless and insensate to pain. A riot of unliving berserkers, terrified animals and surprised Hunters had filled the streets, and screams, curses and cries of agony had filled the air.

Without a thought for Holok, she'd drawn her swords and plunged into the fray. The risen corpses moved slowly, but each had to be hacked multiple times before it would stop moving, and so the progress of the battle was slow. All of the servants and several of the Hunters were down by the time Holok emerged to join the fight, and while no more casualties were taken after that, the battle had still raged well past sunset.

She'd cursed him, then, for being so slow. It was not until hours later that she discovered that he had been facing a trial of his own. Now when she looked at him, it was with a mixture of respect and fear. She'd asked him about the battle, and he'd deflected her questions. She'd taken a moment then to return to the antechamber where they'd fought the skeletons and to examine the gouge the sickle had made in the wall after it pierced his hand. It went three inches deep.

She'd also gone back with the intention of looting Shamblemerry's body. It was, to her dismay, gone. Holok had been philosophical about it. "Strange things happen to her kind upon death," he'd said, and would say no more. Then he had exhorted her to see to other tasks, and gone to tend to the bodies.

"Neleh?" he said, his voice breaking through her reverie.

"My apologies," she said, and found that she actually was apologetic, if only for a moment.

"Hmm, yes. As I was saying, if we meet another servant of the Abyss, we don't want to give him any more tools that necessary, though I suspect we won't be seeing Shamblemerry again. At least, not in that form." His voice dropped, and he looked down. "It's kinder than leaving them for the beasts, as well."

Neleh shrugged, minimally. "The beasts have already gotten what they can from most of them, but if you feel this is necessary..." She let her voice trail off.

"I do." Holok's was firm. "Proper respect for the dead is

not the sort of thing one can take or leave. Once the fire burns down, we'll make our next move."

"And that is?" Neleh stopped short of open scorn, preferring to flavor her words with skepticism. "So far, this has not gone as planned."

Holok turned and stared at the fire, pushing diffidently at a flopping arm with the hoe. After a few tries, he managed to push it back into the fire. "We didn't find what we came for, but we did uncover what we need to find. Obviously, the monster responsible for this is no longer here, but he's secondary. I think we want the boy Shamblemerry spoke of to me, not Ratcatcher"

Neleh frowned. "Why not hunt Ratcatcher instead? Surely this is what your omen foretold. We should find the butcher, and we make him pay for all of this."

"No. It is tempting, but it is not why we are here. Precious little in this place makes sense, and I have no desire to follow trails that divert us from what we're supposed to be doing. Avenging murders is all well and good, but I'd rather prevent the ones that will follow in the child's path if he lives."

"What sense is there to make of this?" Neleh demanded as she strode around the fire. "You're clutching at straws. We were called on to Hunt an Anathema here, one that was powerful enoughto slaughter the villagers and your precious monks. Now we know its name, so we find it and we kill it. There is nothing more sensible than that. The boy you're talking about? Pointless."

Holok shook his head, "Oh, we will find this Ratcatcher and we will destroy him, but later, when our real work is done. My gut tells me that he was drawn here as surely as we were, and by the same thing. Ask yourself this—why did the Deathknight ask us for the boy? That is the question the whole affair balances on. One would think that if he were nothing, Shamblemerry would not have asked for him, and if he were allied with the Abyss, they would already have him. That's the only way this makes sense."

"It does not need to make sense," Neleh said. "We just need to do our jobs. Finish with the bodies. We'll ride as soon as the ashes cool."

Without waiting for a reply, Neleh walked off. Holok watched her go, sadly, then returned to tending the fire. There were a great many bodies to burn, which would give him a great deal of time to think about what he might actually be dealing with here. One thing was clear, and that was that Kejak's instructions were woefully inadequate. Whatever the omens had foretold at Qut Toloc had already come to pass, and Holok had an unpleasant suspicion that he would be learning far more than he liked about what had transpired.

With a grunt from Pelap, another corpse landed on the fire. A shower of sparks went up and Holok roughly prodded dangling limbs back into the flame, thankful for the distraction.

"The boy," he said to himself, absently. "The key is the boy. Find him first, and all else will become clear." And then he lost himself in the rhythm of tending the fire, at least for a little while.

Chapter Thirty-One

After the Wyld Hunt passed, Yushuv kept to the swamps and meadows as much as he could. Panic whispered in his ear that the Hunt would be coming back for him, and that he'd do well to avoid the road when they did. He stayed parallel to it as best as he could manage, though. The notion of finding the dagger was still with him, and the roads were his best hope for that.

Malaky had the dagger, and Malaky was a Guildsman, after all. He covered a beat from Boneford to the big river cities. If he came back this way, he'd do it along the road leading back to Yushuv's former home, and Yushuv couldn't afford to be too far from the road in case the man did.

As he walked. Yushuv thought about Malaky. The Guildsman had always paid as much attention to the children of the village as he did to their elders, making sure to ask them if they'd found anything interesting the catacombs. He'd made a tremendous fuss over keeping their secret, as if their parents had not run the boneways themselves, years before.

Malaky also told stories, and that was the real reason the village's children loved him. On his infrequent visits, he had delighted in terrifying them with tales of what happened to bad little boys and girls who ran away from their villages. Some, he averred, were eaten by spirits. Others were taken off by wild beasts, or things that used to be wild beasts before they'd stumbled into the strange places where the old, weird magic still reigned. But worst of all, he'd whisper as he leaned forward at his rapt listeners, his traveling cloak draping over his bony arms like a shroud, were those poor, poor children who were caught by slavers and sold to the Fair Folk. The stories he spun then were enough to drive the younger children away screaming in terror, and in one case Shemsi, the blacksmith's apprentice, had to be physically restrained from assaulting the man because the tales had given his younger sister nightmares.

Yushuv's father had told him, rather too emphatically, that the factor's stories were only stories; but Yushuv knew better. He'd come across Malaky once when the man was in his cups, slumped up against the temple wall with a hardened leather bottle of wine in his hand. Yushuv had been all of five years old then, wide-eyed with curiosity and blessed with the sort of solemnity achieved only by Immaculates and the very young. He'd tiptoed up to where Malaky sat and asked, "Are the stories true? Do the Fair Folk really do that to people?"

Malaky had cracked one eye open and gazed up at him with an expression Yushuv couldn't recognize. "No," he finally croaked. "They do something worse." He'd speak no more after that, pretending to be asleep when Yushuv peppered him with follow-up questions.

Eventually the boy had wandered off, filled with a healthy determination never to be taken captive by slavers. Malaky had left town early the next morning, and didn't return for almost a year. Yushuv's father had looked oddly at his son for some time after that, but never said a word.

A sudden thought struck Yushuv, and he stopped. Malaky would come back. Malaky always came back. If he searched for Malaky, he might miss the factor entirely, as Malaky was fond of spending time in those same village taverns that Yushuv was making a point of avoiding. And truth be told, he had no idea where Malaky went once he left the village. He'd seen maps twice or thrice, but the neat lines on parchment seemed to have little in common with the terrain he'd crossed thus far.

But if he waited here, by a road he was certain Malaky was sure to travel, then sooner or later the factor would come. Yushuv looked around. The land was swampy, but not desperately so. There was game here, and enough dry land for him to make some sort of camp. The road was nearby, but screened behind a row of trees rising from the mire. He could see it, and not be seen himself. It seemed in all ways an excellent and sensible plan.

It was not until much later that Yushuv wondered if the plan had indeed been his own, but by then, it was too late to move on. *Perhaps tomorrow, I'll reconsider,* Yushuv thought, and then drifted off to sleep. *In the morning. Perhaps.*

Chapter Thirty-Two

The ghosts were waiting for Ratcatcher when he rode through the citadel's gates, Wren in tow. Throngs of them lined the courtyard, waiting silently as he dismounted and bodily lifted Wren from the saddle. "Can you walk?" he asked. Wren nodded, and Ratcatcher dropped him roughly on his feet. "Good. Follow me. Stay close, or the dead men will have your blood, and I'll have another explanation I need to make to the Prince." He grasped the rope that still bound the monk's wrists and dragged him forward.

Behind him, Wren saw the surviving hounds being led off, as other silent figures tended to the horses and removed Ratcatcher's saddlebags. Most had the pallor and shambling gait of the walking dead, and those who did not looked as if it were only a matter of time. Overhead, low clouds scudded clockwise across the sky, and beneath them huge silhouettes that most probably belonged to vultures circled.

Ahead, the great iron doors of the main citadel itself were flung open. Pelesh the Exchequer, clad in his dusty rags, stood upon the black marble steps before them with a faint smile on his face. "Greetings, Ratcatcher," he said as they approached. "I trust your journey was a successful one?"

Ratcatcher smiled grimly, and held aloft the weapon he'd taken from Wren. "I'd say so, Pelesh. Would you care to examine it?"

"Of course, of course." Pelesh rubbed his hands together in anticipation, and for an irrational moment Wren was reminded of a spider. "It must be appraised, its true worth brought to His Majesty's attention—"

"Fine," said Ratcatcher, and plunged the dagger firmly into Pelesh's belly. The Exchequer's eyes widened in shock, and he staggered backwards gasping. His hands went to his stomach, and he stammered. "You...you didn't..."

"No, I didn't." Ratcatcher held up the weapon, reversed. No blood marked the blade. "Just the haft. You're fine, my dear, dear Pelesh."

Trembling, Pelesh lifted his hands from his gut. They were clean. "You play a dangerous game, Ratcatcher," he gasped, and straightened up in stages.

"I play to win, Pelesh. I have the dagger. I have," and he gave Wren a vicious shove, "the priest. And I have managed to overcome the annoyance of being given short shrift by a tight-fisted ancient with a veritable talent for backing the wrong horse. Give Shamblemerry my love, Pelesh. I'm taking some presents to the Prince." He walked off into the citadel and, after a moment, Wren followed. Pelesh's eyes met Wren's for an instant, and the hatred Wren saw there made him recoil.

"The wheel turns," Wren distinctly heard him mutter, and then a vicious tug on his leash sent the priest sprawling into the darkness.

The corridor leading to the Prince's throne room was long and dark, memorable to Wren primarily for the arrogance with which Ratcatcher shouldered aside any others traversing it. The massive doors to the chamber were unguarded but shut, and the Deathknight pounded on them confidently with a mailed fist. The sound echoed hollowly beyond, and then faded into silence.

"So what now?" Wren asked wearily. His legs ached, and he suspected that the bites he had taken from the hounds were beginning to fester. If he were lucky, he thought, that would spread and take him quickly, sparing him the pleasures of the Prince's torture chambers. "Do you hand me over to the Prince, and then go on your merry way?"

"Merry's not one of my favorite words right now," Ratcatcher retorted. "No, I am going to make a formal presentation of you and the dagger to my prince. I have no idea how long he's wanted the toy, but he's wanted you ever since Talat's Howe, and he tends to get vindictive when he's forced to wait for things he wants. As for what he's going to do to you, I have no idea, but I expect it will be unpleasant and lingering. I'd pray for quick death, priest, if I were you."

"I've always been a terrible priest," Wren said, but weakly. Then the doors swung open, and there was no more time for talk.

The Prince sat on his throne, toying with his mace the way a jester might wave a prop. He wore white today, startling in its brightness and trimmed with small beads of obsidian. With a languid gesture, he motioned Ratcatcher forward, and peered down at him as if awakening from a dream.

"Ratcatcher? So soon, I see. Who is that wretch trailing behind you? I've little patience with your follies these days, you know."

Ratcatcher strode forward and bowed low. Wren followed, haltingly, and the doors whispered shut behind them. "I bring gifts for you, my prince. I have been successful in my endeavors for you, and have brought you the fruits of my labors."

"So you have the boy?"

"The boy?" Ratcatcher's eyes widened in surprise and alarm. Clearly, this was not going the way Ratcatcher had anticipated, and Wren stifled an urge to laugh aloud.

"The boy you left alive in Qut Toloc. You were supposed to find him. Have you?"

"No, my prince, but—"

"Ah. Then perhaps you have the sword?"

Ratcatcher stammered, desperation in his voice, "No, my prince, not the sword, either, but—"

"Let us tally your accomplishments, then. You do not have the boy, for whom I sent you. You do not have the sword, to which the boy was to lead you. You do, however, have a ragged priest on a leash, and the priest, I might add, is bleeding from the ankle onto the floor of my throne room. It is no wonder I sent another to tidy up after your messes. It looks as if I'll have to do the same here."

"Your Majesty, if you would only give me leave to explain—"

Again, the Prince cut Ratcatcher off with an airy wave of his hand. "I suppose I had better. Otherwise, your pet will bleed to death in front of me before I find out why you brought me such a sorry-looking thing. You may proceed."

Ratcatcher bowed low, lower than he had before. "I thank you, my prince." Wren could feel the impotent rage bubbling off his captor, as well as the helpless devotion he felt to the Prince. It briefly occurred to him to pity Ratcatcher, but only briefly. Pity, he decided, was better reserved for himself.

He looked up, and saw that Ratcatcher had approached the throne. He knelt, and proffered up the dagger.

"My prince, may I present you with this gift? It is more precious than rubies, more powerful than—"

"Yes, yes. Ratcatcher, you wax theatrical at the oddest times. It is a dagger. Is it *the* dagger?" The Prince leaned forward, a terrible hunger in his eyes.

Ratcatcher swallowed. "It is, my prince. I had it from a Guildsman named Shotan Fong, who in turn had it from a trader named Malaky, who had it from the boy. Once it came into my possession, I thought it best to bring it to you at once, rather than risk it in such unworthy hands as mine."

"A wise choice," the Prince said, wryly. "Place it in my worthy hands instead."

"Of course, my prince."

"Of course indeed..." The Prince laid his mace before the throne and turned the blade over in his hands. "Orichalcum. Is it not lovely? Does it not hold the very light of the accursed sun in its blade? Could not this dagger lay low entire hosts—if wielded by the right warrior? Oh, Toloc, you ancient bitch, how sorry your shade must be to see this."

The Prince stood, and thrust the dagger aloft. A golden light poured from it, illuminating the chamber. Brighter and brighter it shone, until Wren was forced to look away. He heard, rather than saw, Ratcatcher scrabbling at the floor, begging the Prince to make it stop. And he sensed, rather than heard, the Prince's unkind laughter.

Abruptly, the light faded, and all was dark again. "An excellent gift, Ratcatcher," the Prince said soberly. "I am well pleased with you."

"Thank you, my prince," the Deathknight replied, his voice faint. "I am honored to have served you."

"Then serve me once again, and explain the thing on the leash." The Prince strode down the steps and over to where Wren stood. "He does not bow. He does not speak. He does not try to escape, which shows at least a modicum of wisdom. But there are many, many Immaculates in the world. Why bring me this one?"

"It's Wren, my prince. My other gift to you."

"Wren?" There was silence for a moment, and a beatific smile spread across the Prince's face. "Oh, you have done well indeed, my little hound. Wren!" The Prince stepped back and spread his arms in welcome. "I am so glad to have you as my guest, Most Inquisitive Initiate, Most Thoughtless Assassin, Most Unfortunate of Men. I have been waiting for you, What do you think of my citadel? Is it not majestic? Does it not fill you with awe and dread? Answer me!"

Wren stood still, stood silent. Slowly, an expression of rage crept over the Prince's face. "Answer me," he said softly, and took a step forward. Wren said nothing. "Answer me," the Prince cried again, more loudly. Again, Wren kept silent. "Answer me!" Wren closed his eyes, sought his center, and clenched his tongue between his teeth.

"Answer me!" The Prince's blow caught him on the side of the jaw and sent him spinning to the floor. He tasted blood, but made no effort to rise. In an instant, the Prince was standing over him. "I am the Prince of Shadows. No man mocks me with silence. No man averts his gaze from me unless I wish it. Now answer me, or I will carve the Immaculate Texts on your liver and slice off your eyelids so that you might study them better. Answer!" Without waiting, he leveled a savage kick at Wren's ribs, and the priest doubled up in pain. The Prince extended his hand, and the mace that had lain at the foot of his throne flew through the air. He caught it, tested its heft, and stared down.

Wren opened his eyes. He saw the mace descend, saw it clearly enough to count every fold, every place where the metal had been hammered. He saw the fury on the Prince's face and the irresistible power of the swing. Then it hammered into the floor beside his head, shattering the marble and scoring his cheek with razor-edged fragments.

Abruptly, the Prince's demeanor changed. He whirled, leaving the mace on the stone. "You're brave, Wren. This is admirable. It is also foolish. Ratcatcher?"

"Yes, my prince?"

"Punish him."

"Yes, my prince."

Wren struggled to a sitting position, but could go no further. He looked up into Ratcatcher's pitying face. "You should have answered, you know," the Deathknight said, and then the blows started to fall like hail.

"That was crude, Ratcatcher," the Prince observed idly after Wren had at last succumbed to unconsciousness. "I would have expected more delicacy from you, and perhaps a better technique."

Ratcatcher shrugged slightly. "Sometimes the simplest ways are the best. He's not permanently damaged."

"No, he's not. Have him taken to Unforgiven Blossom to have his wounds tended, and then place him in a cell. There are mysteries to this priest, and I want answers to them. Why would Kejak send him to Talat's Howe when he is, really, nothing? And how did such a nothing kill Sandheart? I expect that unraveling this onion of a man will take some time. I want to make sure he is healthy enough to endure the process." Abruptly, the Prince looked up. "Did you grow fond of him while you were traveling, Ratcatcher? I heard what you said to him before you commenced the noble task of pummeling him."

Ratcatcher shook his head, and examined the state of his fingernails. "Not so, my prince. He was irritating company, and tried to escape repeatedly. I simply find it amusing to be able to tell an Immaculate monk the course of wisdom."

The Prince laughed politely. "An excellent jest. Now, you are dismissed. See to it that Wren wakes up caged. We'll visit him soon enough."

Ratcatcher bowed. "Yes, my prince." The doors opened before him, and he stepped out, calling for slaves to do the Prince's bidding.

Feebly, Wren stirred. The Prince rose, curious, and peered at him. "Brave priest. Dead priest. You'll serve me either way, and make reparations for what you've cost me. Heal quickly, little man. I've no patience with you anymore."

Chapter Thirty-Three

"Do we ride?" Holok shouted over at Neleh. Behind her, the other four surviving Hunters sat, mounted and in single file. Only Holok could ride next to the lead Huntswoman, an honor he frankly did not relish much.

"As soon as Your Most Immaculate self is ready to go, yes, we go." Neleh's chestnut gelding was stamping nervously, and most of the woman's attention was focused there.

"Excellent." Holok flicked his reins and, without waiting, started back down the dusty road leading from Qut Toloc. "We will have better luck hunting elsewhere."

Neleh cantered up to him, the chestnut clearly relieved to be moving. "Do you know where we're going?" she asked in a low voice, not wanting the others to hear. "I'll follow you this once, but this has not been the pleasure trip we were promised. If the boy doesn't turn up within a week, we go back to hunting Ratcatcher. Do you understand?"

"The role of the Hunt is not pleasure," he said benignly. He caught her expression and, before she could rebut, continued. "The key is the boy, I'm convinced. They want him, therefore we should want him. He's on foot, and he's probably never left the village before. That means he's most likely hewing to the road, and moving at a walking pace. He's slow, and he is out in the open. We can find him. I know we can."

"I hope you're right," Neleh replied mournfully. "I just hope we're not following this road until it loses itself in the Ice Wastes."

"Not to worry. If we follow it that long, we've already failed. He's not too far. I can sense it."

"Can you really?" Her face was a mask of shrewd curiosity.

"Literally? No. But there are other ways," he said, and smiled in a way that made Neleh's teeth ache. Good humor from the priest worried her.

"I will do my best to be supremely impressed later," she said wryly, and dropped back in line. Chuckling, Holok rode on.

Chapter Thirty-Four

Wren awoke on the floor of a cell to discover that he was wet, cold, and missing at least two teeth of which he had been moderately fond. Spitting out blood, he opened his eyes and sat up, and was mildly surprised to discover that it didn't hurt nearly as much as he thought it would. Flickering torchlight from down the corridor illuminated the cell's dimensions, and so he gingerly rose to examine them.

The room itself was small, with a ceiling so low that Wren found himself unable to straighten up completely. Hunched over, he walked its dimensions—ten paces deep and three across, a bare hole gouged out of the living rock. At the back of the cell manacles had been set into the stone floor with massive bolts. The black iron of the chains was rusty with a combination of disuse and dried blood, and Wren felt it was prudent not to examine the cuffs themselves too closely. If his captors had wanted him chained, they'd had plenty of opportunity to arrange it while he had been unconscious.

The stone of the cell was the same black as the exterior of the citadel, pitted and scarred and marked with a thousand small fissures. None was large enough to offer hope, and a trickle of water ran through the network of cracks. This dripped down to puddle on the floor before flowing away to who-knew-where, ensuring that any sleep Wren managed to obtain would be uncomfortable at best. The steady plip-plip-plip of water striking the floor was already beginning to grind on his nerves, and he suspected that if he stayed here more than a few days, he'd find it maddening.

The cell's mouth was wide enough for two men to pass through, and barred with a heavy gate that sat on thick hinges. The gate itself was made of what looked to be cold iron, cast in the shape of misshapen bones, and the lock, if there was one, escaped his detection. There was enough space between the bars for Wren to extend an arm nearly to his shoulder, but there was nothing for him to grasp. The corridor, near as he could tell, was wide enough for four soldiers to march abreast, and carved from the same stone as the cell. A thick stench, combining the worst of smoke, rot, and stagnant water, filled the heavy air, and the torchlight was low and wan.

Experimentally, Wren tried the bars of his cell. They were very cold and very heavy, and Wren's best efforts barely produced a rattle. Prodding the walls produced results no more promising, and while a careful examination of the floor revealed where the water drained away, it did not reveal any faults that Wren might take advantage of.

Furthermore, apart from Wren himself and the tattered robes he wore, the cell was empty. There was no bench to sleep upon, no blanket, not even a bucket in which he might relieve himself. Wren could not even hear any other prisoners. For all he knew, he and the torch were the only things in the dungeon, and that once the torch went out it would just be him and the dark.

Thoroughly depressed, he sat down in the cold water and assumed the lotus position. Kejak had always chided him to improve his meditation. Now, Wren thought glumly, he was going to get his chance. With an air of resignation, he closed his eyes and began chanting. The pain of his injuries, the cold of the water, the fear that gnawed at him—all receded as he gave himself up to his meditations. The flesh is transient, he told himself. The spirit is all, the spirit will be raised up by the dragons. To form an attachment to the flesh is to deny one's true nature. To form an attachment to the flesh is to anchor one's spirit when it should soar.

All this he told himself, slowing his mantra so that the toy-drum plinking of the water formed a useful pattern beneath his rhythm. But part of him was still cold, and in pain, and alone.

It was perhaps an hour—or a day—later when Wren opened his eyes again. The Prince of Shadows stood before his cell door, flanked by Ratcatcher and a woman he did not know. She looked somehow withered, as if life had been drained from her too soon, but her gaze was direct and challenging. Ratcatcher stood at the Prince's left, his armor exchanged for gray silk and his arms folded across his chest in imitation of the Prince. He bore no weapons, and the arrogance of his stance demonstrated clearly that he didn't think he needed any.

Between the two stood the Prince. He was garbed in black and deep red, and his gaze was that of a farmer appraising another man's prize cow. His hands were clasped behind his back, and even in the smoky torchlight, his face was pale.

"You're awake," the Prince said. "Good. That will make this easier."

Wren rose as best he could. "And what would this be? Torture? I would suppose that's more productive when I can speak."

The Prince laughed insincerely. No one else did. "My dear priest, may we dispense with the false bravado? There is no point to it. Your life is mine now. You'll live as long as I want you to, as well as I want you to, and sooner or later, you will do exactly what I want you to. If you persist in playing the fool, you will live poorly yet briefly, and I'll feed your corpse to my hounds. If you act as a man with one foot on the path to enlightenment should, then your stay here will be pleasant, longer, and perhaps even fruitful. The decision, of course, is yours."

Wren shook his head. "I fail to see what you want from me. I'm a monk, and not much of one. You'd learn more of the Order from a thousand others."

"I'm not interested in the Order," the Prince spat. "I am interested in why you are so important to it. You have barely passed the First Coil. Your devotion is slipshod, your career erratic, your attempts at simple meditation appalling. And yet, you continue to turn up in the most interesting places. Ratcatcher told me that Fong was *very* eager to see you again—unusual for a simple priest. And then there is the question of what you were doing in Talat's Howe. A hunting trip gone awry, perhaps? Were you seized by uncontrollable wanderlust? I'm not as clever as a monk, little bird. You'll have to tell me."

"I don't know." The words sounded hollow, even to Wren, but he clung to them. "I don't know what you're talking about."

Ratcatcher smiled evilly. "I believe His Majesty asked you to cease the games, Wren. Your amusements caused me a great deal of pain, and I haven't begun to pay you back."

"That is quite enough, Ratcatcher. Thank you." The Prince's voice was mild, but Ratcatcher's jaw snapped shut with remarkable speed. "Now, Most Dreadfully Caged Postulant, would you please do me the honor of not treating me as if I were stupid. I know you were at Talat's Howe, Wren. You killed someone very dear to me there, and she is never, ever coming back. This is something that I find irritating. Furthermore, you then proceeded to brag about how clever you were by leaving us your token, and then you managed to evade us entirely. Because you were so clever in doing so, I even said some unkind things to Ratcatcher here that were completely unjustified. You owe many debts, Wren. Sing, and they will be wiped away."

Wren spread his arms in a gesture of sincere regret. "I wish I could, but all I could tell you is how one insignificant priest lives in insignificant temples. And sea travel. I could tell you a great deal about sea travel as well."

"You're not amusing, Wren," the Prince said, and snapped his fingers. "Bow."

"I will not—" Wren began, and then a terrible, crushing weight descended on his shoulders. He struggled, but it forced him ever downward until he stumbled forward and found himself on his knees. Above him, the Prince looked down speculatively and stroked his beardless chin.

"Not quite what I had hoped, but kneeling is just as good, I suppose. You give pitiful homage, you know."

Wren looked up. The ceiling of the cell had buckled downwards, reducing the height of his cell by half. A fine black dust showered down on him. When he experimentally prodded at the stone above him, it refused to give.

"I can bring it lower, you know," the Prince added conversationally. "I can make it so that you have just enough room to lie down, and then I'll snuff the torch. Would you prefer to stare up at that in the dark, or to lie half-drowned on your belly and pray that the stone doesn't snap your spine? There's really no need to torture you, you know. You're an intelligent man. As long as you know what I could do to you, I don't actually have to do it. Ponder that, Wren. Ponder it in the dark."

The Prince turned on his heel and walked off. Ratcatcher followed, shooting Wren a poisonous glance as he did so.

The woman glanced after them, then strode up to the bars. "The stars tell me that you will not die tonight," she said in a husky whisper. "They refuse to show me tomorrow. I would advise cooperating with my prince." Then she, too, turned and was gone. An instant after she vanished, a hiss announced the dousing of the torch. Light fled, and with it, Wren's hope.

"You'll need another man, Kejak," he said to himself, then sat down with his back against a wall. Chilled to the bone and beyond, Eliezer Wren closed his eyes and slept.

Chapter Thirty-Five

Holok stopped his horse and raised his hand. "Quiet," he said, very softly.

Neleh reined in, and behind her, the surviving Huntsmen did so as well. She looked around, and was profoundly unimpressed by what she saw.

To the right, a small cliff rose up from the roadside. Shattered piles of rock lay at its feet, and a few scrub trees clung precariously to its surface. A quick glance told her that nothing human could have climbed it, and few things that were inhuman would have even made the attempt.

To the left, the land fell away rapidly into a dismal-smelling fen. A row of trees off in the distance gave promise of sturdier ground, but otherwise it was a sea of tall grass, taller reeds, and standing water. The road itself had been covered in crushed stone from the cliff face by some enterprising soul. No doubt this allowed the track to hold its shape against the encroaching swamp, but it also meant that the surface of the road held no footprints. All in all, it looked like any of a hundred stretches of road the Hunt had seen since leaving Qut Toloc and, given enough time, it would no doubt look like a hundred more.

"He's here," Holok muttered, finger raised to test the wind. "Somewhere nearby. He's here."

Neleh rode forward. "How can you be sure?"

"I just...know." Holok sounded genuinely surprised. "Normally we rely on auguries in situations like this, but this time, I can feel him. It's like something cold in my gut."

"Are you sure that's not Taenat's cooking? We've been on this miserable road for days. We've seen nothing, not even a footprint. We've stopped in every pisswater hamlet and village and roadside hostel, and no one's seen a lone boy. There hasn't been a Guild caravan through, so we know that slavers didn't get him. There hasn't been so much as a missing chicken from a farmhouse. In short, we have seen nothing, nothing at all to indicate that the boy passed this way. Furthermore, we have only the word of a half-mad Deathknight, whose corpse conveniently vanished, that the boy exists at all! And yet you have steadfastly led us along this muddy little ribbon of a road, convinced that you knew where the boy would go, and now you say your gut tells you he's in the swamp? Are you mad? Is your hand infected, and has the sickness spread to your brain? Did Shamblemerry curse you? We've lost him, I say. Let us return home, and then send a garrison in force to Qut Toloc. It's better than this pointless chase!"

Holok turned to her, his face very pale. "Are you finished?" he inquired mildly. "If this is what you wish, you—and the other members of the Hunt—are free to go. I will proceed alone. However, if you are willing to trust me a single hour longer, I think I can lead you to our prey. Just..." He paused, tilted his head, and sniffed.

"What?" Neleh's voice dripped annoyance. "Don't tell me you think you're a dog now."

"Neleh, I would have given a great deal for some silence from you just now. Do you smell anything unusual?"

Experimentally, she sniffed. "I smell the swamp," she said flatly. "Nothing else."

"That's odd. I smell smoke. Wet wood, too. Precisely the sort of fire I'd make if I were trying to remain hidden. Try again."

Her eyes widened. "You're right. It's faint, but it's there."

Holok nodded. "And we are here. Have the rest of the Hunt dismount quietly and casually, as if we were stopping for a meal. I want as much surprise as possible. Something in all this is rotten, and I want us to have every advantage."

Neleh nodded, then wheeled her horse around. "We're stopping here for luncheon," she called loudly. "Tie the horses to that outcropping there." More quietly, she added, "And make ready. He's here."

"Are you sure?" Taenat was openly skeptical.

"There's a good chance. And if not, we go home."

"Good enough for me." Taenat shrugged and prepared to dismount, when a sudden sound from the marsh distracted her. "What's that?"

A cloud of birds exploded upwards from near the tree line, scattering into the sky. Neleh cursed. "That's him. Move. Move!"

"He's running. Spread out! Off the road!" Holok was already off his horse and moving into the marshy fields as he spoke. His steps were crane-light as he sprinted from hummock to hummock, eyes scanning the tall grasses in front of him.

Behind Holok, the other members of the Hunt dismounted grimly, drawing their blades but saying nothing. They fanned out along the road before stepping into the swamp, spacing themselves a dozen yards apart and sweeping forward in Holok's wake. One by one cloaks of blazing light enveloped them, making them seem like sinister will-o-the-wisps as they sought their prey. Unlike in Qut Toloc, there were no glad cries, no boasting as they leapt to the hunt. Instead they moved forward with terrible and inexorable purpose, cutting deep swaths in the marsh grass as they went. In their wake, small fires flickered and smoldered, and belched forth wet, dark smoke.

Holok ran on ahead of them, his feet barely seeming to touch the ground. Birds burst forth from the cover of the reeds as he approached, thundering up into the sky as he strode through them, heedless. There was clear sign of passage here for him to follow, bent reeds and broken twigs, and he bent to it like a hound on the scent. "This way, you fools!" he bellowed, and pressed on. The Huntsmen came after him, sweeping forward swiftly and silently.

Yushuv saw them coming. The woman's shouting had alerted him, but even before that, he had known they were here. A subtle twisting in his gut, a sour taste to the air, a throbbing pain on his brow—all told him that he was being hunted. And so he had doused his fire and tried to creep off into the deeper swamp, but the birds had betrayed him. He wondered if he had offended Raiton somehow, then put the thought out of his mind. The Huntsmen coming for him were trouble enough.

Instinctively, he reached back and counted the arrows in his quiver by touch. There were thirteen. It would not be nearly enough.

At his belt still hung the knife he had taken from the tomb, its edge wickedly serrated and thirsty for blood. Experimentally, Yushuv took it in his hand and hefted it. It was light, no heavier than the twigs he and his friends had pretended were swords just a few weeks ago. Tentatively he thrust with it, the air whistling with the blade's passage. It felt good in his hand, and he imagined what it would be like to use it, to drive it into an enemy's guts and twist. He could almost feel the hot spurt of blood on his hand, the whoosh of breath from his enemy's lungs as the shock of the wound hit, the terrible slow tearing as he pulled the knife out so that it might seek another belly or throat.

Those were not his memories, Yushuv knew. He had never stabbed a man, never so much as cut a friend during childish play. He had killed animals for food, but never with joy and never for pleasure. But he could feel the knife's hunger, remember the savage joy of striking down countless foes. He knew how to use the knife now, knew how he could face a man with a sword and surprise him with it. When they came for him, he could make them pay.

Looking around, he spotted an island of dry ground rising from the marsh behind him. It was steep, rising perhaps six feet from the mire. It would serve as a good place to make his stand. The hillock was steep enough that it would be hard for his foes to scale it, and small enough that they could would have to come at him singly, or at best in pairs.

Thirteen arrows, he thought. *I can't kill them all. But maybe I can kill enough.* With a resigned shake of his head, he stuck the knife back through his belt and started climbing. Crumbling handfuls of soil slid from between his fingers, but within seconds, he had attained his perch. It was covered in stiff reeds, tall enough to hide him, and for that he was thankful. He squatted down, nocked an arrow, and waited. His targets would be along soon enough.

Holok broke through a thin fringe of trees and gazed around. The land here was flat, marked by long, low pools of dirty brown water. A breeze from the west made lazy ripples in the marsh grasses, and in the distance a single tuft of land poked up above the sea of green.

"There," Holok said quietly, his eyes narrowing. Then, louder, "He's there! Hurry!"

The Huntsmen swept past him, gaining speed as they went. A startled snake burst from cover as they went by. Reflexively, Neleh decapitated it and continued on without slowing. Before it had finished thrashing, she had forgotten its very existence.

"Converge on that hill. He's hiding there." Holok advanced more slowly now, more cautiously. Ahead of him, those Hunters who bore shields raised them. "Careful, he may have a bow."

As if in answer, an arrow came whistling through the air. It struck Shiresh's shield above dead center and splintered, and Shiresh himself let out a curse. "The arrowhead came through my shield," he shouted in disbelief. "Ware the archer!"

The others crouched low and advanced, drawing the net tight around the hill where Yushuv waited. Those with shields pressed forward. Those without held back. In the rear, Holok stood, arms crossed and face stern, and urged them on.

"Pah!"

Yushuv could not resist an exclamation of dismay, even as he reached for another arrow. He had but twelve left, and he had been clinging to the hope that he'd be able to drop an enemy with a single shaft. The shot itself had been perfect, and would have taken the target through the eye had his shield not been raised. How had they known to find him here? How had they known to seek him at all? He thought back to the raiton's words and grimaced. There were other powers in the world. If they could make birds speak and the dead tell tales, surely they could find a boy with a bow.

Twelve arrows left. He peered out through the reeds and saw his enemies advancing in a semi-circle. There were five of them closing in on him, three in the first rank and two in the second. The man he'd shot at was moving slowly, cautiously, while the other two with shields were advancing more quickly. That was good; any flaw in their plan worked to his benefit. Behind them came two women, one with a pair of swords with which she wove shining patterns of silver in the air. The other held a javelin poised for throwing, and gripped a long, curved knife in her off hand.

In the distance Yushuv could see a monk, bearded and frowning. Unlike the slender aesthetes and jolly priests he had known in the village, this man carried himself like a warrior born. His eyes met Yushuv's for a second, impossibly, and he felt a shock of recognition. This was his true enemy, this sad-eyed but implacable man, and the five figures that closed on Yushuv were nothing more than the man's tools. He could kill them all, kill a hundred like them, and still the monk would keep coming.

You won't kill them all, boy, he heard the man whisper, and then wrenched his gaze away. With a warrior's cry, he stood and loosed another arrow.

Holok staggered backward in shock. The Anathema had seen him, had somehow known him for what he was.

And just a boy! A child, fresh to power—he should be an easy hunt. Confused, alone; he could not possibly have learned to harness his strength. And yet, a shuddering fear told Holok that this would not be the case.

"Rush him, you fools," he found himself whispering. "It's just a boy, only a boy." And then the arrows started raining down like molten gold, and it was too late.

Neleh heard the twang of the bowstring and looked up. Honed by a hundred battles, a veteran of a dozen Hunts, she could clearly see the single arrow leaping from the bow up on the hillock, could see in her mind's eye the arc it would take, could anticipate just how to strike to cut the shaft down in mid-flight. Confidently she crouched in a ready stance, her swords already coming forward to pluck the arrow from the air.

Suddenly, it shimmered. As she watched in horror, it flickered and caught like a wisp of straw in a bonfire, blazing with a golden light. In its wake other arrows followed, converging on her like a swarm of angry hornets. The air screamed as they flew, and she could sense the terrible exultation behind them.

She struck down one and its fragments hissed and guttered in the muddy water at her feet. Another took her in the throat. Two more pierced her arms and a half-dozen took her in the chest. The stench of cooked meat filled the air, and her last scream died as a choked gurgle. Writhing like a drunkard's marionette, she fell, shuddered for the last time, and lay still. Around her the dancing sheets of light dimmed once, twice, a third time, and then went out.

"Eleven," said Yushuv grimly, and bent his bow again.

Chapter Thirty-Six

A lone in the dark, Wren dreamed.

He dreamed of light, and he dreamed of warmth. He dreamed that cold water did not lap around him, and that his ankle did not throb with the hot poison of infection. He dreamed that he was whole and strong, and cloaked only in golden light.

Wren dreamed. Around him, the rats that infested the Prince's dungeons raised their heads and chittered to one another fearfully. The roaches and centipedes and great befanged spiders that spun thick webs between the bars of the cell doors ceased their skittering and tasted the air, waiting. The few serpents that could abide the cold hissed, and curled their bodies in ways that ancient memories told them would bring the pleasure of warmth. Above them, swarms of bats whistled and shrieked, raising a din that made the hounds in their faraway kennel howl and whine.

Wren dreamed. The water he lay in grew warm in his dream, heated by the sun like the lazy creek he had played in as a boy near Cherak. He could see the fish swimming lazily against the current, fat and slow and easy prey for a boy with clever hands. He could see the ancient weeping willow whose branches made mock-swords for his epic battles against other children. And he could see the creek receding in the distance for the last time after his father sold him to the Guild, for that was a better place for a boy with quick hands and quick wit to be.

Wren dreamed. Above him, Ratcatcher paced nervously. He strode to the window of his chamber and looked out, fearful that he might see Shamblemerry returning in triumph, and that he would once again be cast from the Prince's favor. Pelesh had sent him poisoned wine that morning as a gift, and he pondered passing the gift along once his rival returned. Surely she would not partake, even as he had not, but if he could convince her that it came from the Exchequer, her ally...

Wren dreamed. In his dream, there was light, the light of the sky over a Guild caravan where he labored as a young man. They had been impressed with him, with his wit and his skill, and he had risen quickly. Fong had taken him under his great flabby wing, and mentored him. Promises were made that one day he would rise to great prominence in the Guild, that he would have vast wealth and power if he obeyed Fong and those whom Fong called master. He remembered silks and gemstones, furs that came downriver from Rubylak and overland from Crystal, coffles of slaves bound for Fair Folk outposts and brightly colored fabrics traded from eastern barbarians. Most of all, he remembered the clinking of jade and gold passing from hand to hand, and how its music fascinated him.

This was not meant to be, he heard a voice say, and in agreement he nodded.

Wren dreamed. In his dusty room, Pelesh stared nervously at the locked door and waited for the sound of an armored fist pounding on it. Candles, a wasteful number of candles, illuminated the gloom, and thick trails of wax spattered his once-immaculate desk. Coins lay scattered in reckless heaps, and an inkpot bled its contents onto the floor. He had not known what had possessed him to send the wine, save fury at the way he had been played the fool on the citadel steps. But he had been played the fool before, and always smiled and nodded and worked his revenge later. This fury was new to him, and he did not like it. It devoured his caution, and caution was what had kept him alive for so many years. Eyes wide and fingers twitching, he stared at the door.

Wren dreamed. He dreamed that he was in peaceful silence, the silence of a temple when a hundred monks meditated in perfect harmony. Kejak had plucked him from the Guild somehow, had wooed him and cajoled him and somehow ensorcelled him. He had replaced the vision of wealth with one of something greater, and had made him feel as if he bore the weight of ages on his shoulders. Kejak had honed him into a blade and told him that he was to be used to excise the cancers of the world. He was made a monk, but in name only. His studies were haphazard, his focus diverted. There was always another deed to perform for Kejak, another relic to uncover or bargain to subvert or man to kill, and the promise of enlightenment that had seduced him from trade grew more and more distant.

This was not meant to be, the voice called again, and Wren cried out in his sleep.

Wren dreamed. Unforgiven Blossom watched her orrery with confusion, her elegant features crumpled into a scowl. She had tended Wren's wounds as best she could, and had intensely disliked doing so. She had disliked dealing with the arrogant Ratcatcher even more, and found herself hoping that the Prince's mercurial favor would shift again, soon. Above her, the planets and stars of the orrery swooped and hovered, but their paths seemed oddly frantic, their orbits unstable. She could find nothing wrong with it, but still the machinery moaned and whined with each orbit, and the floor groaned under its weight. Never before had she seen it like this, and she was deeply troubled.

Wren dreamed. He dreamed of motion, of the last few days of nightmare with Ratcatcher. Once again he saw the hounds dying, staggering and collapsing. He heard the cries as their packmates tore at their still-cooling flesh and grinned with bloody muzzles. He felt the rope at his wrists, the tightening in his throat as his horse lagged too far behind Ratcatcher's. He saw the Prince's citadel rise in the distance, and felt the panic that spurred him to one last, feeble escape attempt. He heard Ratcatcher's sad laughter as the man caught him effortlessly. Ratcatcher had not even bothered to punish him, knowing that worse punishments lay ahead. He was a prisoner, and he was doomed, and then the vision faded.

This is not meant to be, the voice said, commanding now.

"What is?" asked Wren in his dream, and heard nothing.

Wren dreamed. Shamblemerry sat in the dark underneath Qut Toloc, holding a half-devoured rat in her hand. Her breathing was ragged and harsh, and the pain in her throat was jagged every time she drew breath. The priest's blood still marked where he had caught her, and she had vowed to wear it as a badge of shame until she could kill him. It was cold in the ossuary, and she shivered. Cold had never bothered her before. This was another indignity to lay at the feet of the man who had defeated her, another item to be added to his bill. He would pay, she vowed. She sat and hugged herself in the dark, and swore vengeance. She would seek him now, she told herself, if only it were not so cold....

Wren dreamed. He dreamed of himself, free and powerful. He dreamed of casting down those who had used him, of walking away from Kejak and the Guild and Ratcatcher, of finding a cool stream laden with fat, slow fish that he might catch once more with his hands.

This might be, the voice told him. *But not yet.*

"When?" Wren demanded.

Soon, the voice replied. *Behold, I take you from the house of my enemies and I Exalt you. I raise you up from the dust and loose the prisoner from his bonds. Go forth and do my bidding.*

"No!" Wren cried. "Not anymore!" But the dream faded.

He awoke to a moment of golden light, one that quickly dimmed to black. Before him the cell mouth gaped open, and he crawled toward it. His hands found the remnants of the door, melted and cooled into a puddle of iron. Shuddering, he eased out into the corridor and stood. His forehead throbbed, but he felt no other pain.

I Exalt you, the voice whispered faintly.

"Oh, no." Wren shook his head, tears pooling in the corner of his eyes. "This can't be."

I Exalt you.

"You make me an abomination!" Wren cried out.

As you understand things now. Your understanding will change. I Exalt you.

"No!" Wren shouted, and stumbled off into the dark as fast as he could. The echoes of the voice followed him, but the spiders and serpents remained behind.

Chapter Thirty-Seven

Taenat was halfway up Yushuv's hill when a shimmering arrow took her through the breastbone. It pierced her jury-rigged armor as if it were the sheerest silk and spun her around. She fell and tumbled down the hill, the arrow snapping off as she did so. Shiresh leaped past her, his daiklave singing as it cut the air, his armor shining in the sun. One hand caught a tussock of grass and he pulled himself upward, calling out a challenge to the coward who hid from honest battle.

Taenat rolled on her side and struggled to stand. Pain seared through her as she propped herself up on her right elbow, and hefted a javelin in her left hand. Gazing up, she could see Shiresh's ascent, hear his battle cry. He seemed unstoppable, a warrior from the days when the Anathema had been cast down. Streamers of orange flame trailed behind him, and the light reflected from his blade. Another moment, and he would attain the crest of the hill.

She saw the boy, then. He rose from the weeds, and he was stern and terrible in the way that only children who kill without remorse can be. His bow was drawn, and even as she cast her javelin with all her might, she knew it was too late. Silent as the grave, he loosed the arrow, and then he turned to look at her.

The shaft took Shiresh in the eye and exploded through the back of his helm. In that instant she mourned him, mourned the beauty of his face that had been destroyed, mourned his laughter, mourned the voice he would raise in song as they rode, mourned the touch of his hand that she would feel no more. Then he tottered backwards, his life's blood fountaining in the air as he fell, and he was gone.

Too late, the javelin took the boy in the shoulder, slamming him back off his feet. The impact tore his eyes from hers, and she was thankful for that. There had been something cold and deadly in his gaze, and Taenat wanted no more of it. She heard him cry out in pain, and was startled when the sound reminded her that this monster they fought was a child.

With a titanic effort, she forced herself to her feet.

One javelin remained to her, and she leaned heavily on it. There was a taste of blood in her mouth and a stabbing pain in her chest that told her she had very little time. Ignoring both as best she could, she surveyed the field of battle. Pelap's corpse lay behind her, eyes wide in surprise. He'd tried to take the hill from behind while Taenat drew the archer's fire, and had failed. Three arrows in his chest and another in his belly attested to that. In the distance she could see Neleh, and beside her lay the ruin of Shiresh. She'd heard, rather than seen, Shattered Ivory die earlier. Of Holok, there was no sign. She cursed the priest for a coward, even as she had cursed him at Qut Toloc, and then limped toward the hill.

No arrows greeted her as she climbed it. She slid once, when her foot found a patch of soil that had turned muddy with Shiresh's blood. The pain of the misstep blinded her for a moment, and she waited until her vision cleared before she continued upwards.

At last she reached the tall grasses that marked the top of the hillock. Most of the weeds had been tramped down during the course of the battle as the boy moved back and forth, and she nearly stepped on his bow as she hobbled forward. The boy himself lay in the center of the cleared area, the javelin beside him. He had pulled it out, it seemed, but then collapsed. The wound to his shoulder still bled profusely, and the red blood had stained much of his tunic. His eyes were closed, and his face was handsome, in a boyish way. If he'd lived to manhood, he might have broken hearts. It was almost a pity he would never do so.

Gritting her teeth with the effort, Taenat lifted the javelin that supported her. She found herself wobbling slightly, but at this range, she could hardly miss. "Good-bye, monster," she said, and began to bring her arm down.

His eyes snapped open, and Taenat knew then that it was a

trap. With blinding speed he snatched a knife from his belt and threw it. The javelin thudded into the earth by his head, and the knife took Taenat in the heart. Her mouth opened in shock, and bright blood flowed out. She sank to her knees, clutching at the wound and whimpering. "How?" she murmured once, and collapsed.

"I was running out of arrows, you see," Yushuv said, and reached for his knife.

Chapter Thirty-Eight

The door was ten feet high and six across, and looked as if it had been hewn from a single piece of found iron. Its surface was rough and cold, and smelled slightly of rust and the damp. A great handle in the shape of a beast's head had been set in the door, and a heavy bar of ebony wood had been laid across it so that it might not be opened from the other side. The door's hinges were also of iron, and were the size of a man's two fists placed one atop the other.

No archway surmounted the door, and the black stone of the wall was blank otherwise. No sign marked what the doorway led to, though there was no dust before it on the floor. There was merely the door itself and its bar, and beside it a single flickering torch.

Wren took the torch from its sconce and examined the door more closely. Here and there he saw claw marks, mute evidence of times when some monstrous thing or other had hewed at it. There were stains on the door, some of them clearly blood and some less identifiable. The metal of the door was cold and, even through its vast bulk, Wren could hear strange, echoing sounds that seemed to be a mix of screams, laughter and the relentless tide of a devouring ocean. Curious, he returned the torch to its sconce and placed his hands on the massive bar that held the door shut. It was cool, but not unpleasantly so, and he was suddenly filled by a desire to see what the door concealed. Perhaps safety could be found behind it, or even a route out of the Prince's citadel. Such might explain why the door was hidden here, and why it was so heavily barred.

Something about that logic bothered Wren, but he was too tired to examine it closely. His head ached and he felt ill, and the knowledge of what he had become gnawed at him. His devotion had been a spotty thing at best, but to be made Anathema? His training taught him that he would do best by the world to find a knife and slit his own throat. But life was sweet, and freedom was sweeter, and the urge to live overwhelmed any such notions any time they arose.

Still, he dared not hope. Anathema in the bowels of the Prince's domain was still a dead Anathema, he knew. Soon his captors would return to his cell to see if they could humiliate him more, and they would find the evidence of his new patron's handiwork.

His new patron? Wren paused for a moment to consider that. Even if he escaped, his life as he knew it was over. He could never return to Kejak or the sanctity of the temple. Once the keenest of hunters, he had instead become the hunted.

It would be best, then, he decided, to make a start on this new life before he was hunted through the damp and nitre of the Prince's dungeons. He had already spent what felt like hours stumbling through the dark, traveling ever downwards. Up was light and life, but up also led to the Prince and his minions; regardless of what his dream had told him, Wren knew that he was overmatched. So down was the only way to go, past cells filled with old corpses and older bones, past storerooms that had held trade goods before the shadow had fallen on the city of Thorns, and past lightless corridor mouths that promised nothing but the endless sound of water falling onto wet stone.

It was at the very bottom of the Prince's dungeons that he found the door. The light of the torch had drawn him, and it was not until he was close that he saw what the low flame illuminated. It astonished him. He could not imagine the strength required to move something so massive, and he felt a sudden surge of pity for the smith who had crafted the door's hinges and handle. No doubt the man had been killed to protect the secret of this place; of that Wren suddenly was sure. No doubt Wren would be swiftly dispatched as well if he were found here, or indeed, if he were found at all. Filled with a surge of panic, he adjusted his hands on the bar and pushed.

"You would regret that," a quiet voice said from the shadows.

Wren whirled, dropping into a rough approximation of

a crouch. "Who said that?" he called, scanning the darkness anxiously.

"It is one of the perils of standing in the light when all around you is dark," the voice continued, and now Wren recognized it as belonging to the woman who had accompanied the Prince and Ratcatcher. "One cannot see, but one can be seen. It makes one a target." There was a whistling sound, and suddenly a long pin with a tortoiseshell handle quivered in the metal of the door, a miniscule distance from Wren's left ear. He fought to keep himself from shuddering.

"Who are you?" he bellowed, his eyes trying futilely to pierce the dark. "Show yourself."

Unforgiven Blossom stepped forward into the light, bemused. She wore a shift of deep blue, belted at the waist with a gray sash, and her hair was piled atop her head in an elaborate coif held by a half-dozen pins. "You may cease shouting, if it would please you to do so. I assure you there is no one here save my unworthy self, and I am quite capable of hearing you. My name is Unforgiven Blossom, and I mean you no harm."

"I am sorry to doubt you, madam, but I find that hard to believe." Wren felt some of his old bravado seeping back into him. "You serve the Prince, do you not?"

She nodded. "As his oracle, and occasionally as his physicker and scribe. Nowhere in my duties is the task of tracking down runaway prisoners, or of serving as His Majesty's executioner. He reserves that pleasure for himself. As such, I have no duty to him in this matter. If he wishes you found or slain, there are others to whom that task will fall. For myself, I find you curious, and would speak more with you before you are flayed."

Wren quirked an eyebrow. "Flaying? Is that what is planned for me?"

"Initially, yes." Unforgiven Blossom's voice took on a singsong tone as she recited what was undoubtedly an oft-spoken list. "Flaying, followed by a bath in salt water, followed by torment with hot coals, and then time with the hounds. You are a most esteemed prisoner. Normally the Prince does not plan such elaborate torments for his prisoners."

"I think I may have killed someone he liked," Wren said

guardedly. "He seemed most eager to make my acquaintance."

Unforgiven Blossom smiled. "Ah, Sandheart. Yes, he was most wroth when he returned from that expedition, though all others who knew Sandheart were not. She was not well-loved, even for one already dead."

"Already dead?" Wren's brow furrowed in suspicion. "What does that mean? Was she ill?"

The astrologer shook her head. "You misunderstand me. Sandheart's soul had already descended to the Underworld and returned to the lands of the living. Several times, if memory serves. She was fond of possessing the bodies of young women, as I recall, and several of the other nemessaries found that frustrating. Also," she added primly, "Sandheart never knew when to shut up. However, that is no longer an issue. It would seem that the ground beneath Talat's Howe was ensorcelled so as to make it impossible for any nemessary slain there to rise again. Such is the true reason the Prince was so wroth with you. It was not because Sandheart was destroyed, though she was the Prince's favorite. No, it was because he was not the one to pronounce her doom. They—we—are all the Prince's, you see. His to create, his to dispose of as he wishes. Taking that away from His Majesty makes him very angry."

"Ah. Would you believe me if I told you that I had no idea the mound had any spell on it other than the lockstone that guarded the entrance? I won't apologize for leaving behind my little presents, though." Wren caught himself being defensive, and with an effort forced his tone back to bantering. "I've got a problem with being followed, you know."

"I know." Unforgiven Blossom chuckled, the sound of it lower than Wren would have expected. "Having followed you down here, I am quite aware of your tendencies. Now, tell me this—what *did* you find in Talat's tomb? The Prince said merely that you had looted it, and made no mention of what he sought. Jade, perhaps, or gems?"

Wren considered, then decided that he would lose nothing by telling the truth. "The tomb was empty except for a single coin. It was a joke laid for us by the ancients. I left the tomb more full than it was when I arrived. Poisoned darts on tripwires, and

I left my signature for the ages. I did not know for certain I was being followed, but it seemed sensible to take the precaution."

"And you made yourself a much greater enemy than you could have imagined. You seem clever, in such small ways."

The insult stung. "More clever than Sandheart, whatever she might have been."

"This is true," she replied with prim precision. "And it is also true that there are fish in the sea, and worms in the dirt, and beetles eating corpses that are more clever than Sandheart is right now, and that many of those fish and worms and beetles will outlive you."

Despite himself, Wren laughed. "True. So I have given you an answer." He turned and gestured. "You owe me one. What lies behind that door?"

She frowned. "The deeper Underworld. The passage leads to the Labyrinth at the heart of all things, the maze gnawed by the dead gods from the dreams of creation. They still slumber in vaults beyond this door, awaiting the day when they are summoned to wakefulness and destruction. Some sleep uneasily. It is best not to risk disturbing them."

"Ah." Wren slumped, his back to the door. "So I cannot go forward, and I cannot go back, and I am sure that if I tried to flee from you now, one or both of us would regret it." He lifted his head, defiance in his eyes. "So, Unforgiven Blossom, what do you propose I do?"

She stared back at him. "I propose that you walk with me to my orrery. I will brew tea there, and we will discuss the order of the heavens, the proper interpretation of the Immaculate Texts and the possible explanations for why the one who calls himself Ratcatcher is such an ass. Eventually, the Prince will find you there, and will remove you from my custody, but in the interim you will have had pleasant and informative conversation. And tea."

Wren bowed, chuckling. "I haven't had a better offer all day. Shall we?"

"We shall." She reached past him to pluck the pin from the iron door, and saw for the first time the mark on his brow. "Oh. This may change things."

"What?" Wren was instantly alert and defensive.

"There is a looking glass in my chambers. It will serve to explain. Let us go from this place. It is cold here, and I am old."

"But you will outlive me," he said, and took her hand. Together, they walked out of the torchlight, and up into the Prince's citadel of shadows.

Chapter Thirty-Nine

There were precisely seventy-seven steps leading from the top of the tower where Ratcatcher dwelt to the ground floor of the citadel, and another seventy-seven leading down into the dungeons where Wren was being kept. There were deeper dungeons below that, and the Prince had often made light of the fact that his domain was three times as deep as it was tall. Ratcatcher had found the witticism amusing once, and had resolved to use it himself someday when he, too, was lord of a citadel such as this one.

Perhaps this very one, his ambition had whispered, and he had not put the thought from his mind as quickly as he might have.

Torch in hand, he descended into the depths of the citadel. The Prince had dismissed him curtly after the unsatisfactory interview with Wren, and the thoughts that had troubled him afterwards were deeply unsettling. The thought of taunting Pelesh crossed his mind, but it lacked savor. And so, the notion of visiting Wren emerged, and after much debate he decided to indulge it.

The route to Wren's cell was a relatively brief one, and the way was paved in black cobblestones. Occasionally Ratcatcher found the Prince's choice of color scheme oppressive but in a dungeon, it made a certain amount of sense. All of the other torches here were extinguished, and he resisted the urge to relight them. The damp in the tunnels soaked into the wood, and torches that remained too long gave forth foul, thick smoke when lit. As the new shape of Wren's cell ensured that Ratcatcher would be the closer of the two to the ceiling, additional smoke was something he wanted nothing to do with.

Coming around a bend, he stopped abruptly. A snake lay

in his path, doing something that looked for all the world like basking. It was perhaps six feet in length, banded black and yellow and red, and it regarded Ratcatcher lazily through hooded eyes. Its tongue flicked out once, then it slowly moved off into the darkness of one of the cells.

Ratcatcher waited a moment for the snake to depart, then knelt. The stone where the serpent had been resting held the comforting warmth of a rock that had received a morning's sunshine. "This is very disturbing," he said to himself, and rose quickly so that he might complete his errand.

As he did so, a swarm of bats descended from the ceiling, shrieking. One hurled itself onto his torch, dousing it and filling the air with the stench of burned meat. This drove the others into a frenzy, and Ratcatcher found himself buffeted by the swarm. He swiped ineffectively at them for a long moment, then called upon his power and bid them begone. They scattered and, grim-faced, he continued onward. Briefly he considered going back for another torch, but it seemed wiser to press onward. He could imagine the laughter if Pelesh or one of the others caught him, forced to retreat by a stray bat. And so he went on. Rats scuttled out of his path, and things that were most probably insects crunched under his boots. Never had he seen the dungeons so full of life, and it disturbed him on a deep and abiding level.

The last turn loomed ahead. He took it, calling out softly, "Wren?" There was no answer. Ratcatcher repeated himself more loudly: "Wren?" Still, there was only silence. "Damn it, Wren, are you there? Wake up. I could be whipped for this, you know," he added petulantly.

The words echoed once, then vanished. Irritated beyond speech, Ratcatcher strode over to Wren's cell, and brought his gauntleted fist across where the bars of the cell should have been. The racket, he thought, would surely rouse the priest from whatever slumber or meditation he was currently indulging in.

Instead, he felt nothing. Frantically, he waved back and forth. The gate was gone. He dropped to his knees and stared into the gloom. The cell was empty. The door had vanished and so had the prisoner.

With as much dignity as he could muster, he crawled

backwards and stood. "Wren!" he bellowed. "I don't know how you did it, Wren, but I will find you. Pray you break your neck in the dark first!" Unsurprisingly, there was no reply.

Ratcatcher waited a moment, indecisive. Then, as the sound of his shout died, he fled back up toward the stairs, there to relight his torch and to seek help, discreetly.

Chapter Forty

The bleeding had mostly stopped by the time the woman with the javelins stopped breathing. In truth, the wound in his shoulder was not that deep, but it had bled profusely, and he was relieved when it slowed to a trickle. Carefully he wiped the knife on the grass, then stood. The monk was still out there somewhere, and Yushuv knew that he, not these broken corpses, was the true enemy here.

He did not have long to wait. A minute passed, and then the Immaculate came striding out from under the trees. He barely seemed to touch the mud and water below him as he walked, and Yushuv could see that his hands bore no weapons.

At the base of the hill, Holok leapt, and rose effortlessly toward the crest where Yushuv stood. White light surrounded him as he flew, and he landed gently next to Taenat's body. Yushuv saw that his left hand was bandaged, and that blood had soaked through the wrappings. He looked down at the corpse with a mixture of pity and regret, and in that instant Yushuv stabbed at him.

Without turning his head, Holok caught Yushuv's wrist and twisted it until he dropped the blade. "That was foolish, but I suppose you had to try it. Do you feel better now?" Yushuv squealed in pain, and with a deft shove, Holok sent him sprawling. "I'm sorry, boy. That was unkind of me."

Yushuv dove for the knife, but Holok caught him under the chin with a solid kick. The boy's head snapped back and he rolled on his side, moaning softly.

"Is this what you want?" Holok asked, bending down to take the blade in his hands. It was a horrid thing, and thin gobbets of meat still trailed in the serrations along the cutting edge. "It looks old. The right Guild trader might give you a fortune for it. I'm less generous." He took the dagger between his hands and closed his eyes. The blade snapped, and he dropped the fragments to the ground. "That should save us from any more of your awkward attempts to stab me, I think."

Yushuv glared at him, eyes bright with hatred. "I killed the rest of them, you know," he said.

"Yes, yes," Holok replied. "I saw you do it. Your artistry is remarkable. It's why I didn't intervene. Well, that and the fact that Neleh would no doubt have been very upset had I saved her life again. Once in a fortnight tends to test the limits of gratitude, I find." He looked over and, for the first time, saw Yushuv's expression. "Surprised? Yes, I would be, too. It's all new to you, isn't it? Unfortunately, it won't get much older. I have to kill you." More gently, he added, "You do know why, don't you?"

"Because I killed them?"

Holok shook his head. "You did what every fox would do to the hounds, if it got the chance. No, it's not that at all. It's that you're dangerous, child. You have a power in you that's been cursed."

"I never wanted power," Yushuv said petulantly. "I just wanted to grow up like my father."

"Power finds you. And this power will grow, and it will twist you. It matters not how good you are now. It's beyond you, I'm afraid. You're not strong enough. No one is. Look around. You've killed today, boy. Does that bother you? Another few years and it will be armies you're laying low, and the dead will number in their thousands. And the worst part of it will be that it will bother you not at all."

"I think you're lying."

Holok sighed. "I wish I were. I have no wish to be here, either. It's always hard killing children."

"It's harder doing the killing." Moving like an old man, Yushuv stood.

Holok frowned. "No, it's not, and it gets easier every time. That's what brought us to this endgame. Make your peace with your deeds, boy. I'll give you that much time."

Yushuv looked around. There was no escape. He could fling

himself into the marsh below, but no doubt the priest would flutter down beside him. Attack had proved futile. There was nothing left but to die.

The palm of his good hand itched. For an instant he wished he still had the knife. Even broken, it was worth something; a death with dignity, perhaps, or a last stab at life.

"Come to me, boy," Holok commanded, not unkindly. "I'll cause you no pain, though the Huntsmen's ghosts will no doubt howl at me all night because of it. It's time for this to end."

Yushuv took a hesitant step forward, and then another. All his thoughts were on the knife. He could feel it tugging at his hand, pulling it closer. The two belonged together. They had traveled together, drawn blood together, killed together. Now, of all times, they should not be apart.

"This Hunt ends now," Holok said quietly, and prepared for the final blow. Yushuv closed his eyes.

The knife leapt into his hand, momentarily a single entity once more. More out of reflex than plan, he jutted his fist forward and encountered something soft and warm and yielding. Holok cried out, hoarsely, as the blade took him in the side, and Yushuv stood before him, blinking in astonishment.

"What have you done?" Holok gasped, and then screamed. Astonished, Yushuv pulled back his weapon. Once again, it was broken, the few inches near the tip missing and the rest of the blade sticky with blood.

Holok stared at the boy, who suddenly seemed very young. The child stared at his knife in horror, and then looked up to meet Holok's eyes. Then, wordlessly, he ran, stumbling down the hill in a windmill of arms and legs. In an instant, he was gone, and only broken reeds marked his passing.

Quickly, Holok cupped his wound with his good hand. It was bleeding profusely, which was not a good sign, and he could feel part of the blade moving within the wound. *I had broken that knife,* he thought muzzily. *Strange that I've been stabbed with it. The dragons laugh at us.* He sat down, hard, and shivered. Focus was key here, or he would bleed to death in a matter of minutes. Still holding his side, he began to chant a calming mantra, one that slowed the heart and eased pain. If he could endure this, he could find a safer place to remove the fragment of metal, and perhaps to begin to heal. But if he did not slow his bleeding now to give himself that chance, then the Hunt died here, with him. And with the power the boy had displayed, that could not be allowed to happen. His life was not his own, Holok knew. Otherwise, he would never have fought so hard to preserve it.

A hundred yards away, Yushuv lay in the tall grass, shivering. His strength had given out here, and he could go no farther. His quiver still on his back, a broken knife in his fist, he clutched his knees to his chest and quietly sobbed. Once he tried to stand, but he could not. There was no strength in his legs, no will in his heart to go on.

Suddenly, he felt very sleepy. A part of his mind screamed at him to get up, to flee the priest on the hill as quickly as he could, but its voice was drowned in the gentle hum of slumber.

Wounded and alone, Yushuv slept.

Chapter Forty-One

The hammering on the door of Unforgiven Blossom's chambers was thunderous. She looked over her shoulder at the door, set down her teacup, and said politely to Wren, "Will you excuse me?"

"Of course," he replied, and sipped delicately. She had brewed the tea herself, pouring fragments of black leaves into boiling water, then serving the tea in delicate porcelain painted with the graceful image of soaring gulls. The tea itself was flavored faintly with apricot, and the steam that wafted up from it gave a pleasant and healthful scent. The tea tray itself was carved from mahogany, and it rested on a table inlaid with agates and soapstone. Both Wren and Unforgiven Blossom sat on cushions of black silk stuffed with silk rags. Beside them the orrery swooped and danced, its aches and groans mysteriously gone.

Unforgiven Blossom stood and walked to the door. Wren paused a moment for politeness' sake, then stood as well. He had no doubts as to what the pounding presaged, and while the futility of his position was apparent, a small part of him insisted on not going without a struggle.

Besides, he had no wish to spill Unforgiven Blossom's tea.

As Unforgiven Blossom opened the door, Wren strolled over to the orrery and examined it. It was a marvelous piece of work, and he cheerfully confessed to himself that he had not the faintest idea how it worked. It was easy to tell, however, what each of the whirling bodies represented. Here was Mars, angry and red and swooping low with each pass. Venus soared overhead, tracing delicate arcs high in the air. Stars, celestial clouds and comets, all danced intricately before him.

"—have informed the Prince, and now I am informing you.

Wren has escaped, and he is quite dangerous." Ratcatcher's voice could be heard clearly, equal parts command and panic. "I am here as a courtesy to warn you, and to ask if you've seen him."

"I believe he's over by the orrery, if you must know." Unforgiven Blossom's answer was bland, but Wren could sense an undercurrent of gleeful malice directed at the looming figure in the hall. "He's been having tea."

"Please tell me that you're joking." Ratcatcher sounded exasperated. "Wren killed Sandheart, and while I think we should fete him like a prince for doing so, the fact remains that he is extraordinarily dangerous."

"He's also extraordinarily underinformed on the Immaculate Texts for a monk, but that is water beneath the bridge," Unforgiven Blossom retorted. "If you refuse to believe me, move along so that we may finish our discussion. If you wish to attempt to retrieve him, he is inside. However, you may find him changed."

"Changed? How?"

"He now bears what I believe is a Zenith Caste mark, though you may choose to examine it for yourself more closely. However, I expect he will not be amenable to such a procedure. You may wish to ask him yourself."

"If you're lying to me, woman—"

"I never lie. Shall I tell you what I see in the stars for you, Ratcatcher? I promise you, that will be the truth. Are you brave enough to hear it?"

Wren turned, mildly amused. Unforgiven Blossom stood before the door, holding it open halfway. Ratcatcher was in the hallway, half-attempting a peek inside while trying to hide any intention of doing so. He seemed completely cowed by the woman before him, his manner equal parts bluster and frustration. As he watched, Ratcatcher shook his head, vehemently.

"I'll hear nothing of the future from you, witch. You'll twist it to suit your needs. Now let me inside."

She gestured to the orrery. "As you wish."

Ratcatcher said, "Thank you," in frosty tones, and stepped

forward into the room. His gaze swept over the tea table, then went to the orrery, and his face contorted in a mixture of astonishment and rage. "You..."

"Black suits you," Wren said, and flung a porcelain spoon he had palmed at him. Ratcatcher sidestepped, and the spoon shattered against the wall. Unforgiven Blossom shrieked, "No!" and slammed the door, even as Ratcatcher leapt at Wren and the monk dodged and spun away.

"I can't kill you, Wren, not without the Prince's permission. But I can make it very difficult for you to run away again." Ratcatcher crouched low and closed, arms spread wide in a wrestler's stance. "I'll snap every bone in your legs like they're green twigs."

"Only if you can catch me," Wren replied, and leapt straight up. Ratcatcher charged, but Wren passed over him, spinning halfway to face him as he landed. Ratcatcher turned and snarled; Wren leaned down and picked up the cushion he had lately been sitting on.

"My apologies about the spoon," he said, "and I'm afraid I'm going to need to borrow the cushion." Ratcatcher threw a punch and Wren deflected it with the silken pillow. "If I make it out of here, I'll buy you another one." Ratcatcher swung again, and Wren caught the blow on the cushion directly in front of his face. He snapped his hands forward, catching Ratcatcher's fist in the cushion, then twisted right with the clear intention of breaking his opponent's wrist. Rather than resist, the Deathknight threw himself into the motion, flipping in midair and pulling his hand free as he did so. He landed awkwardly, and Wren took advantage of the opening to land a series of kicks on Ratcatcher's side. As the last blow landed, the Deathknight fell to his left, overbalanced. With a curse, he hit the floor and rolled to his feet by the table, eyes bright with the joy of battle.

Rather than press his advantage, Wren stepped back. He risked a quick glance at the door and saw Unforgiven Blossom still standing there, impassively. He had no idea whether she would hinder or assist him if he fled, and so decided not to chance it.

A howl from Ratcatcher and a crash of broken porcelain

brought Wren's eye back to the fight. The Deathknight had lifted Unforgiven Blossom's tea table, and the delicate bowls and teapot had slid to the ground. "Catch this on a cushion," he shouted, and hurled the table forward.

Wren tried to dodge, but his foot found a puddle of spilled tea and he tumbled to the floor. That saved him, as the table went soaring overhead and crashed to the ground perilously near the bottom of Mars's miniature orbit. "Touch the orrery and I'll have your head, Ratcatcher," Unforgiven Blossom called out matter-of-factly, and then it was Ratcatcher losing his footing and Wren leaping to his feet as the Deathknight stumbled past.

"I'm truly sorry," Wren called out, and leapt as high as he could. With a thud, he landed on the sphere representing Jupiter, and smiled to see the look on Ratcatcher's face as he scrambled up. "I'm afraid the heavens themselves don't want you to beat me," he catcalled, then fell forward as a minor comet impacted solidly with the back of his neck. He tumbled down and landed on Mars as it swept upward, the impact of his landing nearly bending the metal arm that supported the planet, and then was carried away from Ratcatcher again as he rose unsteadily to his feet.

"Riding in circles? There's nowhere you can hide from me, priest," Ratcatcher snarled, and leapt onto the orrery. His feet scrabbled for purchase on the massive silver globe that served for Luna, and he grinned a wolf's grin as it rose to intersect with Mars's orbit.

"I'm willing to test that," Wren replied, and launched a side kick at Ratcatcher's head. The Deathknight ducked under it and threw a blow that connected with Wren's ankle, sending him sprawling across his perch. Ratcatcher raised his fist for another blow, but instead took a stylized constellation made of crystal and marble in the gut as it swung over Wren's prone form. The impact knocked Ratcatcher backwards, and he clutched madly at the constellation as it swept him along in its arc. His feet clanged off a series of smaller celestial bodies, even as Wren slid down from Mars and landed on a slow-moving construction of wire and gems that represented a nebula. He felt the wire bend ever so slightly under his weight, and winced.

Ratcatcher hoisted himself onto the constellation, ducked Venus as it swooped past, and leapt down onto the Unconquered Sun itself. His boots scored the globe's surface and, rather than land cleanly, he slid down the side onto one of the many arms supporting the planets' orbits. With an ominous creak, it bent.

"No!" Unforgiven Blossom's face was a mask of horror. "Ratcatcher, what have you done?" Even as he leapt upwards toward Mercury, Jupiter grazed a pair of comets that normally it would have passed over safely. Knocked out of their alignment, the comets rebounded solidly into Luna, which shrieked its protest and began wobbling. Ratcatcher's eyes widened in fear as he balanced precariously, then Venus smashed into a series of constellations and burst into green-tinged flame.

Wren hurled himself to the ground as Ratcatcher slid, his hands gripping at Mercury in desperation. He swung through a half-orbit, then Venus caught his left arm at the elbow with a sickening crunch. He cried out in pain and let go, falling onto the Sun itself as a deluge of shooting stars fell upon it. They pinned him there, and he howled as his legs were struck hammer-blows by the wildly careening moon. White bone shone through where his left leg had been twisted, and blood gushed and spattered on the floor.

Wren came shakily to his feet as the flames from Venus raced down its supporting arm and spread. "I am deeply sorry," he said to Unforgiven Blossom, still standing before the door with a stricken look on her face, "I truly am." And to his surprise, he truly was.

"I'll kill him," she whispered. "I will kill him." Without thinking, her hand went to her hair, and she pulled forth a long, wicked steel pin. "This one is for his right eye. I'll leave it there as long as it takes him to die."

Abruptly, she straightened and caught Wren with her stare. "You. Go. The Prince will find you soon enough. I'll not have it be here."

Wren bowed." You are, as always, gracious. I thank you for the tea."

A smile quirked the edge of her mouth. "A pity you will be dead soon, and that we did not finish our discussion. Give my regards to Ratcatcher when you see him in the Prince's private hell. He'll be there, waiting for you. Now run, priest, like you've never run before."

"As always, I am your servant," he replied, and opened the door. He bowed, sketchily, and then ran. He could hear the clamor of troops from the direction he assumed was the courtyard, and going up offered the chance to be trapped in a tower.

"Down it is, then," he muttered to himself, and set about retracing the steps he had taken with Unforgiven Blossom. The sounds of pursuit rose behind him, and he pelted down the stairs into the dungeon below. A pair of unliving guards posted at the stairwell's bottom turned to face him as he descended, but before they could bring their halberds into position he was between them, landing a staccato rhythm of blows that sent both sprawling. As one tottered he grabbed the man's halberd and plunged it into his chest, pinning him to the floor; then spun and did the same for his partner. They writhed piteously, but Wren paid them no heed as he took the torch from their watch station and descended deeper into the maze.

He knew where he was going, of course. His path had been set from the moment he'd left his cell. Another unliving guard rose up out of the dark, and without hesitation he plunged his torch into its eyes. There was a sizzling sound and the scent of rotten meat cooking, and then Wren was past it. It shrieked and dropped its weapon to claw at its face, but the flames caught and it sank to the floor as its own funeral pyre.

Wren did not look back. Another twist, another turn, another flight of stairs down, and a rivulet of water splashing around his feet told him he was racing past his old cell. A cry to his left warned him of more pursuit, and he sped onwards, praying he remembered the way. In the distance he heard thin screams, and he found himself hoping it wasn't Ratcatcher. If the man's agony could carry this far, then the torments he must be facing would be unimaginable.

Down he went, and then down again, and the path seemed as familiar as those he'd walked as a child along the creekside. Ahead he could see the door. The same torch, or one very much like it, still guttered next to it, and he could see where he had budged the bar on the door in his previous attempt. Fear, he suspected, would lend him strength now. He threw himself into the final sprint, even as he heard iron-shod boots clattering down the stairs behind him. *How has the pursuit gotten so close?* he wondered, and then the Prince's voice rang out and he had his answer.

"Don't be foolish, Wren. You're not ready for what's behind that door."

Wren ignored him, leaning his torch against the cold stone wall and getting a grip on the ebony beam. "I'm not ready to die, either," he muttered, and lifted with all his might.

"Do not ignore me, Wren. Go behind that door and death will seem like a mercy. How lightly do you value your soul, Immaculate?" The Prince strode forward, and with each step swallowed more of the light. Wren's torch guttered and died, and the other sputtered and burned low.

"I'm not...Immaculate anymore!" Wren shoved upwards, and the beam moved. It slipped from his grasp, falling to the floor with a thunderous boom, and the Prince cursed. His anima billowed out behind him and he raised his hands, crackling with veins of purple lightning as he advanced.

"No, you are not. But you still will not pass through that door," he said calmly. "You are forfeit to me. I will not permit this, not until you are ready."

Wren laughed, a mad sound. With a lunatic's strength, he grasped the beast-headed handle. The door swung open easily, and beyond it a black abyss yawned. He stepped backwards and placed himself in front of it. "You won't permit me? Wait, it's another joke, just like Talat's tomb!"

"That was no joke, Wren, and neither is this. You're mine now, body and soul, and I'll not have you throw yourself away. I'll not allow it."

"Not allow? Shall we bring all of those who claim me here to debate what I can and cannot do? You can't stop me, you know, not unless you kill me. Well, Your Majesty? Will you strike? I've had too many masters to surrender myself to you."

"Damn you!" the Prince roared, and lightning arced from

his fingertips. Spinning, Wren threw himself backwards, into the dark. The Prince's magics passed harmlessly overhead, but by then he was falling, falling down into the dark.

He thought once of the torch he had left in the sconce, and once of the scent of apricot tea, and then Eliezer Wren gave himself up to the endless night.

Gently, the Prince of Shadows closed the door. It clanged shut softly and without any undue fuss. With one hand, he lifted the heavy ebon bar that Wren had barely managed to hoist, and he slid it back into its track effortlessly. The fallen torch he picked up, and relit it with the smoldering flame that lingered in the other. He moved very precisely, every action carefully controlled. Then, carefully and precisely, he took the lit torch in his hands and snapped it in two. The burning fragments fell to the floor, and their flames whooshed out within seconds. The only glow was the angry throbbing of the Prince's anima, which pulsed around him like a living thing.

"Ignore me, will he? I'll have his soul anyway. We'll see who wants to barter for it."

So muttering, the Prince turned his back on the boundaries of his domain, and went forth to see what was left of Ratcatcher.

Chapter Forty-Two

On the other side of the line of trees from where he'd last seen Yushuv, Holok took three inches of steel out of his side. The pain was blinding, or would have been had he not been taught to mask it and hide it away. Such were the benefits of the discipline of the Order, and Holok was thankful for them.

With his good hand he drew forth the blade's tip, moving slowly lest the barbs catch and tear more of his flesh. At long last it slid into his palm, and he cast it into a pool of muddy water. Blood had power, but he had no wish to carry that blade with him back to the Palace Sublime. It would sink here, and be lost forever.

With effort, he tore strips of cloth from his robes and bound his gut as tight as he could stand. Deep within he could feel the warmth that meant healing had begun, but he still moved slowly. He had no desire to bleed to death now, after all of the work he had done to restore himself.

Resting against a smooth tree trunk, he replayed in his mind the battle. So much more made sense now. The boy's power was immense. Clearly, Ratcatcher and then Shamblemerry had been sent to bring him to the Prince of Shadows and thus under the spell of the Abyss. They'd failed, and now the boy was loose, pursued by not only the Hunt but the powers of darkness as well. It would be impossible to find him, Holok suspected. He'd go to ground and wouldn't emerge until he accidentally orchestrated some sort of catastrophe. And all the while, the Prince of Shadows would be hunting him.

Clearly the Prince must not be allowed to find the boy. The deaths of the Huntsmen, while regrettable, were of little consequence. The Dragon-Blooded were like grains of sand on a beach, innumerable. Such had been the logic when Kejak and his brothers in the Bronze Faction had raised the banner of rebellion against the Solar Exalted, and such was the logic now.

He lurched to his feet, painfully, and spat a gobbet of bloody phlegm into the same pool into which he'd discarded the knife blade. His concentration had long since lapsed, and the agony of his wound was upon him. The horses, he hoped, were still on the road. He staggered forward slowly, each step burning like another stab. He'd strike south to find the river and take the horses back with him, yes. He'd book passage at Great Fork or Lookshy or Nexus, alerting the Order there to see to Qut Toloc, and return to the Imperial City. He'd bring the matter to Kejak and the Mouth of Peace, and give neither of them any peace until they granted him an audience. They both must know what kind of power was now loose in the world. It was now vital to turn every effort to the pursuit of the boy.

Somehow he traversed the last hundred yards of swamp and collapsed on the road. The horses were still there, and as one they stared at him, quizzically. He chuckled softly, then hauled himself to his feet and set about the laborious task of untethering them. His mount whickered quietly as he cupped its muzzle in his hand and then mounted, wincing.

"We're going home, boy," he said. "Slowly, but we're going home." He clucked to the horse, and obediently it started forward.

A sudden thought struck him that perhaps he should stay and search further for the boy, but the pain in his gut argued against that. The child had stabbed him, and then run. Surely he was long gone. There was not even a sense of his presence any longer, just gnawing agony.

Home was the best option, Holok decided. And with luck, it might remain his home even after he reported his failure.

Chapter Forty-Three

Yushuv awoke on the back of a horse, draped across it like a sack of meal. His shoulder hurt, and he could feel that it had been bandaged. "Where am I?" he asked. Panic filled him and he scrabbled for his knife. It was gone.

"Easy, boy." The man in the saddle before him was as big as the monk he'd fought in the swamp, and carried himself the same way. Like the priest, his head was shaven, but he wore intricately decorated armor that no Immaculate would ever don. "You're safe. Relax, or I'll throw you off the damn horse."

"Who are you?" Yushuv sat up, nearly fell off the horse, then found his unsteady seat.

"I'm called Dace. I've been looking for you for weeks. Raiton didn't hide all of the signs, you know. I have a friend," for a moment, he sounded vaguely uncomfortable, "who reads the skies. She warned me that I should be searching for you. A damn long way I came, too, and what do I find? You, half-dead in the mud, and dead Huntsmen all around. You had one arrow in your quiver and a broken knife in your hand, and something had beaten you within an inch of your life. Good thing I came along, or you'd have been wolf fodder."

"One arrow...where's my quiver? Is the arrow still there?"

Dace laughed. "Oh, have no fear, mighty hunter. Your bow and your quiver are safely tucked away. They'll be making the journey with you."

Yushuv gave a sigh of relief. "That's good to know. Where are we going?"

Dace turned and smiled, and Yushuv saw on his brow a mark similar to, but unlike, his own. "We're going someplace safe, where you can be taught what you are and how to use what you've been given. Until then, you're always going to be at risk, and you'll be a danger to those around you. I'm to be your first teacher, but I won't be your last."

"Teacher. Hmm." Yushuv looked up. Overhead, at the limits of vision, he thought he could see the shape of a great raiton, silhouetted against the sun.

And in his mind's ear once again he could hear raucous, croaking laughter.

The epic continues in book two.

About the Author

Richard Dansky is a twenty-plus-year veteran of the video game industry. He has written for games including The Division, Splinter Cell: Blacklist, Outland, and many more. GHOST OF A MARRIAGE is Richard's eighth novel. He has also published a short-fiction collection titled SNOWBIRD GOTHIC. Richard has numerous tabletop roleplaying game credits, and was the developer on the critically acclaimed WRAITH: THE OBLIVION 20th Anniversary Edition. He lives in North Carolina with his cat and an ever-changing roster of books and single malt scotches.

Curious about other Crossroad Press books?
Stop by our site:
http://www.crossroadpress.com
We offer quality writing
in digital, audio, and print formats.